HOW TO WIN AT HIGH SCHOOL

HOW TO WIN

AT HIGH SCHOOL

OWEN MATTHEWS

HARPER TEEN
An Imprint of HarperCollinsPublishers

YP
matt

For Jay, BJ, Jesse, Angele, and Brianna—my Windsor crew

HarperTeen is an imprint of HarperCollins Publishers.

How to Win at High School
Copyright © 2015 by Owen Laukkanen
All rights reserved. Printed in the United States of America. No part of this book may be used or reproduced in any manner whatsoever without written permission except in the case of brief quotations embodied in critical articles and reviews. For information address HarperCollins Children's Books, a division of HarperCollins Publishers, 195 Broadway, New York, NY 10007.
www.epicreads.com

Library of Congress Cataloging-in-Publication Data
Matthews, Owen, date.
  How to win at high school / Owen Matthews.
    pages cm
  Summary: Partly for the sake of his brother, Sam, who is paralyzed, Adam decides to go from high school loser to god by selling completed homework assignments, buying alcohol, and arranging for fake IDs, but before the end of junior year, he realizes his quest for popularity has gone way too far.
  ISBN 978-0-06-233686-6 (hardback)
  [1. Popularity—Fiction. 2. High schools—Fiction. 3. Schools—Fiction.
4. Conduct of life—Fiction. 5. Dating (Social customs)—Fiction. 6. Brothers and sisters—Fiction.] I. Title.
PZ7.M4256How 2015   2014022683
[Fic]—dc23   CIP
                                                                       AC

Typography by Ellice M. Lee
15 16 17 18 19 CG/RRDH 10 9 8 7 6 5 4 3 2 1
❖
First Edition

I.

Adam Higgs is a loser. That's the first thing you need to know.

2.

It's junior year.

The first day of school. Our boy Adam, five foot—I dunno—six? A hundred and forty pounds. Messy brown hair and a zit on his chin.

First day at Nixon Collegiate, doesn't know a soul.

3.

That pretty girl standing beside Adam? The blonde in the tight shirt?

That's Steph, Adam's sister. She's a freshman. By the end of the day, she'll have about a hundred new Facebook friends.

By the end of the day, Rob Thigpen will offer her a ride home in his daddy's mint twin-turbocharged BMW 335i.

Rob's a junior. He's in Adam's English class. He won't be offering Adam a ride home anytime in this lifetime.

4.

Nixon Collegiate.

You don't know it, but you know it.

You've never been there, but you know exactly the kind of school I'm talking about. Sunny. Clean. Kind of looks like a country club, with a big green lawn in front. Parking lot's so full of late-model imports, they should valet park.

And the girls, man.

Our boy Adam Higgs dawdles as he crosses the front lawn toward Nixon's doors. Takes in the view like a starving man at a Vegas buffet. It's still summertime pretty much, even this far north. That means it's still halter-top season.

Girls everywhere.

Blondes, brunettes, redheads. Tall and small. Short skirts and long legs and tight designer T-shirts. They're camped out on the lawn with their noses in their iPhones; they're pulling into the parking lot in convertible Benzes; they're watching a group of tanned, muscular boys throw a football around.

Steph's watching the boys too.

One of those boys is Rob Thigpen. He's surfer-preppy cool, shaggy blond hair and a pastel polo shirt. He pauses the football game to watch Steph cross the lawn.

Adam's too busy taking in the girls to notice. But the girls aren't returning the favor.

Adam's small. He's unremarkable. His clothes are

off-brand, Walmart.

Girls can smell "loser" a mile away.

Adam's a loser.

He's also a virgin.

Neither is likely to change anytime soon, not here at Nixon.

5.

The second thing you need to know is: Adam Higgs has a history.

This is his first day at Nixon. Freshman year, sophomore year, he went to Riverside, across town. Kind of an average school. Bricks and mortar. Not so many iPhones. *No* BMWs.

He was a loser at Riverside, too—nearly flunked out.

(Not so much because he's stupid. It's more, you know, who *cares?*)

Adam's dad is a decent guy. He worked at the Chrysler plant until the Chrysler plant shut down. Now he sits at home and cashes his measly settlement checks. He has a bad back anyway. Most days, he doesn't get off the couch.

Some days, he doesn't bother with pants.

Adam's mom is an administrative assistant. She works three times harder than her boss and makes about 10 percent of his pay. She doesn't complain. Adam's dad does. Adam's dad has time to complain. It's his luxury. Adam's mom needs the job, though. It's not like her husband's settlement is paying the rent.

6.

Third thing: Adam has an older brother too.

    Adam's brother's name is Sam. Sam Higgs. He's twenty-two years old and he works at the Tim Hortons doughnut shop across from city hall. He lives in an apartment a few blocks from the doughnut shop. Somebody from the hospital got Sam his job.

    (Sam's obsessed with being independent.)

7.

Fourth: Adam's brother is in a wheelchair.

He wasn't always.

Adam's brother was a really good hockey player when he was a teenager, assistant captain of the Riverside school team. Some people thought he could maybe turn pro.

Then this asshole from Nixon hit him into the boards from behind. Sam fell face-first, fucked up his spine.

So much for hockey.

So much for *walking*.

Sam's in a wheelchair now.

8.

Adam goes to visit Sam a couple times a week.

Sometimes they watch movies—*Scarface* is their favorite.

Sometimes, hockey games—

(You would think Sam would kind of have a hate-on for hockey, seeing as it pretty much ruined his life, but not so much. Sam's still the biggest Red Wings fan Adam knows.)

—and sometimes Adam takes Sam down to the river and wheels him along the trail and they look at pretty girls and watch the freighters drift by,

but mostly,

Adam and Sam hang out in Sam's room in Sam's apartment, watching funny videos on YouTube and playing PlayStation, and Adam listens to Sam talk about his glory days in high school.

9.

See, Sam Higgs never had a problem in high school.
(Until the accident.)
He was taller than Adam.
Better-looking.
Athletic.
Sam got his looks from the same lottery-ticket gene pool
as Steph, but Adam?
Adam, not so much.
Adam looks a lot like his dad.
And these days, Adam's dad looks a lot like,

well,

a *loser*.

10.

Sam Higgs could have been a god in high school.

He could have been *the man*.

He was well on his way to *owning* Riverside High.

Sam made the hockey team freshman year.

Sam had scouts watching him as a sophomore.

Sam was dating junior cheerleaders. Going to the right parties.

Sam Higgs was groomed for success.

(Until, well, you know.)

The thing is, if everything had gone the way it was supposed to, Adam is sure that not only would *Sam's* life be different—*his* life would be different too, guaranteed. When your older brother's a hockey star, you have it made. You don't even have to try. You're just a god by association.

But Adam's not a god.

Sam was never *the man*.

Nothing turned out the way it was supposed to.

II.

Now Sam lives in a shitty little apartment. He's still good-looking, and he's funny, and he plays wheelchair basketball, but he's not the man anymore. He's just some guy in a wheelchair.

Sam doesn't tell Adam how unhappy he is, how

cheated

robbed

frustrated

he feels. He doesn't tell Adam how sad he gets when he thinks about the accident and everything that came after it, when he thinks about what a waste his life is, but Adam knows.

Adam can see it.

Adam feels pretty fucking sad about it himself.

12.

Anyway, that's the home life. A mom who busts her ass and a dad who kinda sits there. An older brother who can't walk anymore. And Steph.

Steph is pretty. She's fun. She plays volleyball and served on the activities committee at her middle school. Steph has nearly seven hundred Facebook friends.

Adam has one real-life friend.

Not enough to justify a Facebook account.

Adam's one friend is a guy named Brian O'Donnell. He's a chubby stoner back at Riverside and even his friendship status, most days, is uncertain.

Mostly, Brian's just a dude. He shares his joints with Adam when they cut class. Sometimes they shoot hoops after school. Maybe they eat lunch together. It's not like they're hanging out on weekends, though. No slumber parties. No Xbox. No chasing girls.

They're not BFFs.

Anyway, Brian goes to Riverside, halfway across town. And Adam, by virtue of strange and unhappy circumstance, finds himself at Nixon.

Brian's not around.

Adam's alone.

Nobody at Nixon even knows who he is.

13.

Nixon is weird. Adam figures this out within a couple of days.

Mostly, it's rich kids.

There's Rob Thigpen and his daddy's BMW. There's Paul Nolan, whose parents are doctors. He anchors the swim team.

(Nixon Swim: pride of the school. Undefeated at Regionals the past twenty years. Paul Nolan: Nixon swim god.)

There's Alton Di Sousa, starting point guard on the basketball team. Still a junior, but already seeing offers from Division One schools.

There's Jessie McGill. She's dating Paul Nolan. Tall, gorgeous brunette. She looks like that movie star, you know the one. The one who looks like the pop singer.

There's Leanne Grayson and Janie Ng. The original BFFs. Their dads work together, some biotech firm. They vacation together in Maui.

And then there's Sara Bryant. Sara Bryant rolls into school every day in a cherry-red Porsche convertible. Her dad's the personal-injury lawyer you see on all the billboards. Big, cheesy smile. Thousand-dollar suit. A full office of rich mahogany and leather-bound books in the background.

("Sam Bryant: Help me to help you win the settlement you deserve.")

Sara *freaking* Bryant.

And she's beautiful—your prototypical California blonde,

somehow marooned up here in the Rust Belt. But not for long, though.

She's going to be in movies.

Everyone knows it.

She already has an agent and everything.

Sara *freaking* Bryant, it turns out, is Adam Higgs's lab partner. Physics, second period. This would be good news, except that she sits beside him and texts on her iPhone and files her nails and does everything except talk to Adam Higgs.

She doesn't even know his name.

But Adam knows her name. He knows every popular kid's name. And every day when Sara Bryant breezes into physics and sits down beside him, he watches her and waits. Waits for her to notice him. Waits for a smile. A kind word.

Anything.

He's still waiting.

14.

How Adam Higgs came to be at Nixon Collegiate with all these rich kids:

Easy.

His dad was laid off.

His dad was laid off and his measly settlement checks couldn't cover the mortgage, even with Adam's mom busting her ass.

Adam's parents owned a nice house. East side of town. Three bedrooms upstairs. A finished basement. An aboveground pool and parking for two cars.

Too expensive.

The real estate agent didn't even try to sound hopeful. "Bad timing," he told Adam's mom. "The plant's closing. Nobody's buying houses right now."

What are you going to do, though?

They took a bath.

Packed up the nice East End house and migrated westward, to Remington Park. Sounds decent, right?

Wrong.

I mean, it's not dangerous or anything. Just, you know, the houses are small.

Really small.

One-story bungalow thingies with one bathroom and

shitty little kitchens. Peeling linoleum. Paper-thin walls.

Adam can hear his mom and dad arguing—

(About Sam, mostly, because:

- Adam's mom doesn't think Sam should live on his own, but:

- Adam's dad says there's no room to keep him in the house, and:

- anyway it's not like he's *completely* a cripple, and:

- this is usually the point where Adam's mom starts to cry.)

He can hear Steph's awful pop music, loud and clear. And she's wearing headphones, two rooms away.

Every morning, there's a line outside the bathroom. The hot water runs out about two showers in. You're third in the shower, you're freezing.

Remington Park.

The new 'hood.

Just so happens, a couple streets in the Park fall into the Nixon school zone.

Just so happens, a few poor kids each year get signed up for Nixon.

Just so happens, Adam Higgs is one of them.

15.

Sam doesn't have much to do but work at the doughnut shop and think about how great his life was back when he could still walk.

He's always talking about how amazing high school used to be. How every year at Riverside just got better.

The parties.

The girls.

The relentless adulation.

"It's unbelievable," he tells Adam. "Freshman and sophomore years were okay and all, man, but junior year is where it really gets dope. You'll see."

Adam just laughs. "Yeah, right."

"I'm so fucking jealous of you," Sam tells Adam. "I could have been king of that school."

Adam just laughs.

Sam laughs too. But it's kind of a hollow laugh.

16.

It gets to Adam, you know? It just feels like such a waste.

    (After the accident, Sam:

        - left Riverside

        - spent months in the hospital

        - spent *years* in rehab

        - stopped going to parties

        - stopped dating pretty girls

        - stopped *winning*.)

    (Hell, even his friends stopped coming around eventually.)

    And meanwhile, here's Adam, as able-bodied as can be, a loser. Two years of high school wasted. Another two years left to waste.

    Adam looks at Sam and feels like they're supposed to trade places. Like the universe would be a better place if Sam Higgs was a junior at Nixon and Adam was just some mope selling coffee at a drive-thru—

    (Cream and sugar?)

    And the worst part is, Adam knows Sam feels the same way.

17.

Adam Higgs is sick of being a loser.

That's the last thing you need to know.

18.

So, some kids, they get sick of being a loser, they take things to the extreme. Maybe they bring a gun to school. Or maybe they hurt themselves.

(It's not like Adam has never thought about it.)

Real talk? High school is hard. It's hard for everyone. It's especially hard when you're the kid nobody likes, when you're getting your ass kicked by some Neanderthal every day, when you can't get a date to save your life.

When the only way to make it through the day is to cut out and smoke a jay in peace somewhere, and even then you're watching your ass for the vice principal because he already suspended you once this year and the next time they're talking about kicking you out.

So yeah, Adam's thought about going drastic. Couple problems with that strategy, though:

a) He doesn't really want to hurt anyone.

b) He doesn't really want to be dead.

That destructive shit, it's the wrong vibe. Not even an option. It's like, you're thirsty, you don't blow up the water fountain. You sure as hell don't slit your wrists.

You're thirsty? You fucking fight your way up to that water fountain and you *drink*, motherfucker. You quench your thirst.

Adam's thirsty.

He's ready to drink.

19.

Maybe you know that movie *Scarface*.

(If not, you have homework tonight.)

It's old, but it's worth it. And if you're into hip-hop, you should know that every rapper's self-styled rags-to-riches mythology mirrors that movie *to a* T.

We all want to be Tony Montana.

You already know that our boy Adam Higgs doesn't have many friends. And what do you do when it's summertime and school's out and your only friend—

(and we use the term loosely)

—is a Pizza Hut delivery driver working nights?

You watch movies, I guess.

You hang with your crippled older brother.

You play Xbox.

Sometimes you jerk off.

Adam Higgs sees Sam twice a week. Adam plays a lot of Xbox. He's never had a girlfriend, so you can figure out how much jerking off he does. And when he's not playing video games or jerking off, he watches a lot of movies. He watches a lot of *Scarface*.

And there's this scene in *Scarface*, right at the beginning (no spoilers), where Al Pacino arrives in Miami and it's beautiful, man—a land of opportunity. Women, wealth, everything a guy could want.

Except it seems like the whole world's against him. Nobody wants to hang with him, give him a job. The women laugh at him.

He doesn't blow up the city.

He doesn't walk away.

He sure as hell doesn't slit his wrists.

No, man, he doesn't do any of those things. He goes to work. Little by little, he takes over the city.

The world is yours.

Say hello to my little friend.

All that jazz.

Fuck suicide. *Scarface* is the answer.

20.

Adam Higgs walks into Nixon on the first day of junior year and nobody knows his name. Nobody knows a damn thing about him except that he's another pipsqueak with acne and shitty taste in clothing.

(And his sister's, like, the hottest freshman girl in the school.)

But forget about Steph for a moment.

See Nixon how Adam sees it:

That long, lush expanse of front lawn, the whitewashed, country-club facade behind it. It's a beautiful, sunny day, not a cloud in the sky, and the flag atop the flagpole is new and crisp, and all you need is a decent soundtrack and this is a killer tracking shot for the movie.

To the right of the school is the football field, the big Nixon *N* on the scoreboard, a bunch of cheerleaders already working on their routines. To the left is the parking lot, all gleaming chrome and cherry paint.

And everywhere—lawn, school, field, and lot—are the students.

Stoners.

Nerds.

Athletes.

Actors.

Band kids.

Skaters.

B-girls.

Baseheads.

Punks.

Post-punks.

Goths.

Intellectuals.

Aesthetes.

Gamers.

Smokers.

Hipsters.

Dancers.

Thugs.

Students. Everywhere. In clusters and groups, passing cigarettes and iPhones back and forth. Throwing balls around, Frisbees. Couples holding hands, making out, copping feels.

Normal kids, most of them. Decent kids. Average. They have friends, most of them. They have boyfriends and girlfriends. They go on dates to the movies and shop at the mall, swipe booze from their parents on weekends, break curfew and throw up in the neighbors' azalea bushes.

Normal kids.

But among them walk *the gods*.

You know their names already. Rob Thigpen. Paul Nolan. Alton Di Sousa.

Jessie McGill. Leanne Grayson. Janie Ng.

Sara *freaking* Bryant.

They jog after the football with that lazy, confident air. They wear the hypest fashions. They have perfect teeth, perfect tans, perfect hair. They *are* perfect.

There's not a girl at Nixon who doesn't want to fuck Paul Nolan. There's not a guy who wouldn't give his left arm to be

Rob Thigpen. These are the popular kids. These are the charmed ones.

These are the people Sam would have become.

(Until the accident.)

These are the exact polar opposites of a loser like Adam Higgs.

21.

So that's what our boy sees when he walks up to Nixon on the first day of junior year.

Adam is two years into a four-year high school career. He's wasted two years already at Riverside High getting spat on and shat on by the popular kids. He's sick of it. And he's sick of having to lie when Sam asks him about school.

("You dating any girls yet?")

("Been to any parties?")

("Well, are you making any friends, at least?")

(Uhhhh, no.)

(Sorry, Sam.)

(Oh, yeah. Tons. *sarcasm*)

The point is, Adam's sick of underachieving. He's sick of feeling like a waste of space and energy. He's sick of Sam looking at him like he's a failure, like Sam's the hungriest guy in the world, but it's Adam who's sitting at that Vegas buffet.

Adam wants to be popular more than he wants anything in the world, and not just for him, but for Sam, too, to maybe give a little bit of meaning to Sam's life, maybe cheer him up a little.

Adam's been thinking about this a lot. He's been watching a lot of *Scarface*. He's been listening to a lot of hip-hop. He rolls into Nixon like he's Tony Montana on day one in Miami—

(some runt)

(some loser)

(some funny-looking nobody)

—looking around at a world of opportunity and calculating just how he can make it all his own.

Adam's ready to make Nixon his own.

He's ready to make Sam proud of him.

He's ready to claim what should have been his all along.

He's ready to become a god.

22.

So how do you take over a high school?

(*Take over?* Sounds violent. Invasive. Destructive connotations. Let's rephrase: How do you *win* at high school?)

Winning.

Like an Xbox game: Unlocking achievements. Racking up a high score. Attaining god mode. Basically becoming THE MAN.

Winning.

("Junior year's where it all begins, man.")

Adam doesn't sleep at all that first week at Nixon. He racks his brain, trying to work out a Tony Montana strategy, and every day that passes feels like a waste. Unforgivable. It's time to take action.

The popular kids are rich. They're good-looking or they're good at something. Sports. Music. None of this describes Adam.

He's never played an instrument.

He's terrible at sports. (*Airrrrrrr-ball.*)

And he's not rich. Not in the slightest.

Adam figures he's probably not going to make the football team. He's not much of a swimmer, either. And he doesn't have a guitar. But at least he can *look* like a popular kid.

Look like a popular kid, *be* a popular kid.

Dress for the job you want.

Pick up the swag.

Hashtag YOLO.

At the very least, trash the fucking mom jeans.

Okay, so step one: Adam gets a job.

23.

Brian O'Donnell is pretty sure he can hook Adam up with a job at Pizza Hut.

"Working in the kitchen or something," he says. "You want?"

Adam shrugs. Making pizza isn't glamorous, but none of the cool stores in the mall will even call him back, not with that hair and that outfit—

(and don't even ask about the résumé, because it's not like Abercrombie & Fitch gives a *fuck* about thirteen-year-old Adam Higgs's *PennySaver* route)

—and it's not like Adam has the connections to, say, land a job at his doctor parents' office, filing paperwork and eating candy bars for twenty bucks an hour like some of the popular kids, so he just shrugs and tells Brian, "How hard can it be to make pizzas?"

Short answer: it's not hard.

Shorter answer: immaterial.

The manager doesn't want Adam making pizzas. He wants Adam bussing tables. Not that Adam cares. Same wages. Less responsibility. Less potential for cataclysmic screwups.

So Adam works. Three or four nights a week, he clears tables for minimum wage. Pizza trays, soda glasses. He cleans baby puke off a high chair. It isn't glamorous. It isn't even particularly lucrative. But it gets Adam out of his mom jeans.

Step one: achieved.

24.

Abercrombie.
Aéropostale.
American Apparel.
Armani Exchange.
Banana Republic.
Billabong.
Burberry.
Campus Crew.
Cheap Monday.
Club Monaco.
Gap.
Gucci.
Guess.
H&M.
Hollister.
J.Crew.
Lacoste.
Levi's.
LRG.
Naked & Famous.
Nudie Jeans.
Pure Blue.
Ralph Lauren.
Rag & Bone.

Topshop.

True Religion.

Zara.

Yeah, you aren't buying much of that on those Pizza Hut wages. But Adam hits the mall anyway. Cashes his first paycheck. Picks up a couple shirts and a new pair of jeans and bam, the paycheck's exhausted. Barely enough left over for a Happy Meal.

It's a start.

Adam lies awake all night. The proverbial tossing and turning. Can't focus his mind, keeps looking over at his new gear hanging on the doorknob, just waiting to be worn. Wakes up the next day and pulls on the new jeans, the fresh polo, and rolls into math class, first period—

(The school year at Nixon: First semester, four classes, September to January. Second semester, four new classes, February to June.)

—and right away, this kid beside him, Darren something, looks over and gives him a nod.

"Hey, man," Darren says. "Sweet shirt."

Darren's an okay guy. Kinda bland. Kinda average. An okay guy, anyway. And he noticed Adam's new clothes, which is cool.

Adam gives Darren a nod back. "Thanks," he says. "I just picked it up yesterday."

"Looks sharp," Darren says. The math teacher, Hawkins, walks into the room. Darren and Adam watch him fiddle with the attendance sheet. Then Darren leans over again. "You going to Sara Bryant's party this weekend?"

Whoa.

Double-take.

Party?

"I don't know yet," Adam says, shrugging, nonchalant.

"Are you going?"

Darren shrugs too. "Maybe," he says. "I might have plans that night, though."

"Yeah, I feel you," Adam says.

Darren leans closer. "Okay, truth? I don't even know where Sara Bryant lives. I figured you might know or something."

Adam debates this. *Bluff or no?* "Nah." He shakes his head. "I have no idea."

The bell rings. Hawkins clears his throat. Starts in on the lesson: sine, cosine, tangent.

Adam isn't paying attention. He's thinking about the party.

It's just about all he can think about.

25.

Sam's eyes light up when Adam mentions the party.

"Oh yeah," he says. "The parties are where it all goes down, buddy. You have to go."

You *have* to go.

You just *have* to.

26.

You probably figured this out already, but,

                                 our boy doesn't get to many parties.

      I mean, birthday parties? Yeah, back in the day. Cake and ice cream and balloons and shit, sure. Someone's backyard, a swimming pool, McDonald's, Chuck E. Cheese's.

      Parties, though?

      Like, *real parties?*

      Kegs and red plastic cups and sloppy make-out sessions, cops and bongs and hookups?

      Nah, man. Only on TV.

      Never in real life, not for a guy like Adam. The old Adam, anyway. Riverside Adam. Adam 1.0.

      Nixon Adam, though, he's Adam 2.0: Bigger and Badder. He's changing his life. Already got the fresh gear to prove it. So you can see why he's pumped for this party.

      And he's pumped, all right.

      Second period, physics class. Sara Bryant breezes in—

      (a girl like Sara Bryant—she doesn't *walk* anywhere. She sure doesn't *run*.

      No, man, Sara Bryant *breezes*.

      Like she's in a different world.

      A more advanced plane of existence.

      Like the concept of time doesn't apply to life-forms on her level, like she's evolved beyond your petty concerns.

She *breezes.*

She knows Mr. Powers, the physics teacher, is going to hold up the class until she's sitting down anyway.

(And he totally will; he'll stand at the front of the room and let his eyes linger on that short skirt, those long legs, just like every other guy in the class—and half the girls.) Sara Bryant *breezes* into physics class, my friend.

Like she's better than you.

Because she is.)

So Mr. Powers waits until Sara Bryant is settled in beside Adam to start the lesson (Newton's Laws).

And Adam curses because he got here early, *rushed* over here like a regular chump, like a loser, to make sure he caught Sara Bryant before the lesson started.

(Forgetting, of course, that Sara Bryant operates by her own clock, and she's never on time.)

So he can't ask her about the party. Not before class, anyway. And he has to sit through Mr. Powers's very long, boring lecture about gravity and acceleration, glancing across the lab workstation at Sara Bryant every couple of minutes, listening to her giggle as she texts with Jessie McGill across the room, catching a whiff every now and then of the Marc Jacobs perfume she wears every day like it's her personal scent—

(which it might as well be)

—waiting, just *waiting*, to ask about the party.

And finally the bell rings, cutting Powers off midsentence, and everyone's on their feet and stuffing books into their backpacks, and Sara Bryant has her nose in her iPhone and she's standing and *breezing* away and it's Friday, damn it, and Sara's not in any more of Adam's classes and he needs an answer *now*, and he kind of panics and gets desperate and just says her name—

"Sara"

—except it comes out more like a shout and half the kids nearby turn and look at him, this weirdo new kid who dresses funny and never says much and suddenly has the *gall* to talk to *Sara freaking Bryant* in that tone of voice.

Sara stops. She looks back at Adam. Cocks her head.

"*Pardon?*"

Adam knows he's screwed up.

Everyone's watching.

"Hey," he says. Softer. Not quite so desperate. "What's up?"

It doesn't help. Everyone's still watching. And Sara Bryant is not impressed. She arches an eyebrow. Doesn't say a word.

Shit.

Adam can't even look at those piercing blue eyes. "You, uh, having a party tonight?"

Whispers all around. Someone laughs. Adam feels his face go red. *Not cool. Not cool at all.*

Sara Bryant frowns. "Who'd you hear that from?"

"Uh"—Adam pauses—"around. It's around."

"Around where? The school?" Sara Bryant casts her gaze across the classroom. Instantly, eyes are averted. Kids pretend to go about their business. "Who knows about this?"

Nobody answers.

She looks at Adam again.

"Everyone," Adam says.

"Jesus Christ." She pulls out her phone and starts texting, rapid-fire, furious. Fingernails rapping like bullets against the iPhone glass. "It's not a party," she says. "It's a *get-together*. I'm having a few people over, that's all."

Adam nods. "Oh."

She punches at her phone. Looks up. "Dude, I don't even know who you are."

"Adam," Adam says. "My name is Adam Higgs."

"Well, *Adam*, just so it's clear," she says, "this party? Is *invite-only*. And you're not invited."

Then she *breezes* out of the room.

And that's that.

27.

Embarrassment.

Mortification.

Social suicide.

The whole grade knows who Adam Higgs is now. He's not just some anonymous guy. Some new kid with a zit on his chin.

No.

He's the weirdo who got shut down by Sara Bryant in physics class.

He's worse than anonymous. He's a LOSER.

Certified.

Guaranteed.

Grade A.

And just when he's thinking it can't get any worse?

It does.

28.

Saturday night.

(Because if you think our boy Adam made it to that party, you need to go back and reread that last bit.)

Adam's working at Pizza Hut. Clearing tables. Some snot-nosed ten-year-old's snot-nosed birthday party.

(He's in a bad mood. See above.)

There's giggling from across the restaurant. Adam looks up and—

(*Oh shit*)

—the gang's all here:

Paul Nolan.

Janie Ng.

Leanne Grayson.

Alton Di Sousa.

Rob Thigpen.

Jessie McGill.

And, yes—

Sara *freaking* Bryant.

The gods. The goddesses.

They're all here, huddled around Leanne's phone. Flipping through pictures. Jostling for a view. Laughing.

Basically, living the charmed life.

"Best. Party. Ever," says Paul Nolan.

"I'm so fucking hungover," says Rob Thigpen.

"You drank half a fifth of vodka, you moron," says Janie Ng, giggling. "What did you think would happen?"

"I can't believe how many people showed up," Leanne Grayson tells Sara. "Are your parents going to be cool with it?"

"Long as they didn't see it on the news," says Alton.

Sara smacks him. "*Shut up.* It wasn't on the news." She looks around the table. "And you assholes better help me clean up before they get home."

Groans. Laughter. Leanne passes her phone around. The gods all stare at the screen, their eyes goggling. More laughter. Alton and Rob Thigpen slap five.

Adam stands there and tries not to look obvious. It doesn't work. Sara makes him. "*Oh shit,*" she whispers. "*That's the guy.*"

The gods stop with the laughing. With the slapping five. They all look at Sara.

Sara's not looking at the phone.

She's looking at our boy.

Our boy, Adam Higgs, loser, where he stands across the restaurant, hands-deep in a bucket of dirty pizza plates and empty soda cups, still clearing that snotty ten-year-old's table, trying not to let on that he's listening.

Trying not to let on how pissed

upset

angry

depressed

he is that Sara Bryant's little get-together turned into the biggest party of the year, and *he wasn't invited.*

(And now Sara Bryant is looking at him.)

(And the rest of the gods are staring at him, too.)

He's blushing.

He can feel it.

The whole restaurant gets about fifteen degrees hotter.
He's screwed.

For a moment, nothing happens. Then Paul Nolan speaks up. "Hey, man," he says. "C'mere."

Adam hesitates. Like a serial killer on death row when the cell door opens that final time. He knows he has to walk, and to walk means to die.

They all walk, eventually.

Adam is no exception.

He walks like his legs have a mind of their own. Crosses the restaurant to the gods' table. Leaves the dirty dishes behind.

Janie Ng looks him up and down. "Hi there," she says. She giggles.

"Hi," Adam says.

Leanne Grayson nudges her, and they both collapse into laughter. Adam stands there and takes it. Wishes he was dead.

"Hey, man," Paul Nolan says. "What's your name again?"

Adam clears his throat. "Adam," he says. "Adam Higgs."

"You missed the party, Adam," Jessie McGill says. "Biggest party all year. Where were *you*?"

"Biggest party all year," Rob Thigpen says. "Your sister was there. You had better things to do, though?"

Something about the way Rob Thigpen says it, the way the whole table laughs. The way he leers when he mentions Steph. The cocky smirk on his face—

(Something about Rob Thigpen, period.)

(The guy is an asshole.)

(He looks like the kind of guy who spends his summers on the Kennedy compound in, like, Martha's Vineyard or whatever. Gleaming white teeth, perfect hair. His daddy's BMW. Rob Thigpen is a spoiled brat.)

(But there's something else, too, something Adam can't

put his finger on. Something about Rob Thigpen that makes his Spidey sense tingle.

Could be just that he's probably hooking up with Steph.

Could be something else entirely.

Adam's not sure yet. But it bugs him.)

Right now, Adam would give just about anything to knock that smirk off of Rob Thigpen's face.

Except he knows he could never actually do it.

Because all he *really* wants is to be the one smirking, for a change. To be the one at the table. A god.

He knows he wants to win.

And right now, Adam's losing.

Adam doesn't do anything. He stands there in front of them and laughs along, like he's in on the joke. Like a jester in the king's court.

"Guess I had something else going on," he says.

"Like *what?*" Sara Bryant's voice is breaking now, hysterical. *"Cleaning dirty pizza dishes?"*

Everyone laughs. Funniest joke ever. Adam keeps his smile pasted. What else can he do?

"But seriously, though . . ." Rob Thigpen waits for the table to calm down. Fixes Adam with a stare, earnest. "It's great to meet you, Adam," he says. "I just have one question."

"Yeah," Adam says. "What's up?"

Thigpen pauses.

Wait for it. . . .

Wait for it. . . .

"I was wondering—" Thigpen picks up his glass and rattles the ice. "Could you get me another Pepsi, man?"

Laughter.

Applause.

Drop curtain.

End scene.

29.

Later that weekend, Adam finds Steph.

Asks her: "You went to Sara Bryant's party on Friday?"

Steph's texting. She doesn't have an iPhone either—

(doesn't even have a job)

—but she has a cell phone and it's better than nothing—

(which is exactly what Adam has).

Steph stops texting. She looks up at Adam. "Oh yeah," she says. "Rob said he saw you at Pizza Hut yesterday. Great service, by the way."

Adam brushes this off. "Why didn't you tell me you were going?"

"What, to the party?" Steph makes a face. "Maybe because I didn't know I had to check in with you every time I did something."

"They're juniors. They're in *my* grade."

"Yeah, but Rob's *my* friend."

Adam thinks about Steph riding home in Rob's daddy's BMW. The hugs good-bye. Rob's wandering hands.

Some *friend*, he thinks.

"You have your own friends, Adam," Steph's saying. "Who's that fat guy you always get high with?"

"He lives halfway across town. And he's not fat."

Steph shrugs. "So get a bus pass. Don't put this party thing on me. You can't get invited, that's your problem."

"Yeah," Adam says. "Whatever."

She looks at him. "Just quit trying to force it," she says. "What's so great about hanging out with Rob Thigpen and his buddies, anyway?"

Adam looks at her.

Tries to think of an answer.

Something witty and all-encompassing.

Fails.

"Everything," he says finally. "Just everything."

30.

"So did you make it to that party, or what?"

Sam and Adam are watching the hockey game on TV. It's the intermission and Adam is getting more Doritos from Sam's cupboard. He pauses when Sam asks the question. Keeps his nose in the cupboards, pretends like he's rummaging.

"Uh, no," he says. "Had to work."

"Shit," Sam says. "Really? You couldn't get the night off?"

Adam turns around. Shrugs. "Guess they needed me or something. Lame, right?"

"What about after?" Sam says. "The Hut's not open that late. And parties don't really start until like eleven or midnight anyway. You could have just swung by after work."

Adam pretends like he's looking for a bowl for the Doritos. "Yeah," he says. "I know."

Sam doesn't say anything for a long time, and the TV just blares some stupid car commercial, and Adam can tell that Sam's looking at him, watching him pour the Doritos into the big bowl, waiting for him to come back to the couch and sit down.

Adam takes his time, but it's not long enough.

Sam's still looking at Adam when he sits down. Looking at him like he'd do anything for a day in Adam's shoes.

(*Take them*, Adam thinks.)

"You don't like parties, huh?" Sam says after a while. "That's cool."

"No," Adam says. "That's not it. I do, I just—"

He stops.

(*I'm just a loser*, he thinks.)

"I was tired," he says.

Sam sighs. "You gotta get out and do this stuff, Adam," he says. "Do the fun stuff while you can. It's not going to be like this forever."

Adam looks into the bowl of Doritos, like that toxic blend of monosodium glutamate and delicious chemical cheese can save him.

"It's not always going to be this way," Sam says. "It's not always going to be just parties and girls. It gets taken from you before you even know what's happening."

Sam pauses. "Hey," he says. "Look at me."

Adam wrenches his gaze from the bowl and looks at Sam. His withered, useless legs. His shitty apartment with its millions of safety bars and emergency nurse buttons. The wheelchair with the squeaky wheel in the corner.

"Even if you don't fuck around and get paralyzed, man, it's not going to be high school forever. Sooner or later, you're going to have to go out into the real world.

"And the real world?" Sam says. "The real world fucking sucks, Adam. You have to get out there and do it. You have to take what you can—everything you can—*while you can*. Understand?"

Adam does understand. He wants it. He wants to take it, just like Sam is saying. He just doesn't know how, exactly.

It's fucking frustrating.

31.

Monday morning. Math class.

"Looked for you at Sara's party," Darren says, sliding into the seat beside Adam. "You didn't make it?"

Adam closes his eyes.

It's too early for this.

"Like two hundred people showed up," Darren says. "There was a Facebook blast and everything. It was crazy."

"Yeah," Adam says. "So I hear."

"What's your cell number?" Darren says. "Next time, I'll text you."

Good luck, Adam thinks.

Then he thinks:

I need a cell phone.

More $$$.

More Pizza Hut.

More dirty dishes.

Then Adam thinks about Sam in his apartment, staring at the TV, thinking about all the lost chances he never got, wondering why his little brother is such a big fucking pussy.

"When's the next one?" he asks Darren. "I'll be there for sure."

"Next party?" Darren frowns. "Dunno. They don't happen all *that* often. Man, you should have seen it. Janie Ng and

Leanne Grayson—"

"There's gotta be something," Adam says. "What's going down this weekend?"

Darren shakes his head. "I dunno, man. Probably the usual. I guess everyone's going to Crash."

And just like that, Adam knows what he has to do.

32.

Crash.

33.

Downtown is a wasteland.

Empty storefronts.

Second-run movie theaters.

Sketchy restaurants.

The bus station.

Homeless men.

And Crash.

("In my day it was Voodoo," Sam says. "The crazy shit I got up to in there, Adam, you don't even know.")

It's not Voodoo anymore, though.

Voodoo's still around, Voodoo and a million other little bars and nightclubs, but we don't care about them. The Nixon kids don't even think about them. Crash is the spot now.

Crash is the hype joint.

Crash is where the gods hang out.

It's a dive.

It's a shithole.

It's a dank, sweaty room with a DJ and strobe lighting and a couple of stripper poles in the corner.

It ain't Studio 54, or even CBGB. It's just Crash.

As in: Crash and burn.

As in: Car crash.

As in: I'm wasted, man, let's find somewhere to (Crash).

The bouncers are corrupt. They hardly check IDs. The drinks are dirt cheap and the clientele is hookup friendly. Paul Nolan's been known to score university girls there. Leanne Grayson picked up a hockey player. Rumor has it Alton Di Sousa got with some drunk Miss America wannabe in a bathroom stall a couple weeks back.

No one batted an eye.

It's *that* kind of joint.

Crash.

34.

Friday night, Adam heads for Crash.

It's a long walk from Remington Park—

(Adam thinks: *I really need a car.*

More $$$.

More Pizza Hut.

More dirty dishes.)

—but the bus service is spotty this time of night and it's not like Adam has the cash for a cab.

And nobody—*nobody*—gets a ride to Crash in their mom's beat-up old LeBaron.

So he walks. Dodges douchebags in Camaros cruising the strip. Drunk girls in tube dresses shivering in the October air, scarfing down greasy pizza. Crash sits on the end of the block like an oasis, a little neon box with a long line out front, a throbbing bass, and a loud, laughing mob.

Adam hesitates when he sees it.

Almost turns around and walks home again.

Then he thinks about Steph and that sly little smile. Thinks about Sam. Thinks about another two years as a loser.

Fuck that.

Hashtag seize the day.

Adam squares his shoulders. Wades into the mix.

35.

Steph is at the front of the line, clinging to Rob Thigpen's arm. Sara Bryant and Paul Nolan are beside them. Jessie McGill's flirting with the bouncer.

Adam ducks back, suddenly aware of:

- His ten-dollar Walmart haircut.
- The pimple on his cheek.
- His crappy Payless shoes.
- His absolute loner status.

(There are people everywhere, all of them drunk, all of them happy, all—*absolutely all*—of them having fun. None of them are alone. The minute they notice Adam standing by himself, he's shark bait.)

Adam watches Steph and Rob and Sara and Paul and Jessie *breeze* into the club. As predicted, the bouncer doesn't ask them for ID. They just disappear through the front doors, into the strobe lights, the fog, the laughter, the screams, the music.

Adam walks to the back of the line.

He's nervous.

He kinda wants to go home.

But he's thinking about Sara Bryant's party last weekend and how everybody was there, even Darren—

(who isn't even that popular)

—and just about the only junior at Nixon who didn't get an invite was, hey, Adam Higgs. He's not going back and telling

Sam he bugged out again—couldn't even make it through the front door.

So.

He walks to the back of the long line and stands there, alone, staring through the club's foggy windows at the chaos inside—nervous, yeah, but hell, a little excited, too.

There are girls in there, man.

Drunk girls.

In tight dresses.

Adam waits a *long* time.

(Can you blame him? He's a virgin. He's never even kissed a girl. And if history has established any concrete human laws, it's that men will suffer anything if there's a chance they'll get some action out of it.)

So he waits.

Finally, he's at the front of the line. The bouncer lets a crowd of girls through and clips his rope back into place and looks Adam over.

Holds out his hand.

Says: "ID."

Adam blinks. "Uh, what?"

The bouncer sighs. "ID, man. Identification. Proof of age. Show me something."

"What?" Adam looks around. "You didn't ask anyone else for ID."

"They look legal," the bouncer says. "You don't. You have ID or not?"

The line's jostling behind Adam now. People are getting antsy.

(*Who's this loser holding up the line?*)

Adam digs in his wallet, trying to bluff. The bouncer watches him. The line shoves him forward.

He's got nothing.

He's about to say something to the bouncer, beg him, *plead* with him to let him in the club, when:

Sara and Paul and Jessie and Rob—

(yeah, and Steph)

—stagger out of the club, laughing, shoving, hugging, all of them wasted. They *breeze* past Adam and then—

(*shit*)

—Sara notices Adam. Smiles, wide, her eyes swimming. "*Heeeey*," she says. "Adam, right? That's your name?"

Someone pushes past Adam and into the club. In the back of Adam's mind, he realizes the bouncer didn't check *their* IDs—

(*asshole*)

—but he doesn't care. Fuck the club. Fuck Crash. Sara *freaking* Bryant remembers his name.

"Hey, Sara." He steps out of line toward her. "How's it going?"

Sara reaches out her arms. Wobbles a little. Steadies herself. "I'm so drunk," she says. Then she looks at Adam. "What are you *doing*? Why aren't you *inside*?"

Adam looks back at the (asshole) bouncer. Shrugs. "Couldn't get in," he says. "Where are you guys going now?"

Paul and Jessie and Rob and—

(yeah, and Steph)

—are already in a cab. "*Sara*," Rob calls out the open door. "Get your ass over here."

"We're going to Paul's place," Sara says. "After-party."

"Nice," Adam says. "Cool."

Rob Thigpen climbs out of the cab. Grabs Sara by the waist and drags her to the curb. Looks back at Adam. "Cab's full," he says, shrugging. "Sorry, Pizza Man."

"Pizza Man!" Sara shrieks. "Adam, you're a pizza man!"

"I guess so," Adam says.

Paul Nolan steps out of the cab. Picks up Sara and hauls her inside. "Say good night, Sara," he tells her.

Sara sits. "Good night, Sara," she slurs. "Good night, Pizza Man."

Paul closes the door. The cab speeds off. Adam stands on the curb, watching it go.

Watching Steph in the passenger seat, staring straight ahead.

Like she doesn't know him at all.

36.

Nightmares.

This whole Pizza Man thing, it could be a disaster.

An earthquake.

Volcano.

A nuclear bomb.

Adam knows how this story goes. "Pizza Man" catches on. Soon the whole school picks up on it. Not too long after, Rob Thigpen takes his lunch money.

Paul Nolan puts his head in a toilet and flushes.

Adam Higgs becomes a punch line. A walking joke. And he'll have to pretend to laugh about it while the whole goddamn school tortures him, while they look at him and point and whisper, "Pizza Man," like he's a leper or something.

He's been down this road before. It's not pretty.

This is what keeps him awake all weekend.

It's what keeps him locked in his room, hiding out from his parents and—yeah, from Steph.

(*Especially* from Steph).

Adam's shot is blown, his opportunity wasted. He'll be a loser forever now, and Sam will smell the stink of failure on his clothes like BO.

Sam will hate him for blowing this shot. For not even giving him a couple of years of crazy high-school exploits to live through vicariously.

Pizza Man.

Adam can see the future, and the future is bleak.

It's a long,

       brutal

              weekend.

37.

As he's lying awake Sunday night, though,
      tangled in sheets,
            Adam realizes
                    it's not so bad.
See, Tony Montana—
      (*Scarface*, remember?)
                —he was insulted too. He was
                    picked on
                    laughed at
                    rejected
                    kicked to the curb
                    and
      he still took over Miami.
      He still *won*.
      Adam's going to win too. He just has to get back on his
feet.
      Fast.

38.

So, Monday afternoon, our boy rides the bus out to Brian O'Donnell's house on the east end of town.

Brian's dad is an accountant or something. He lives in a new suburb, a pretty nice house. A house like Adam's family used to have, before his dad got laid off.

Adam knocks on Brian's door and Brian comes out and they walk to the park and smoke up. Adam tells Brian about life at Nixon Collegiate.

"It's like a private school," he says. "Everyone's parents are doctors and lawyers, and, like, rich. I can't keep up."

"*Snobs.*" Brian takes a hit from the joint. "Everybody at Nixon's a snob."

"Does it still count as being a snob if you really are better than everyone else?" Adam says.

Brian passes him the joint. "That's bullshit, man. They're not better."

"I just need a way in," Adam says. "I'm sick of being background noise."

"Forget those guys. None of it's real, anyway. In a couple years we'll be out of school and none of this will matter."

Adam shakes his head. "No. I've been a loser my whole life. I'm sick of it." He passes the joint back. "I just need to make a change."

Brian takes another hit. Looks out across the park and

exhales. "Anyway," he says. "How's your brother? He still living in that place downtown?"

"Yeah," Adam says. "He'll probably be there forever. He needs a fucking nurse to come by and help him whenever he wants to take a bath."

Brian shakes his head. "Imagine if that was your life," he says. "I don't know if I could do it, man."

"Yeah," Adam says. "Me either."

They smoke in silence for a while. Then Brian finishes the joint. Crushes it beneath his shoe. "They're not just going to wake up and, you know, *like* you," he says finally. "Those Nixon kids? You want to fit in? You have to earn it."

"How? I can't afford all the clothes and the phones and stuff," Adam says. "I don't have a BMW. I can't—"

"It's not about the *stuff*." Brian looks at Adam. "Look, you're a nobody. I'm sorry, but there it is."

"Yeah," Adam says. "I fucking know."

"You want them to respect you, you have to get their attention. Demonstrate value somehow."

Makes sense, Adam thinks.

Demonstrate value.

But how?

"I could phone in a bomb threat," he says. "We'd all get the day off school."

Brian nods. "Not bad. It's dangerous. Dangerous is sexy. It won't last, though. A week later, they'll forget you again."

Adam thinks some more.

Nothing.

He looks at Brian. "So what do I do?"

Brian shrugs. "I don't know, man. But if you really want this, you're gonna have to go big."

39.

Go big.

    Adam knows Brian's right.

    You don't get to be the boss without taking a few chances.

You don't win by playing it safe.

    Pizza men don't earn respect.

    Go big.

    Or go home.

40.

Here is how Adam Higgs begins to take over Nixon Collegiate.
    (Whoops—
    there's that phrase again,
    Take over.)
    Here is how Adam Higgs begins to win at high school:
        It's an accident.
            (But not really.)

41.

Mr. Powers—

(You remember Mr. Powers. He's the physics teacher who's always checking out Sara Bryant's ass as she *breezes* into his classroom.)

—gives out lab assignments every couple of weeks. They're brutal. Basically, you work with your partner on an experiment

and then there's an essay,

and you do that part on your own time, with your lab partner.

Each assignment is worth 5 percent of your final grade. And it's always—

(*always*)

—a pain in the ass.

It's a pain in the ass at the best of times, but when you're Adam Higgs—

(Pizza Man)

(LOSER)

—and your partner is Sara *freaking* Bryant, it's a serious ordeal.

Because Sara *freaking* Bryant doesn't trouble herself with meeting the likes of Adam Higgs after school or—god forbid—on a weekend, so the experiments pretty much just don't get done. And the essays are pretty half-assed themselves. Sara and Adam have handed in two assignments so far. They've pulled:

- 40 percent on the first one.

- 40 percent on the second.

They're crapping the bed.

Girls like Sara Bryant don't crap the bed. It's unseemly. Undignified. Not cool. But it's just as unseemly to hang out with Pizza Man. This is a problem.

Adam has a solution.

Powers hands out the third assignment a couple weeks after Crash.

A couple weeks post–*Pizza Man*.

The whole class groans. They hate these assignments. Sara Bryant's got her hand up. "Sir?" she says. "Do we *have* to work with our lab partners? Why can't we just partner with our friends?"

Across the room, Jessie McGill takes up the cause. "Mr. Powers, this is unfair."

Sara's making these doe eyes at Mr. Powers. Batting her eyelashes. Licking her lips. Jessie McGill's doing the same. Adam figures he's got about a minute and a half before the old perv blows his wad and caves to the girls' demands. Crumbles like a cardboard cruise ship.

And Adam doesn't want that.

Adam *wants* to work with Sara Bryant.

Adam has a plan.

"Wait," he tells Sara. "I'll do it myself."

Sara frowns at Adam. "One sec," she says. She turns to Powers and bats her lashes again. "Sir?"

"*Sara.*" Adam goes to nudge her. Bails at the last second, as he contemplates the horrendous social ramifications of touching Sara *freaking* Bryant without her permission.

"Just listen to me," he whispers. "I'll do the whole project myself. You don't have to do a thing. I'll just do it, okay?"

Slowly, Sara puts down her hand. Turns to stare at him. "What, you'll do the whole thing?"

"And I'll get an A," Adam says. "Swear to god."

Jessie McGill is frowning at Sara from across the room, trying to get her attention. She still has her hand sky-high. She's wearing a low-cut top. Powers is going to melt in her hands.

"Fuck it," Adam says. "I'll do Jessie's, too."

42.

Jessie McGill's lab partner is a quiet Iranian girl named Nadja. She's unconvinced.

"You're just *doing* Jessie's assignment?" she says to Adam when he catches up to her after class. "She's not even your partner."

Adam gives her a grin like, *Don't ask questions.*

Like, *Everything will be fine.*

"I know," he says. "It's weird. Just work with me."

Nadja shakes her head. "I'm supposed to work with Jessie. She's my lab partner. I don't get it."

"You don't have to get it," Adam tells her. "Let's just do the damn assignment and be done with it."

"I don't think so," Nadja says. "I'm going to do it myself. This is weird."

43.

Whatever.

Nadja can do her own thing.

Adam busts his ass on Sara's assignment, anyway. Figures Nadja and Jessie can work out their own arrangement. Figures it's probably for the best he's just doing one assignment.

Between Pizza Hut and Sara's homework and sleep, he doesn't have time for much of anything else.

He manages to make time to watch hockey with Sam, though. "I'm working on something," Adam tells him. "It's going to be big."

So, okay, Friday.

Adam rolls into class with the finished assignment. Finds Sara and Jessie waiting for him. "Where's our stuff, Pizza Man?" Sara wants to know.

Adam hands Sara the assignment. "Voilà."

"Is it good?" Sara wants to know.

"Better than anything else we've done this year," Adam tells her.

"What about me?" Jessie says.

Adam gestures across the room to where Nadja is unpacking her backpack. "Your partner wouldn't work with me," he says. "I'm sorry."

Jessie frowns. "So what does that mean?"

"I don't know. Ask Nadja."

Jessie spins on her heels. Marches over to Nadja. They exchange a few words and then Nadja takes her own paper out of her backpack. Hands it to Jessie. Jessie reads it. Nods and smiles.

Nadja glares at Adam across the room. Adam grins back.

Assignment complete.

Win.

44.

Physics class, Monday morning.

Powers walks the aisles, handing back the assignments. Drops Adam and Sara's paper on their workstation. "Great work, you two," he says. "Good to see you're finally putting in some effort."

Sara reaches for the paper. Adam snatches it away. Scans it. Flips to the mark: 91 percent. A solid A.

"Holy crap," Sara says. "You crushed it."

"Not bad, huh?" Adam says.

Sara picks up her iPhone. "Nice work, Pizza Man," she says. "I owe you one."

45.

"She said she *owes you one?*" Sam says. "And she's really hot?"

"So hot," Adam tells him. "Like, smoking hot. Tall and blond and, like, stacked. She's going to be a movie star someday."

"Holy shit." Sam grins at him. "And you're in, right? You're in."

Adam grins back.

"Yeah," he tells Sam. "I'm in."

Value: demonstrated.

Sara Bryant: impressed.

Mission: accomplished.

46.

Brian shakes his head.

"Won't work," he says. "Won't ever work."

Adam takes the joint from him. "Why not? She owes me. She said it herself. Plus, she knows I'm a nice guy now."

"Girls don't like nice guys," Brian says. "That's the first thing you gotta understand."

It's Wednesday. Adam and Brian are hanging out behind Pizza Hut, stealing a joint, hoping the manager doesn't come out and catch them. Adam's been coasting ever since Monday morning.

Except now, Brian's seriously killing his high.

"Come on, though," Adam says. "She failed the first two assignments. I'm saving her ass."

Brian pulls out his iPhone. "What'd you say her name is?"

"Sara Bryant," Adam tells him.

Brian brings up Sara Bryant's Facebook page on his iPhone. "Yeah," he says, shaking his head. "You're screwed."

Adam frowns at him. "What the hell are you talking about?"

"A girl like this?" Brian turns his screen so that Adam can see Sara Bryant's profile picture.

Her headshot.

Professional.

Model-esque.

"A girl like that?" Brian says. "Every guy in the school wants to do her a favor. She's like a movie star who gets all her clothes for free because she's famous and shit. You hand her a T-shirt, you ain't getting noticed, man. You're busting your ass for nothing."

Adam thinks about it.

Realizes Brian's right.

Shit.

"So what do I do?"

"What I've been telling you." Brian finishes the joint. "Show some balls."

47.

Show some balls, huh?

Okay.

The next time Mr. Powers hands out a lab assignment, Sara Bryant doesn't beg and plead to work with Jessie McGill.

No.

She flashes Adam that all-American smile and bats her eyelashes. "So, Pizza Man," she says. "You want to handle this?"

Adam looks her in the eye. Takes a deep breath.

(*Show some balls.*)

Here it is.

"Yeah," he says. "I'll do the assignment."

Sara nods like she knew it was coming. Like she's already counting on the A. "Thank you so much," she says. "You're the best."

"I'll do it," Adam says. He's not finished yet. "But you're going to pay me for it."

What?

Sara Bryant's smile disappears. She cocks her head. "I beg your pardon?"

Adam holds her gaze. Inside, he's dying. Outside, though, he's cool.

Really cool.

Ice-freaking-cold.

"Think about it," he tells her. "You know I do good work.

You don't want to do the assignment, but you want the A, don't you?"

"I'm not going to fucking pay you to do my homework," Sara Bryant tells him. "Who the hell do you think I am?"

"Ten bucks a page," Adam replies. "And a twenty-dollar bonus if I get us another A."

Sara's glaring at him now. No more flirty smiles. No more big, blue doe eyes, filled with the promise of fantasies brought to life, if only you'll do Sara Bryant—

(Sara *motherfucking* Bryant)

—this favor.

No. She's glaring at him now. She's *pissed*. "Are you retarded?" she says. "I'd never—"

Then the bell rings. Catches Sara in mid-rant. Throws her off. She looks around, helpless. Disbelieving.

Adam stands. "Think about it."

And he walks away.

Boom.

48.

Balls.

Adam walks from that physics classroom fully aware of three things:

a) There's a good chance he's just turned Sara *freaking* Bryant into an enemy for life.

b) Money for homework is the kind of crazy scheme that gets kids suspended.

c) What happened in that classroom is the ballsiest thing he's ever done. One way or the other, he's going to make a name for himself (and it ain't gonna be Pizza Man).

Adam works harder on that assignment than he's ever worked before.

It isn't easy.

He's a smart enough kid, but it's not like Adam was a model student before he came to Nixon. He spent the bulk of his time getting high. And it's not like the Higgs residence is a sanctuary devoted to academic rigor.

Adam's family has a fifteen-year-old computer sitting smack in the living room. Five feet away, Steph is watching *Gossip Girl* reruns.

Chuck Bass is hooking up with two underage debutantes.

It's distracting.

Still, he works hard. Busts his ass. Steph peers at him from the couch. "You never do homework," she says. "What's your game?"

"No game," he tells her. "Just a little experiment."

He slaves away on that paper. Stays up all night. Polishes it off and brings it in on the due date. Sara Bryant, for once, is there early. She watches Adam walk into the classroom—

(blue eyes fixed on him the moment he walks through the door).

"You do the assignment?" she asks him.

Adam shows her the paper. "Uh-huh."

Sara Bryant visibly relaxes. "Good work," she says. She smiles at him. Almost—

(but not quite)

—the all-American smile. "I knew you'd come through."

"Best paper I ever wrote," he tells her. He shows her the title page. Keeps it just out of her reach.

Acceleration, by Adam Higgs, it reads.

Sara frowns. "What is this? Where's my name?"

"Figured I did all the work, I should get the credit, right?" Adam tells her. "Five pages times ten bucks a page is fifty bucks. You ready to deal?"

Sara stares at him. The smile is gone. "This is extortion," she says, glancing at Mr. Powers's desk. "This is bullshit. This is—"

"This is capitalism," Adam tells her. He's struggling to keep the shake from his voice. "You don't want to do the work, and you know it. I can get you the grades. You can spend your time doing whatever it is that you do. It's a win-win. Think about it."

Sara looks around the room again. She looks:

helpless

frustrated

mad.

"Let me see the paper," she says. Adam hands it over and she flips through. "You swear this is good stuff?"

"Better than a zero," Adam tells her.

"You know you're a real asshole?"

He shrugs. "Whatever it takes."

She flips through again. Hands it back. "Five bucks."

"What?"

"Five bucks a page."

At the front of the room, Powers starts picking up the assignments. Adam gives Sara his poker face. "Ten bucks a page. Plus twenty dollars for the A."

Sara says nothing. Sara thinks it over. Sara watches Powers coming up through the aisles.

This is it, Adam thinks.

She takes the bait

or

she rats me out.

He waits. Can't breathe. Watches Sara as Powers gets closer.

Come on, he's thinking. *Come on, come on.*

Powers is two desks away. Sara swears. "Fine," she says. "Ten bucks a page, you little shit."

Adam doesn't flinch. "Cash," he says. "Now."

Sara glances at Powers again. Reaches into her purse and pulls out three twenties. Shoves them into Adam's hand. "Happy? Put my fucking name on the fucking paper, Pizza Man."

Adam takes another copy of the paper—this one printed with Sara's name—from his backpack. Hands it to Powers in the nick of time. Then he takes out his wallet and pockets the

twenties. Hands her a ten-dollar bill. Gives her his best approxi-
mation of an all-American smile.

"There you go," he tells her. "Thank you, come again."

Balls.

49.

Balls or no, Adam sweats that assignment.

    Adam's terrified.

    What if Sara Bryant rats him out?

        What if Powers somehow grows wise to the scheme?

            What if?

                What if?

                    What if?

50.

Mr. Powers hands the assignment back. "Even better than the last one." He lets his eyes wander down Sara Bryant's body. "Glad to see you're waking up, Ms. Bryant."

Sara gives him that smile, thanks him, waits until he's moved along. Then she checks the grade on the paper. "Holy shit." She flashes Adam the grade.

Holy shit is right.

92 percent.

Holy shit.

"Twenty bucks," Adam tells her. He's earned that bonus. Sara's smile wavers a little, but she reaches for her purse.

"Two things," she tells Adam as she hands over the money. "One, you don't tell anyone we're doing this."

"Duh," Adam says.

She pauses. "One more thing."

"I'm not taking you to prom," Adam tells her.

Sara makes a face. "That's not actually funny." She looks down at the twenty. "We do this again next time, okay? Same deal."

"So long as you pay me," Adam tells her.

Sara hands over the twenty. "*Duh.*"

51.

It works for a while. A couple more assignments. Low-nineties grades. Seventy bucks a pop. Sara pays up gladly now. She's over the weirdness of it. Adam's over the fear.

(Sara's still calling him Pizza Man, but what the hell? She's paying him.)

(Things are happening.)

Then Jessie McGill finds Adam in the hall. "I heard what you're doing with Sara."

Adam freezes. Adam blinks.

Adam puts on his poker face. "I don't know what you're talking about."

"Come *on*." Jessie pulls him into an alcove. Stands so close that Adam can smell her perfume.

It's Candy, by

Prada.

It's intoxicating.

"So what's the deal," Jessie says. "How much is she paying you?"

Adam shrugs. "I gotta get to class."

Jessie puts her arm out. Stops him. She's smiling like this is all one big punch line—

(Which, Adam supposes, it is.)

(He's the Pizza Man, after all.)

"*How much?*" Jessie says again.

Adam looks at her. Adam sighs. "Ten bucks a page," he says. "Twenty bucks extra for an A. You happy?"

He tries to squeeze past her. Doesn't wait for an answer. Jessie doesn't move. "Wait," she says.

Adam sighs again. He's thinking about how much of a pariah he's going to be when word gets out he's extorting Sara Bryant in second-period physics.

But he waits anyway.

It's Jessie McGill.

Jessie bites her bottom lip. Fixes Adam with those big brown eyes. Then she blows his mind. "Can we make a deal too?"

Adam stops trying to get out of there. For a minute, he considers the possibilities.

Two popular girls.

Two *goddesses*.

Then he shakes his head. "Not going to work," he says. "We're not lab partners, and Nadja thinks I'm crazy."

"I'm not talking about physics," Jessie says. "Nadja just does the assignments anyway. I don't even have to ask."

"So, I don't get it," Adam says. "What do you need me for?"

"English," she says. "That Shakespeare essay. We're allowed to work with partners, remember?"

Jessie bites her bottom lip again.

Jessie smiles.

Jessie says: "Will you be my partner, Adam?"

52.

Adam hands in the Shakespeare paper a week later. A couple days after that, Mrs. Stewart—

(the English teacher)

—hands it back to Jessie and Adam.

"Nice work, you two," she says. "You should work together more often."

Jessie McGill takes out her purse and peels off a twenty. "You heard her, Adam," she says. "We should work together more often."

"Whenever you want," Adam tells her. "You know my rates."

Jessie grins at him. "Then until next time, Pizza Man."

53.

Still with the Pizza Man.

It triggers something in Adam.

He leans back across to Jessie McGill's desk. *"Listen,"* he whispers. *"You know anyone else who wants in on this action?"*

"What do you mean?" Jessie says.

"This homework stuff," he says. "You know anyone else who needs an A?"

"You mean, like, you'd do their projects too?"

Adam nods.

(Go big or go home.)

"Ask around," he says. "Paul, Alton, Janie, tell them my rates. If they need something done, tell them to talk to Adam Higgs."

Jessie cocks her head. "Wow, you're quite the little schemer, aren't you?"

Adam grins at her. "Whatever it takes."

54.

"These are seriously hot girls," Sam says. "And they're friends with you now?"

Adam and Sam are eating McDonald's—

(Adam's treat)

—and Adam's telling Sam about Sara Bryant and Jessie McGill while they scarf down Big Mac meals. He gets Sam to look up both girls on his phone. He tells Sam about the scent of Jessie McGill's perfume.

"I'd say we're pretty friendly," Adam says.

"So, what?" Sam says. "She just *asked* you to do that project with her? Just out of the blue?"

Adam nods, eats a couple of fries before he answers.

Adam's been thinking about this, about how to tell Sam about the homework scheme. It's a delicate subject.

See, Sam was an athlete.

He was good-looking and popular.

Sam would never have to resort to some sleazy hustle to make friends at Riverside.

Sam probably won't understand.

So Adam just shrugs. Chews his fries. "She came up to me out of the blue," he tells Sam. "I guess maybe she just likes me."

Sam grins at him. "Hot damn," he says. "Didn't I tell you your life was about to get better?"

55.

A couple days later:

Adam rolls up to his locker, finds Leanne Grayson waiting for him.

"Hey," Leanne says. "Do you know Adam?"

"I'm Adam," Adam says.

Leanne frowns. "Seriously? Everyone just calls you Pizza Man."

Adam sighs.

"I'm the Pizza Man," he says. "I'm Adam, too. What's up?"

Leanne looks around. The hall is mostly deserted. Nobody's listening anyway. "Jessie told me about you," she says.

"Yeah?" Adam's still burning from the Pizza Man thing. "And?"

"And . . ." Leanne trails off. Looks around again, like she's pulling a drug deal or something.

"I wouldn't normally do this," she says. "It's just, me and Janie want to go to Blue Mountain this weekend. First ski trip of the season."

"Ten bucks a page," Adam says. "Twenty extra for an A. What's the class?"

Leanne blushes. "History," she says. "That War of 1812 project for Mr. Shoemaker. I was thinking if you weren't busy—"

"I'm never busy," Adam tells her. "I'll take it."

56.

Adam's lying, of course.

He's busy.

He's really busy.

It's November by now. Teachers are getting squirrely with the projects. He's doing Sara Bryant's lab reports. There's another English essay for Jessie McGill on the horizon.

Adam's got his Pizza Hut job.

(Pizza Man.)

And he tries to see Sam after school, a few times a week. Especially now that this homework scheme is running and he actually has friends—

("friends")

—to tell Sam about.

And then he does his own homework too, if he has time.

He's not too busy to turn down work, though. Especially from someone like Leanne Grayson. But if there's one immutable law about Nixon Collegiate, it's:

wherever Leanne Grayson goes,

Janie Ng goes too.

57.

Janie Ng finds Adam in the hallway. Drags him into a corner. "Did Leanne talk to you?" she says. "About that history project?"

Adam nods. "You're going skiing, she said. So? It's not a group project, is it?"

Janie shakes her head. "No, but I was thinking."

"Yeah?" Adam says.

Janie sighs. "Well, listen," she says. "If Leanne doesn't have to do a project, I don't want to do one either."

"You want me to do yours, too," Adam says. "Two major projects on the same topic and they're due in a week."

Janie grins. Sheepish. "We procrastinated."

Adam mulls it over. Each paper's gotta be about ten pages. That's a hundred bucks each, plus the bonus.

It also means writing three papers on the same subject in a week.

Plus Sara's lab assignment.

Plus Jessie's English paper.

"Fuck it," Adam tells Janie.

"You're on."

58.

Janie Ng loves it.

Janie Ng's thrilled.

Janie Ng *hugs* Adam.

Yay.

"Where's your phone?" she says. "Let me give you my number. Just in case, you know, you need to call or whatever."

Crap.

"It's in the shop," he tells Janie. Lies. "Something's wrong with the battery. I can just find you at school, though."

Janie's face kind of falls. "Well, okay," she says. "Wait, are you on Facebook?"

"Yeah," Adam says.

> (Because somewhere between the lab assignments and the English projects and the Pizza Hut gig, he signed up for Facebook.)
>
> (He has two friends.)
>
> (One of them is Steph.)
>
> (Adam's mom made him friend her.)

Janie pulls out her phone. "Adam Higgs, right?"

"Yeah," Adam says. "How'd you know my last name?"

"I guess I just pay attention." Janie punches something into her phone. Then she giggles. "Did you just get Facebook or something? You have, like, two friends. How is that even possible?"

Shit.

"Yeah," Adam says. "I just got it. I had to switch accounts when I transferred schools because I—"

"*Stalker,*" Janie says.

"What?"

"You had a stalker, didn't you? That happened to Leanne once. She had to get a restraining order."

"Shit," Adam says. "Scary. Yeah, something like that."

"Okay," Janie says. "Well, I added you on Facebook. I'll tell Leanne and everyone to add you, too. That way you don't look like such a loser."

"Ha," Adam says. "Wouldn't want that."

59.

"Sara Bryant and Jessie McGill," Adam's mom says. "I don't know who these girls are, but they're sure good for your GPA."

Steph nearly chokes. "*You* hang out with Sara and Jessie now?"

It's dinnertime. The Higgs family—

(*sans* Sam, who rarely comes over—

> he finds it depressing, he says, and anyway, it's hard for him to get around the house in his wheelchair)

—sits around the dinner table, eating spaghetti. Adam's dad just asked about school. Adam just showed him a couple recent homework assignments, both of which earned him that twenty-dollar bonus.

But Adam doesn't tell his parents about the money. He just shows them the marks in red pen at the top of the first pages.

Steph is incredulous. "How the hell did you manage that, Pizza Man?"

Adam grins at her. "Maybe they have a thing for me."

Steph laughs and laughs.

> She laughs like it's the funniest thing in the world.

> Adam lets her laugh.

He's on a roll.

60.

Progress is being made.

Adam uses the profits from Janie and Leanne's history projects to buy an iPhone. It's the previous generation and he can't afford a data plan, but it's an iPhone, anyway.

It's practically a business expense.

61.

He quits his job at Pizza Hut, too.

Well, he doesn't quit, per se.

More like, the manager calls him into the office for a stern talking-to. The guy's about twenty years old. His acne's worse than Adam's. Much worse. "You've been missing a lot of work lately," he says.

Adam says: "I'm busy. School. Anyway, I always find someone to cover my shifts."

"That's not the point," the manager says. "You're never here. If you're not committed to Pizza Hut, there's no reason for Pizza Hut to be committed to you."

Adam shrugs. "Okay."

"I want you to think about whether you're really committed to Pizza Hut," the manager says. "Come back and see me in a week or so."

62.

Adam takes that week.

He doesn't think about Pizza Hut.

He takes that week and spends it busting his ass on homework assignments for four pretty girls, and for Paul Nolan, who finds Adam at his locker on Tuesday with a math worksheet in his hands.

It's a one-page assignment. Ten bucks. Adam takes the job anyway, because, hell, it's *Paul Nolan*.

Adam busts his ass all week. Then he goes to see Sam.

"You have your whole life to make money," Sam says. "Trust me on this, now's the time to make memories."

Adam trusts Sam. Sam's working at the doughnut shop. He's wearing a silly hat and a goofy-looking tie. He's rolling around clearing garbage from the tables.

(*Doughnut Man.*)

Adam leaves and goes home and does more homework. He doesn't think about Pizza Hut ever again.

63.

Adam's smoking with Brian outside the restaurant. He's just told the manager he's quitting. "I'm sorry," he tells Brian. "I know you vouched for me with the manager and all."

Brian blows smoke. "Fuck that guy," he says. "He's a Pizza Hut manager. It's not like he's the president. You having any luck with that Sara Bryant chick?"

"And three of her friends." Adam makes Brian take out his iPhone and look up Jessie McGill, Leanne Grayson, and Janie Ng on Facebook.

(Then he makes Brian add him on Facebook, for good measure.)

"I think I'm onto something here," he tells Brian. "Like a secret formula or something."

"You gonna hook up with these chicks?"

Adam grins at him. "Maybe."

Brian finishes the joint. Looks at Adam.

(*Even* he *looks at me different now*, Adam thinks.)

"Hot damn," Brian says. "You really found your balls, didn't you?"

Adam grins wider. Adam shrugs.

"Looks like it," Adam says.

64.

You gonna hook up with these chicks?
    You gonna hook up with them, man?
        With Jessie McGill or Leanne Grayson or Janie
        Ng or
            Sara *freaking* Bryant?

You gonna *fuck* them, man?

65.

Adam's thinking about it.

Oh man, is he thinking about it.

Adam Higgs is a seventeen-year-old virgin—

(never kissed a girl)

—suddenly surrounded by four of the hottest girls at Nixon. Four of the hottest girls he's ever talked to.

(Hell, four of the hottest girls he's ever *seen*.)

Is he gonna hook up with them? Even Sam wants to know. Adam shows Sam Sara Bryant's Facebook profile on his computer.

"God damn," Sam says. "You weren't lying."

"Right?" Adam says. "*Right?*"

66.

Sam doesn't meet many girls anymore, Adam's pretty sure. The wheelchair and that ugly doughnut shop uniform scare them all off.

Even his nurse isn't that good-looking.

(She comes by a few times a week to help Sam out with showering and, like, paralyzed-people stuff.)

But Sam's not a virgin. His life isn't that shitty. Adam walked in on him once, just before the accident. He was hooking up with Lesley Taylor, this smoking-hot Riverside cheerleader.

Sometimes Adam thinks about Lesley Taylor and what she and Sam were doing, and sometimes he thinks he'd *still* maybe trade his life for Sam's, even knowing what Sam's life has become.

(He's usually pretty horny when he's thinking this way.)

(But if you saw Lesley Taylor, you'd think about trading your legs for a night with her too.)

(Anyway.)

67.

Anyway, Adam's been thinking about hooking up with these god-desses. He's been thinking about it a lot, if you catch my drift.

But what's a guy like Adam to do? It's not like he's Paul Nolan—

       (yet).

It's not like he's Alton Di Sousa or Rob Thigpen—

       (yet).

He's Adam Higgs.

He's—

       (still)

              —the Pizza Man.

68.

Anyway, before Adam can embarrass himself by asking Jessie McGill—

    (or Leanne Grayson)

    (or Janie Ng)

    (or Sara *freaking* Bryant)

    —on a date,

               well,

                     Victoria Lemieux happens.

69.

It's, like, a Friday.

Alton Di Sousa's at Adam's locker. "Pizza Man," Alton says. "I need you."

Adam looks at Alton. Adam wants to tell Alton his name is Adam, not Pizza Man. But Alton is the starting point guard on the Nixon basketball team. Alton is like six foot five.

Plus, Alton has a job for Adam.

"Economics, man," Alton says. "You know anything about it? Got a lab due on Monday and I totally bailed."

Adam hesitates. Literally the only thing he knows about economics is:

Ten bucks a page beats minimum wage.

But he doesn't tell Alton that. He tells Alton to show him the assignment. It's all gibberish.

Craaaap.

"I'll pay extra," Alton says. "Whatever you need to make this worthwhile. I fucked up the last one and they're saying I can't play ball until I get my average straight.

"I *need* this, man," Alton says.

Adam looks at Alton. From the brand-new Air Jordans on his feet to the big chain around his neck. Alton has money. And Alton *needs* this, man.

Payday.

Except . . .

Adam shakes his head. "Ten bucks a page," he says. "Normal rates."

Adam doesn't fleece him. Adam's thinking long-term. Adam's thinking, *Another satisfied customer.*

"Don't sweat it," Adam says. "Just give me a little warning next time, okay?"

Alton nods. *Okay.*

"Good," Adam says. "Now let me see that textbook."

70.

Oh yeah.

We're supposed to be talking about Victoria Lemieux. She's more important than Alton Di Sousa.

By, like, a lot.

71.

So.

Adam's stuffing Alton's economics assignment into his backpack. Thinking his weekend just got a hell of a lot busier.

A hell of a lot more . . .

economical.

(Sue me.)

Anyway, someone calls out his name. A girl. A pretty girl with long hair, ruler-straight, jet-black.

Victoria Lemieux.

She's a freshman. One of Steph's one hundred new Facebook friends.

"Hey, Adam," she says from her locker. "Where are you running to?"

Adam shrugs. "History," he tells her.

"Oh." Victoria kind of nods, like she's waiting for the punch line. "Cool."

She's cute, Adam notices.

She's really, really cute.

But Adam figures he knows what's up.

"Listen," he says. "I don't think I can help you."

Victoria makes a face. Screws up her nose. It's *cute.* "What are you talking about?"

"You talked to somebody, right?" Adam says. "Sara or Jessie or Paul or somebody? The homework stuff? I just don't think

I could pull off the same stunt for a freshman, you know?"

Victoria cocks her head. Looks at Adam like he just told her he's never heard of Facebook. "I don't know anything about any homework," she says. "I just wanted to say hi. You're Steph's brother, right?"

(*What?*)

Victoria catches the look on Adam's face. Laughs. "Don't people say hi where you come from?"

"Uh, yeah," Adam says.

"It's easy. Just say 'Hi, Victoria.'"

Adam blinks. "Hi, Victoria."

Victoria smiles back. She has an incredible smile. "Hi, Adam," she says. "How are you?"

"I'm good," Adam says slowly. "How are you?"

Victoria laughs. "See?" she says. "You're learning." She closes her locker. "But I have to get to math class. If you hadn't wasted so much time blabbing, we could have talked more."

Adam says nothing.

Adam just stares at her.

Victoria giggles. "See you around, Adam."

"See you," Adam says. "And, uh, *sorry*."

Victoria locks her locker and starts off down the hall. "It's okay," she says, grinning. "You'll figure it out."

72.

Victoria Lemieux adds Adam on Facebook the next day.

"Ugh," Steph says when she catches him creeping Victoria's profile. "I would really appreciate if you would stay away from my friends, Adam."

"She added me, Steph," Adam says. "So suck it."

"Gross." Steph makes a face. "Just don't embarrass me, okay?"

73.

"Victoria Lemieux," Sam says. "Who is she?"

"One of Steph's friends," Adam tells him. "I don't really know her, but she's pretty damn cute."

Sam looks at her Facebook picture. "Yeah, she is."

"Is she as hot as Sara Bryant?" Adam asks him.

Sam shrugs. "I don't know. Do you like her?"

"I think so," Adam says. "She's nicer than Sara Bryant, anyway. By a mile."

"Then go for her," Sam says. "What do you have to lose, right?"

Adam nods.

Adam shrugs.

If only it were that easy, Adam thinks.

74.

It's, like, the next Tuesday. Adam's walking down the hall, passes Victoria at her locker. She's talking to some big, dumb-looking guy. A football player, junior varsity.

(Chad something.)

Big, dumb Chad is leaning on Victoria's locker and grinning down at her, and they're laughing and chattering like BFFs.

Or worse.

Figures, Adam thinks. *She already has a boyfriend.*

A football-player boyfriend.

Adam cruises past. Pretends he doesn't see her. He doesn't get away with it. "Don't be such a stranger, Adam," Victoria calls after him.

Adam turns around. "Oh," he says. "Hey." He gives Chad a nod. Chad nods back, big and dumb.

Victoria laughs. "Why're you being so abnormal? We're Facebook friends now. You can't just ignore me."

Adam gestures to Chad. "Looked like you two were busy."

"What, with Chad?" Victoria pushes Chad away. "This big dummy just likes to make my life miserable. What are you up to?"

Just then, Leanne Grayson wanders by. "Hey, Adam," she says. "What's up?"

"Hey, Leanne," Adam says. Smiles at her as she wanders

off. Turns back around to see:

    a)   Chad's disappeared, and

    b)   Victoria's got a funny look on her face.

"Oh," she says. "I see how it is. Maybe *you're* too busy for *me, friend.*"

"Ha," Adam says. "It's not like that at all."

"You mean you're *not* hooking up with Leanne Grayson? You *don't* want to jump her bones?"

Adam glances back at Leanne. She's wandered away. Didn't hear a thing. "We're just friends," he tells Victoria. "No need to get pervy."

"So, okay," Victoria says. "Whose bones *are* you jumping?"

Adam looks at her. "I don't, uh, jump bones. Do you?"

Victoria rolls her eyes. "It's a figure of speech. It wasn't the real question."

"So what's the real question?"

Victoria shakes her head like Adam has to be the dumbest person in the world. "Come back and see me when you figure it out," she sighs.

75.

(Sidebar:

    That economics thing for Alton?

    A real pain in the ass.

    See, there's an art to forging homework. You can't just write the perfect paper, not for somebody like Alton Di Sousa—

    (career C-student)—

    you have to know your client. You have to know how he writes. You have to know he's never pulling an A-plus in his life, and if you mess up and get him one . . .

                    you're both screwed.

    You gotta throw in typos, grammatical errors, mess up some dates. But you can't fuck up too much, or you won't pull the requisite grade.

    And in this case, if you mess up Alton's grade, he's off the basketball team.

    And it's all

          your

              fault.

    Luckily, Adam *does* know his clientele. He's watched them for months now.

    He *idolizes* them.

    And anyway, he doesn't know jack shit about economics. It's a miracle he passes, but he does.

A B-minus.

Alton gets to keep playing basketball.

Adam gets a new client.

(And a few gray hairs.))

76.

"You never answered my question."

It's Victoria again. In no known universe is Adam getting sick of seeing her.

Of seeing that smile.

She ambushes him in the hall, this time. Sneaks up to his locker and jumps out and surprises him.

(But it's the good kind of surprise.)

"Your question?" he says. "Sure I did. I'm not jumping anyone's bones. I told you that."

"So you're single," Victoria says.

Adam shrugs. "As opposed to?"

"As opposed to dating somebody," she says. "Anyway, that wasn't the real question, and you know it."

Adam shrugs again. "I don't even know what language you're speaking. Is this some kind of code?"

Victoria shakes her head. "Are you really going to make me do this, Adam Higgs? Do I have to spell it out?"

"Spell it," Adam tells her. "I'm clueless."

(He's not clueless, he's just:

in disbelief.

Girls like Victoria Lemieux don't really do this.

Do they?

Do they?)

Victoria looks around. Speaks slowly, like Adam's a

special-needs kid. "Do you ever go to movies, Adam?"

Adam nods. "Sometimes."

"Do you ever take girls to movies?"

Adam shrugs. "Not a lot," he says. Then he catches himself. "I mean, sometimes—"

(Never.)

"Why? Are you . . ."

Victoria: "Wait for it."

"Are you asking me out?"

She claps her hands. "My god, there *is* life in there. You just got asked out by a freshman girl, slugger. How does that make you feel?"

"Not very manly."

"Exactly," she says. "Next time, smarten up. Ask me when I'm free."

Adam asks her.

"Friday," she says. "I like horror movies."

Then she turns and walks off. Halfway down the hall, she turns around. "Make a plan," she calls back. "Facebook me the details. Pick me up at eight."

77.

First date.

Adam spends a week's worth of homework money on a new outfit at Abercrombie & Fitch.

Buys that new Hugo Boss cologne.

He smells . . .

Boss.

Doesn't calm the nerves, though.

This is Victoria Lemieux we're talking about. She has five hundred friends on Facebook. Adam has . . .

Twenty-three.

Huge talent disparity. Adam's out of his league. And he knows it.

78.

"What if I screw everything up?" Adam asks Sam. "What if she realizes what a loser I am?"

They're pregaming at Sam's apartment. Adam's nervous as hell. He's shaky. He's hoping Sam has some last-second tips.

"You're not a loser," Sam says. "And you're not going to screw everything up. Just be yourself. Be normal."

"Those are two totally opposite instructions," Adam tells him. "What if she wants to kiss me? What do I do?"

Sam bursts out laughing. "What do you do if she wants to kiss you? You go with it, obviously. Lean in and kiss her."

"But how am I supposed to know if she wants to or not?" Adam says. "What if she's not cool with it?"

Sam just laughs.

"I've never done this before," Adam says. He's starting to freak out in earnest now. "What if I screw up?"

"You won't screw up," Sam tells him. Sam watches him pace. Sam's grinning wide.

"Damn it, Adam," Sam says. "I'm proud of you."

79.

Adam meets Victoria at the bus loop downtown.

("I don't have a car," he tells her. "*Yet.*")

She's cool with it.

That dope new Italian joint loses his reservation.

("We're sorry, sir, we just can't find you a table.")

She's cool with it.

He takes her to Tunnel Barbecue and they load up on ribs instead. Guzzle Pepsis and get messy.

She's cool with it.

Takes her to a horror movie, something standard. A bunch of teenagers alone in the woods. They drink. They hook up. They die.

She's cool with it.

> (Better than cool, in fact: she's all over it, screaming at the scary bits, burying her face in Adam's coat, gripping on his arm for dear life.)

Adam walks her to the bus loop after the movie. Victoria's bus pulls up. She lingers. Bites her lip. Looks away.

("What do you do if she wants to kiss you? You go with it, obviously.")

Adam leans in and kisses her.

She's cool with it.

80.

Achievement unlocked: First Kiss.

81.

Sam claps his hands. "Damn right you kissed her," he says. "What did I tell you?"

They're on the riverfront trail, looking out across the water at the Detroit skyline beyond. They're just a few blocks away from the movie theater, Tunnel Barbecue, and the bus loop, and the air feels

infused

with Victoria.

(Adam's still buzzing.)

"It was just like you said," Adam says. "She looked at me and I knew she wanted me to kiss her and—"

"And you went with it," Sam says.

"It was so good," Adam says.

Sam grins like he knows exactly what Adam's going through. Like he's loving every minute.

"I told you," he says. "Didn't I?"

82.

Second date.

"So what's the deal with you?" Victoria wants to know. "You're always hanging out with these pretty girls in the hall. Are you, like, a player or something?"

Adam laughs. "Are you kidding?"

"I was talking about you with Steph," Victoria says. "We can't figure it out."

Then she blushes.

"Not that, I mean, you shouldn't be hanging out with pretty girls. Your sister just doesn't seem to think it's your style."

"It's not," Adam tells her. "It's just business."

Victoria frowns. "Business?"

Adam looks at her. Adam pauses.

(Adam doesn't want to tell her about the homework scheme. Not Victoria Lemieux. He's getting the sense she's a good girl.

He's getting the sense that she
would
not
approve.)

So:

"Sometimes I tutor people," he says. "Help them out with their homework, that kind of thing."

"So you're a nerd," Victoria says. "You're just a really big nerd."

"*Fuck no*," Adam says, harder than he means to. "I mean, no, I'm not a nerd."

Victoria laughs. "I take it back, jeez. Didn't mean to insult you or anything, Mr. Big-Shot Cool Guy."

"Ha," Adam says. "I'm not that, either."

(Yet.)

83.

Victoria's story:
  Freshman.
  Only child.
  Both parents work at the Chrysler plant.
          (Adam doesn't say anything when she tells him
          this. Doesn't tell her how lucky he thinks she is
          that her folks kept their jobs. How much he
          envies her life.)
  Victoria's family lives in Walkerville, the old distillery
district down by the river. The trendy part of town.
          (Adam doesn't say anything when she tells him
          this, either. Doesn't tell her about how he lives
          in a shithole in Remington Park. How envious
          he is. What he says is:)
  "Why didn't you go to Walkerville High?"
  Victoria screws up her face. "It's all stoners and burnouts
and losers."
  "Yeah," Adam says—
          (conveniently omitting the fact that he himself
          has pretty much
          always been a stoner
          and a burnout
          and a . . .
                    well, you know)—

"but Nixon's like three miles away."

Victoria blushes. "Okay, confession time," she says. "I was in advanced placement in grade school. They bussed us out of district. All my friends graduated to Nixon, so that's where I went too. I really *am* just a big nerd."

Adam looks at her. "You're not a nerd," he says.

"Oh, no?" Victoria says. "And why is that?"

"You're pretty," Adam tells her. "And popular. People think you're cool. Nerds hang out in the library all the time and play chess and stuff. Nerds don't have any friends."

"Wow," Victoria says. "You've thought a lot about this, huh?"

"Nerds are losers," Adam tells her. "You're most definitely not a nerd."

Victoria laughs. "Okay, Mr. Big-Shot Cool Guy. But *I* don't think there's anything wrong with being a nerd. Popularity isn't everything."

Adam looks at Victoria with her creamy skin and sparkling green eyes and her adorable little smirk.

Easy for you to say, he thinks.

84.

"Steph says you have a brother," Victoria says. "He doesn't live with you guys?"

Adam shakes his head. "He moved out a year ago, I guess," he says. "He's big into independence and stuff. He wanted to be on his own."

"What does he do?" Victoria says.

"He works at the doughnut shop across from city hall," Adam tells her. "He, uh—" He looks at her. "Did Steph tell you about the accident?"

"A little," Victoria says. "Just that he got hurt."

"He's a paraplegic," Adam tells her. "He was playing hockey, against Nixon, actually, and he got body-checked the wrong way. He has to be in a wheelchair now."

Victoria frowns. "That's awful," she says, because that's what people always say, but Adam can see that she means it. "That must be really hard for him."

(*It's hard on everybody*, Adam thinks.)

"It is," he says. "But he's doing okay. He has his own apartment and he does most things himself. I think he's happy."

She looks at him. "Do you?"

Adam pauses. "I hope so," he says.

They're both quiet. Then: "We should see him," Victoria says. "I'd like to meet him."

Adam looks at her. "What, like, now?"

"No," she says, reaching for his hand. "Not now, but sometime. I mean, if you think he would be cool with it."

Adam laces his fingers between hers. Thinks about taking her to meet Sam. Showing her off to him.

"Yeah," he tells Victoria. "I think he'd like that."

85.

Adam kisses Victoria again at the end of their second date. A little longer, this time.

   She's still cool with it.

86.

So things are going well with Victoria—
    (they're going *great*)
    —except

        —except—

            things are going great with the home-
            work stuff, too.

                    Too great.

87.

Adam rolls up to his locker on a Friday afternoon.

Mr. Powers just dropped another lab assignment. Mrs. Stewart has an English paper brewing. And Mr. Shoemaker wants a chapter summary on his desk first thing Monday.

It's the weekend. Everybody has plans.

("I'm going skiing," says Leanne Grayson.)

("Swim meet," says Paul Nolan.)

("I'm getting drunk," says Rob Thigpen. "Screw the rest of you guys.")

They're crowded around Adam's locker like drug fiends, jostling one another, shoving their homework in his face.

(Practically *begging* Adam to help them.)

It's not an unpleasant feeling. But then Adam snaps back to reality.

Sara Bryant's already cornered him about physics.

Jessie McGill's already cornered him about English.

He's supposed to take Victoria out again on Saturday, and he has to visit Sam, too.

But Adam can't tell the gods he won't do their homework. Gods don't know the word *no*. It's not in their vocab.

And Adam isn't going to be the guy to teach it to them.

88.

"I'm screwed," Adam tells Brian O'Donnell.

He should be at home right now, working on homework, but he needs a quick jay and some conversation.

He's stressing, man.

Bugging out.

And he can't talk to Sam about it, because it's all about the homework scheme, which he still hasn't copped to.

(In fact, Adam's supposed to be hanging with Sam right now. He told Sam he had a date with Victoria, told him he was double-booked and had to bail.

Sam was cool with it.

"Call me later," Sam told him. "Give me the play-by-play.")

Brian passes the jay. Brian listens as Adam lays out the situation. "Why don't you just quit?" Brian says. "You got a hot chick who wants to be seen with you. What more do you need?"

"Victoria?" Adam shakes his head. "Way out of my league. She'll bolt the minute the gods forget my name. Besides, I have to do homework to make money to take her on dates."

Brian takes the jay back. "It's like that, huh?"

"It's like that," Adam says. He thinks for a minute. Paces a little. "I need the cash to take Victoria out. But I can't take Victoria out if I'm working too much."

"So cut back," Brian says. "Turn down a few projects."

Adam shakes his head.

Adam has a better idea.

"What I need," Adam says, "is to get paid without doing the work."

Brian laughs. "Don't we all."

But Adam's serious.

Adam has a plan.

89.

Adam slaves away all weekend. Somehow finishes every last assignment. Somehow manages to carve out a few hours with Victoria—

(spends those hours making out with her in the park. Slides his hand halfway up her shirt before she pushes it away.)

Stays up late Sunday night finishing off his own homework and nearly sleeps through first period Monday morning. Barely gets all those assignments back to their owners in time.

Barely avoids disaster.

(*I need a change*, Adam thinks. *Now.*)

Fortunately, change is coming.

Adam is on a mission.

He scours the school all week. He's looking for somebody.

90.

First, Adam thinks:

Maybe Darren.

Darren's pretty cool. Darren's about the only guy who's legitimately nice to Adam at Nixon. Even invites him out sometimes.

("Can't," Adam tells him. "Too much homework.")

But Darren's a B-student. And Darren has friends.

Darren has *a life*.

Darren's unsuitable.

91.

See, Adam has particular needs. He's looking for a loner.

A nerd.

A genius.

A loser like him.

He searches the library, the computer lab, scouts out the debate team and the student council.

It takes all week, but Adam finds the perfect candidate.

His name is Wayne Tristovsky.

92.

Wayne Tristovsky:
>Captain of the Academic Challenge team.
>(Basically a bunch of nerds who meet in the history homeroom at lunchtime to answer trivia questions.)

Wayne Tristovsky:
>Zero friends.

Wayne Tristovsky:
>Perfect.

93.

The truth of the matter is that everyone at Nixon thinks Wayne's a big asshole.

An arrogant prick.

Kind of a douchebag.

He wears Guess and Abercrombie and Lacoste like the rest of the school. But he's too damn smart and full of himself for his own good.

Plus, someone said they saw him picking his nose in math class. And that kind of thing will make you a *pariah*.

Wayne's a loser. Wayne's a nobody. Wayne always eats lunch solo.

Adam corners Wayne in the hall after Academic Challenge practice. Introduces himself. Asks him, "You want a job?"

Wayne looks him up and down. Wayne's eyes narrow. "Do I know you?"

"No," Adam says, "but you want to. I'm the guy who's going to put a hundred bucks in your hand every week. You interested?"

"I'm not selling drugs," Wayne says. "Sorry."

Adam laughs. "I'm not talking drugs, Wayne. I'm talking homework."

"Homework," Wayne says. "What the hell? I don't even—"

"Locker two fourteen," Adam tells him. "After school. Let me show you."

94.

Adam thinks:

- *Maybe I should have sold the program harder.*
- *Maybe Wayne will just blow me off.*
- *Maybe I'm back to square one.*

But he's wrong.

Wayne shows up at Adam's locker after school. He looks a little less arrogant next to the collection of gods and goddesses who join him there.

"One second," Adam tells him. "Gotta deal with my clientele first."

It's another busy day. Alton Di Sousa has an economics lab due. Paul Nolan has a geography paper.

(Adam isn't taking geography, but he swiped an old textbook from Paul's classroom. He's been sleeping with it under his pillow all week. Figures, hey, osmosis.)

(Anyway, nobody's expecting a master's thesis from Paul Nolan.)

So Adam deals with Alton and Paul and the rest of them, and Wayne watches, kind of bored, half interested, like,

What the hell is this?

And then the gods and goddesses *breeze* off and Adam and Wayne look at each other. "Five bucks a page," Adam tells him. "Ten-dollar bonus if you pull an A."

Wayne hems and haws. Wayne isn't so sure about this.

"Twenty pages a week, minimum," Adam says. "That's a hundred bucks, easy."

Wayne's still frowning. Wayne's still not convinced.

Then Janie Ng *breezes* up.

"Hey, Adam," she says.

Adam excuses himself from Wayne. "Hey, Janie," he says. "What can I do for you?"

Janie tells him she's good. "Still coasting off that history paper last month," she says. "Just wanted to make sure you knew about the party."

Adam blinks. Adam doesn't know.

"My parents are going to Vegas in a couple weeks," Janie says. "I figured we might as well celebrate."

"Yeah," Adam says. "Of course we should."

"So you're coming," Janie says. "Right?"

Adam feels Wayne's eyes on him. "Yeah," he says. "Of course I am."

Janie grins, big. "Awesome. I'll IM you the address."

Then she thinks of something. "And bring booze, if you can. My parents are being Nazis about their stash. I'm trying to hook up a connection, but we could always use more."

"Oh, yeah," Adam tells her. "I'm sure I can find something."

"Awesome," Janie says. "Next Friday. Don't bail."

95.

Wayne's in Adam's grill the moment Janie walks away. "Dude, I am *so* in."

(*Yeah*, Adam thinks. *I thought so.*)

"It's not as easy as it looks," Adam says. "You can't just write an essay and hand it in. You're not Paul Nolan. If Paul Nolan hands in a Wayne Tristovsky essay, Paul's screwed. And if Paul's screwed, we're all screwed."

Wayne's hardly paying attention. Wayne's still watching Janie Ng walk away. "Yeah," he says, "but *dude*. Janie Ng just invited you to her party. Do you know what goes on at those things?"

"Sounds like people get drunk," Adam says. "Or maybe they don't. Listen, if you join my team, I can get you in those parties. Who's the hottest junior girl?"

Wayne thinks about it. "Sara Bryant."

"She's your number-one pick?"

Wayne nods. "She's stacked, dude. Why?"

Adam digs around in his backpack. Comes out with an assignment. "This is Sara Bryant's physics paper. Two pages. Ten bucks. This is your audition."

Wayne looks at the assignment. "I can do this."

"Bring it to my locker first thing Monday morning," Adam tells him. "You do good, you're hired. You're hired, you're *in*. Pretty soon you'll have Sara Bryant calling you by name."

"Hot damn." Wayne stuffs the assignment into his back-pack. "Thanks, man. I won't let you down."

"Work hard," Adam tells him. "Work smart. And keep your fucking mouth shut."

96.

Wayne Tristovsky busts his ass.

Wayne Tristovsky knocks Sara Bryant's physics assignment out of the park.

Brings it to Adam first thing Monday morning. Adam looks it over. Thinks, *This is pretty good.* Gives it to Sara. A couple days later, Sara comes back, shows Adam the big red 92 on the front of the page.

Adam lets Sara hug him.

Adam goes back to Wayne.

Adam holds out his hand. Tells Wayne:

"You're hired."

97.

So now Adam has an employee. Wayne's eating it up. Twenty pages a week. Two hundred bucks, easy.

(Plus bonuses.)

Wayne works hard. Wayne keeps his mouth shut.

Wayne looks at Adam like he's a god.

(*Not yet*, Adam thinks. *But soon.*)

Wayne's addicted to the money. To the thrill of rubbing shoulders with Leanne Grayson and Paul Nolan and Jessie McGill.

To the possibility that one day, Sara Bryant will know his name.

Wayne works hard so Adam doesn't have to.

(Adam still works. This homework thing is out of control. New clients every day. Wayne's twenty pages make a nice dent in the workload, but Adam isn't living the life of leisure just yet.)

Adam still works. Adam still gets paid. Adam just has a little more free time to spend with Victoria. And Sam.

And that's a good thing, because:

Janie Ng's throwing that party.

98.

Adam asks Victoria if she's going to the party.

"I might go," she says, shrugging. "If somebody asks me."

"*Somebody*, huh?" Adam says.

"The right guy," Victoria tells him. "I only date nerds."

Adam pulls her close. Adam kisses her in the hallway. "You're coming with me," Adam tells her.

Victoria kisses him back. "Of course I am, dummy."

99.

Adam goes to see Sam. It's been, like, a week or so.

"I'm sorry," Adam tells him. "You didn't mention they piled on the homework in junior year, too."

Sam laughs. "I guess I forgot that part," he says. "I never really focused on homework that much, anyway."

"Yeah," Adam says.

"I kind of wish I did, though," Sam says. "Maybe I wouldn't be working at this goddamn doughnut shop."

"Yeah," Adam says. "So, listen, there's this party coming up. Janie Ng. And I'm definitely going."

Sam doesn't answer for a moment, but then he does. "A party, huh?" he says, smiling. "Big one?"

"Huge," Adam says. "And I need booze."

Sam grins wider. "The eternal problem of the underage drinker."

"Exactly," Adam says. "How did you score your alcohol?"

"Older people," Sam says. "Some of my friends had college friends, or sometimes we'd just hang out outside the liquor store and pay a random to buy for us.

"Why?" he asks. "You need me to pick you up a bottle of something?"

Adam thinks about it. Adam hesitates. Adam's not really looking to get Sam involved. Not with what he has in mind.

"It's no sweat," Sam says. "This is what big brothers are made for."

"Yeah," Adam says. "No, it's okay. I think my buddy Brian might have a hookup."

Sam shrugs. "Suit yourself."

100.

Here's the thing about the party:

It's not just any party.

It's Adam's *first* party.

And Adam knows he needs to make a good impression. Needs to do something special. Needs to shake that Pizza Man thing once and for all.

"You want, like, a forty or something?" Brian says. "Or I can swipe some of my dad's vodka."

"Not enough," Adam says. "I need, like, a carload. This is a party, man. It's huge. I want to show up with *all* the favors."

Brian studies Adam across the schoolyard. They're shooting hoops. Shooting air balls, more like.

(It's something to do.)

Brian takes a shot. It sails over the backboard. "Fuck basketball," he says. "When do you need this stuff?"

"Tomorrow night," Adam tells him. "At the latest."

"You paying?"

"Top dollar. I just need someone who can pick up what I need."

Brian jogs over and picks up the ball. Dribbles a few times. "My cousin's legal," he says. "I'll talk to him. You make him a list, he can pick up the stuff."

"Nice," Adam says. "Tell him just pick up some stuff high

school kids like. Beer, vodka, something for the girls. Tell him to be creative."

Adam shoots. Misses. Brian catches the ball on the rebound. "So who's throwing the party?"

"This girl from school," Adam tells him. "Her parents are out of town."

"Big party?" Brian says.

Adam looks at Brian. Brian's watching him. Adam shrugs. "Not really," he says. "Kind of a get-together, really. You know how it is."

Brian looks at Adam a moment longer. Then he shrugs and shoots again—

(airball).

Brian knows how it is.

101.

Tommy.

(Brian's cousin.)

He's a skinny guy with a raggedy beard and a big goose-down parka. He rolls up to Adam's house in Remington Park in a mean old Ford Mustang five-liter. Climbs out and gives Adam a gangster handshake, pops the trunk to the Mustang and it's filled up with booze.

Beer.

Vodka.

Rum.

Tequila.

Jägermeister.

More beer.

Smirnoff Ices.

Palm Bays.

Even more beer.

(Party time.)

Tommy helps Adam lug the booze into his parents' garage. Walks back out to the Mustang, counts Adam's money. "You need anything else?" he asks Adam. "A little dope or anything? Maybe some pills?"

"Nah," Adam says. "Not this time."

"Make those girls do anything you want, get a couple pills in them," Tommy says. "You know what I mean?"

"I'm good," Adam tells him. "I have a girlfriend, anyway."

Tommy shrugs. Pockets the money. Climbs into the Mustang and drives away. Adam stands there and watches the Mustang drive off. Hopes his parents don't find the booze before he can get it to Janie's house.

102.

Adam picks Victoria up in a taxi. They ride together to Janie Ng's house. Adam pays the driver, pops the trunk. Victoria's eyes go wide. "Did you rob a liquor store or something?" she says.

"Party favors," Adam tells her. "Can you give me a hand?"

Victoria gives him a hand. So does Paul Nolan. So does Alton Di Sousa.

Rob Thigpen sits on the couch and watches.

(Asshole.)

Janie Ng hugs Adam, hard. Tries to pay him. Adam shakes his head.

"You're throwing the party," he tells her. "This is my treat."

Janie hugs him again, presses her whole body up against him. *Breezes* back to the party to spread the good news. Victoria nudges Adam. "She totally wants you."

"Nah," Adam tells her. "She's just grateful."

He's lying, though. He sees it too.

But it doesn't matter. He has Victoria.

She's more than enough.

103.

The gods are in Janie Ng's living room.

Adam and Victoria wade in. Grab a spot on the couch next to Paul Nolan and Jessie McGill. Across from Alton Di Sousa and Sara Bryant.

Right in the middle of things.

Janie Ng walks in with a couple bottles, Bacardi and Cîroc. "Looks like we're getting drunk tonight, y'all," she says. "Adam came through with a *ton* of booze."

Paul Nolan slaps Adam five. "Hell yeah he did."

Alton Di Sousa gives Adam a nod. "Nice work, bud."

Jessie McGill flashes that smile.

And Rob Thigpen,

well,

Rob pulls out the Pizza Man card.

"Where'd you get all that booze, Pizza Man?" he says. "*Pizza Hut?*"

Everyone laughs. Paul Nolan raises a red cup. "To Pizza Man," he says.

"*To Pizza Man.*"

They all drink. Gods and goddesses. They all drink Adam's booze and toast to Pizza Man. Jessie McGill kisses his cheek.

So, why exactly is he fighting it?

"Fuck it," Adam says, raising his own red cup. "To Pizza Man."

104.

They drink. Then they dance.

It's

(get this)

the first time Adam has ever danced
with a girl. I mean, really danced.

Victoria grinds her hips against Adam's. Wraps her arms
around his neck and looks into his eyes. Tilts her head up and
parts her lips like she wants him to kiss her. Smiles when he takes
the bait.

Adam closes his eyes. Feels Victoria's body melt against
his. Thinks, *This is the dream.*

A raging house party.

A pretty girl.

This is what *popular* feels like.

It feels a lot like . . . winning.

105.

"Why do they call you Pizza Man?" Victoria asks him.

Adam shrugs. "Who knows?" he says. "It's just a thing."

"Do you like it?" she teases. "Should *I* start calling you Pizza Man now?"

Adam stops dancing. Catches a glimpse of Rob Thigpen across the room. He keeps looking at Adam. Keeps checking out Victoria.

(Like he can't believe any girl as hot as Victoria would choose Pizza Man over Rob Thigpen.)

(*Something about that guy,* Adam thinks. *Something fucking weird.*)

Adam looks at Victoria again.

"No," he tells her. "No, you shouldn't."

106.

"You want another drink?" Adam asks Victoria. He's on his third or fourth beer.

Victoria shakes her head. Keeps nursing her Smirnoff Ice. Keeps grinding her hips against him.

"You sure?" Adam says. "I bought the stuff. Might as well drink it."

"You just want me to get drunk so you can take advantage of me," Victoria says.

Adam grins at her. "Maybe. Is that so bad?"

She grins back. "You're drunk, you big nerd."

"A little tipsy," Adam says. "Nothing major."

"Damn." Victoria pouts. "I was hoping to take advantage of *you*."

Adam kisses her again. Takes her hand and leads her off the dance floor. "Come on."

107.

They wind up in a study somewhere. A big wooden desk and a wall of bookcases and a big leather couch.

Victoria flops down on the couch. Pulls Adam down beside her. Adam leans in to kiss her. Victoria kisses him. Then she pulls back.

"Do you do this a lot, you big slut?" she says. "Fool around with strange girls at parties?"

"You're the strangest," Adam tells her. "By far."

Victoria hits him. *"Jerk."*

"Seriously? You're the first girl I ever really made out with," Adam says.

Victoria giggles. "You *are* a nerd," she says. "I knew it."

"So I guess you spend all your time making out with strange boys at parties then, huh?" Adam says.

Victoria shakes her head. "I told you, I'm a nerd too."

"Yeah?" Adam says. "So what does that mean?"

"It means you're the first boy I ever made out with." Victoria pulls Adam close again. Slips her tongue in his mouth. Kisses him for a minute or two.

Then she pulls back again. Takes Adam's hand and places it under her shirt. "And you're *definitely* the first boy I ever let touch me here," she says. She kisses Adam again.

Adam closes his eyes and . . .

Adam just goes with it.

108.

Janie Ng pokes her head in the door. "You guys can't be in here."

Adam pulls himself off Victoria. Reclaims his hand from underneath her shirt. Looks sheepishly at Janie from the couch.

"Sorry," Janie says. "My parents don't want anything getting stolen or anything."

Adam swaps a look with Victoria. They untangle from each other, climb off the couch. Fix their clothing and go back to the party.

"Told you she wants you," Victoria whispers. "She doesn't care about anything getting stolen. She just doesn't want us hooking up in her house."

Adam looks at Janie across the room. Janie meets his eye, smiles at him. Adam smiles back.

"Maybe," Adam says.

109.

It doesn't matter what Janie wants. Adam wants Victoria. Adam's pretty sure Victoria wants him, too. But Janie Ng's watching them like a hawk. No way they're sneaking away to fool around again. No way they're catching a cab home, not at this hour—

> (and then they're dealing with parents, who are always a major cock-block.)

Basically, no way they're getting any further alone time tonight.

So, well, they hang out on the couch and get drunker and drunker, listen to the gods and goddesses tell their old war stories, and—

> (and at some point, Rob Thigpen comes back around, with Steph this time, and there's no more room on the couch and nowhere for Rob and Steph to sit, and Rob looks at Adam and it's awkward.

> "Pizza Man," Rob says. "Let us have this couch, dude."

> Adam looks at the couch. There's no more room. And what Rob's really saying is:

> *Get lost, Pizza Man.*

> Adam doesn't move. Rob curls his lip. Rob's about to say something else.

> Then Paul Nolan speaks up.

"Pizza Man brought the booze," Paul says. "Pizza Man sits where he wants."

Rob and Steph look at Paul. Then they look at Adam. Adam gives them a shrug, like

What are you going to do?

And that's when Steph sighs and turns on her heel and drags Rob Thigpen off somewhere else, and boom, just like that

it's not awkward anymore.)

—and soon enough Adam's too drunk to do anything more than cuddle up next to Victoria and tell her how much he likes her, and the last thing he remembers is passing out in Janie Ng's sunroom and Victoria laughing at him between kisses, telling him to shut up and try to get some sleep.

110.

#epicnight

III.

"My friend's cousin hooked me up," Adam tells Sam. "He bought me, like, a shitload of alcohol. All kinds."

Sam looks up from the TV, where the Red Wings are spanking the Montreal Canadiens. "That's why you didn't want me to buy for you," he says. "You knew a guy."

"I knew a guy," Adam says. "And he has a car."

Sam frowns. "I thought you quit your job, though. How'd you pay for this mother lode of booze?"

"I just, you know, had some money saved up," Adam says. "It seemed like a good investment opportunity."

Sam looks Adam over. "So I guess you're pretty much the man after that move, huh?"

Adam shrugs. "I guess so."

He turns back to the TV. Watches the hockey game. Thinks about the party, about all the booze, the gods and goddesses loving him, Victoria all over him, and he knows he should feel like the man, but . . .

He doesn't.

Not yet.

Tony Montana didn't stop when he made his first score. He kept climbing. He stayed hungry.

Adam's still hungry. He's still climbing.

There's a lot more work to be done.

112.

Word gets around.

"*Dude*." Some acne-scarred sophomore buttonholes Adam in the hall, Monday morning. "Who's your hookup, man? I got a drought situation on my hands."

Adam's about to give the kid Tommy's number. Then he thinks about it.

"Make me a list," he says instead. "I'll hook you up."

113.

After school, Adam calls Tommy. Tommy's into it.

"We can basically charge these kids whatever we want," Tommy says. "Let's fucking gouge 'em."

Adam thinks, *Whoa now.*

"Let's not," he says. "I want these kids to like me. Anyway, it's not that hard to get a fake ID."

Tommy thinks about it. Tommy shrugs. "Whatever," he says. "Just make sure you introduce me to some honeys, cool?"

Adam looks at Tommy like, *Honeys?*

Whoa now.

114.

Tommy delivers the booze the next day. Brings it to Nixon in his Mustang and they hand it off to the sophomore in the parking lot after school.

"Tell your friends about us," Adam tells the kid. "If they need drinks we can hook it up, easy."

"I think there's another party going down next week," the kid says. "We'll totally call you."

Adam shakes the kid's hand. Takes his money. Walks back to where Tommy's waiting by the Mustang, watching a couple of pretty senior girls walk to a pink Volkswagen Golf.

"Here you go," Adam tells him. Hands over Tommy's cut of the profits. Tommy stares at it.

It's, like, twenty bucks.

"We gotta bump the price," Tommy says. "This barely covers my gas, man."

Adam looks down at the twenty in his own hand. "Fuck it," he says, handing it over. "Take it all. Soon as people figure out who we are, we'll start making real cash."

"You want to start making real cash," Tommy says, "you gotta start thinking about pills."

He watches the pink Volkswagen drive out of the parking lot. "Pills, man," he says. "The honeys go nuts for that shit."

Adam follows Tommy's gaze. Adam doesn't like the look in Tommy's eyes.

Drug dealing? Adam thinks.

No thanks.

"Just wait until word gets around," Adam tells him. "We'll be rolling in it."

115.

That night, Adam hijacks the family computer. Makes a new Facebook page.

Pizza Man Enterprises.

(Figures after Janie's party, he might as well own it.)

Booze, grades, etc.

Keeps the description vague, like, *If you don't know, ask somebody.* Like, he's not going full retard.

(You never go full retard.)

Then he invites all of his new friends.

116.

By Friday, Pizza Man Enterprises has twenty-five likes.

Four kids send Adam messages asking for booze. A couple more text him for homework help.

Adam tells them all:

"Meet me at my locker after school and we'll talk."

Hits up his locker after last period and the place is a mob scene.

117.

More homework assignments.

    More booze.

    Wayne's clearing four hundred a week. Tommy's in the Nixon parking lot at least once a week. Pizza Man Enterprises has seventy-five likes.

    Adam doesn't get much sleep—

        ("Can't watch the game tonight," he tells Sam. "So much homework.")

    —and neither does Wayne, from the looks of it.

    And it's not like Adam's seeing much of Victoria, between the homework stuff and the party supplies.

    Pretty much all he has time for—

        (if he's lucky)

            —is one date a week.

    A movie downtown.

    Dinner somewhere.

    They fool around in the theater. They make out behind the mall.

        ("You sleep with that girl yet?" Brian asks Adam.

        Adam shakes his head. "Working on it."

        And he is.

        But . . .)

    "Come over to my place," Victoria tells him. "My parents are on afternoons this week. We'll have the whole place to ourselves."

Adam starts to tell her hell yes, he's coming over. Then he thinks about it.

About the three English assignments he's gotta get done tonight.

About Alton Di Sousa's latest econ lab.

About the three senior girls who want Smirnoff Ice for the weekend.

"This week's no good," Adam tells Victoria. "I have a crapload of homework."

Victoria frowns. "You always have homework. Can't you take a night off?"

Adam shrugs. "I gotta keep my grades up."

"I guess so," she says. "You really *are* a big nerd, Pizza Man."

"Don't call me that," Adam tells her. "I told you, I just want to be Adam with you."

"Except you're never with me," Victoria says.

Victoria goes home unhappy. She's feeling neglected. Adam knows this. Adam's unhappy too. But at the same time . . .

People know who he is.

People slap him five in the hall.

Sophomores look at him like he's somebody now.

It's worth it, he thinks. *Keep grinding a little while longer.*

118.

Just when Adam thinks he's about to go insane—
    (from the homework and the lack of sleep and the booze
and the not-seeing-Victoria)
    —Christmas happens.
    Holidays. And not a moment too soon.

119.

Adam pays off Wayne. Wishes him a merry Christmas. Tells him his job will be waiting for him in January. Then he grabs Victoria and drags her to the mall.

It's Adam's first Christmas with money. He buys his mom a cashmere sweater and a couple romance novels.

An autographed Bruce Springsteen record for his dad.

A couple Blu-rays for Steph, and a T-shirt from Hollister. ("She'll love this," Victoria tells him. "She's had her eye on this all year."

"You think Rob Thigpen will get it for her?" Adam says.

Victoria laughs. "I doubt it," she says. "Rob isn't exactly known for being thoughtful.")

Then Adam chases Victoria away, makes her hang in the food court while he picks out her present.

120.

A gold necklace from the jewelry store.

(With a diamond.)

It only costs Adam a couple hundred bucks, but it looks the part. And Victoria squeals when she opens it. "How did you afford this?" she says. "It must be superexpensive."

"I have money," Adam tells her. "I've been working."

"You quit your job, though." She frowns. "Are you, like, a drug dealer or something?"

Adam blinks. "What?"

She waits a beat. Then she bursts out laughing. "The look on your face, Adam. I'm *kidding*."

"Oh." Adam forces a smile. "Yeah."

"You're tutoring, right?" Victoria says. "Somebody said you were helping them out with their homework. I figured that's why you're so busy and stuff."

"Yeah," Adam says. "Tutoring and stuff. Anyway, who cares about that right now? All I care about is if you like the necklace."

Victoria kisses him. "I don't like it," she says. "I love it."

121.

Adam's mom loves her sweater.

His dad loves his Springsteen record.

Steph?

"You seen those movies yet?" Adam asks her. "I heard they were pretty good."

Steph shakes her head. "They're good." She has a funny look on her face. "Yeah, they're good. Thanks, Adam."

"Everything cool?"

Steph cocks her head at him. "I don't know, Adam," she says. "Does Victoria know how you paid for this stuff?"

Adam glances into the kitchen, where his mom is making breakfast. "What are you trying to pull?" he asks. "You don't like your presents?"

"I'm just wondering what Victoria thinks of your little career," Steph says. "I hear you're selling booze now too."

Adam walks over to Steph's pile of presents and pulls out the Blu-rays and the Hollister T-shirt. "You don't want this stuff, say the word."

Steph shrugs. "Whatever. It's probably stolen goods anyway."

"Screw off," Adam says. "What do you want from me?"

"Nothing." Steph grins at him. "I just want you to know that your pathetic little career isn't going to last forever, Adam. And I'm going to be there to laugh at you when it all comes crashing down."

Adam's about to tell Steph to mind her own business. Then his mom pokes her head in from the kitchen. "Christmas breakfast," she says. Then her smile disappears. "Jeez. What the heck's the matter with *you* two?"

122.

Sam comes over for Christmas dinner.

It takes a lot of work to get Sam into the house. There's a crumbling little stoop that Adam and his dad have to lift the wheelchair over, and then the wheelchair is almost too wide for the doorway, and there are a couple of stairs inside the door—

(there's a lot of grunting and muttered swear words)

—and all the while, Adam's mom is watching from the kitchen and trying not to look sad, and . . .

Steph is in the living room texting and pretending not to care, and . . .

Sam looks ashen and kind of tense, like knows he's fucking this up for everyone and he's just kind of fighting to keep it all together, and . . .

Adam was going to do this later, but he can't wait. He goes into his room and digs around and comes back with Sam's Christmas present.

(It's an envelope.)

(Merry Christmas.)

123.

Sam opens the envelope. There are tickets inside. Two (2) of them.

"Holy crap," he says. "Red Wings?"

Adam nods. "They have, like, a wheelchair-accessible area. The game's not until March, but it's the Maple Leafs, so . . ."

"I hate the Maple Leafs," Sam says.

"And what's better than watching them get spanked, live and in person?" Adam says. "I figured we could take the bus over."

"You'll have to talk to Dr. Stevens," Adam's mom says. "Make sure it's okay."

Sam waves her off. "It'll be fine," he says. "There's no way I'm missing this, Mom."

Sam's smiling, now.

Adam's mom and dad are smiling too.

Even Steph looks happy.

(Well, *happier*.)

"Merry Christmas," Adam tells Sam.

"Merry Christmas," Sam tells Adam.

And for the first time in a while, it is.

124.

A few days after Christmas, Victoria calls Adam.

"My parents are working late," she tells him. "And I *know* you don't have homework this time."

125.

Adam's in Walkerville in a minute flat.

     Not really. It takes almost an hour with the way the buses are running. But he gets there. And Victoria's waiting. She lives in this old brick company home a few blocks from the distillery by the river. It's a nice home. Funky. It has character.

     Adam has to push the realization from his mind that it's auto-plant money—

     (the same auto-plant money his dad used to make)

     —that's paying for this place. For a moment, he feels jealous. Then he kisses Victoria and he doesn't care anymore.

126.

Victoria's room looks like Steph's:

    Teddy bears.

    Pink wallpaper.

    Boy-band poster on the walls.

    Adam doesn't really waste much time admiring the decor, though. He doesn't have much of a chance,

        because

                as soon as he walks in the room, Victoria shoves him on the bed, climbs on top of him, kisses him (hard),

                        and Adam stops caring about the wallpaper.

127.

"Mmmph, Adam," Victoria mumbles. "Slow up a sec, kay?"

Adam sits up and looks at her. Moves his hand from the catch on her pants.

(Victoria's on her back, her hair tousled, her clothing askew.

Her skin's flushed.

They're both breathing hard.

Things are

hot

and

heavy.)

"We still have an hour," Adam tells her. "What's the matter?"

"It's not that," Victoria says. "It's just . . ."

She looks away.

"What?" Adam says. "What is it?"

Victoria chews her lip. "I'm sorry," she says, sighing. "I like you a lot, Adam."

"I like you, too," Adam tells her.

"I just"—Victoria sighs again—"I don't want to do any-thing crazy, okay? I don't think I'm ready yet."

"What do you mean, crazy?" Adam says.

"I mean, I don't think I'm ready to have sex with you yet." She leans over and kisses him. "It's not because I don't like you.

I'm just not ready yet, you know?"

Adam nods. "Yeah," he says. "For sure."

"You're not mad, are you? I really like you a lot. And just because we can't have sex yet doesn't mean we can't fool around, right?"

"Of course not," Adam says.

"Good." Victoria leans up and kisses him again. "Then come back here already. We still have another hour."

128.

Mixed emotions.

I mean, Victoria's, like, fifteen. Steph's fifteen, and if Adam found out she'd had sex with Rob Thigpen,

well

he'd probably kill them both.

But still.

Paul Nolan has sex.

Alton Di Sousa has sex.

Rob Thigpen definitely has sex. (Just hopefully not with Steph.)

But Adam Higgs?

Still a virgin.

And that's just embarrassing, man.

129.

Thing is, Adam really likes Victoria.

Like,

Really likes.

They hang out a ton over Christmas break. They fool around in her bedroom when her parents work nights.

("Why don't we ever go to your place?" she asks Adam, when her parents switch to morning shifts and are home all the time.

Adam shakes his head.

Adam thinks, *No way are you meeting my parents. No way in hell are you seeing my shitty house.*

"My dad's always home," Adam tells her. "No privacy there.")

They go to more movies together. They troll the mall. They walk in the park and go skating together, hang out and watch TV shows in Victoria's living room.

On New Year's, they walk down to the river to watch the fireworks at midnight.

(Tommy hooks Adam up with a bottle of champagne.)

They unroll a picnic blanket and sit shivering on the shore, drinking from the bottle and watching the fireworks explode high above the Detroit skyline.

"I've never had champagne before," Victoria giggles. "It makes me feel funny."

Adam smiles too. "It's weird, right?"

"The bubbles," Victoria says, and bursts into laughter. *"They tickle my nose."*

Adam pulls her close, feels the warmth of her body against the cool air off the river. He chucks the bottle away and kisses her again, and as the clock strikes midnight, Victoria pulls back and looks up into his eyes. "I think I might love you," she says. "Is it weird if I say that?"

Adam hesitates. Maybe it's the champagne, or maybe it's the fireworks, or maybe it's something else entirely, but he tilts up her chin and kisses her again.

"It's not weird," he says. "I think I might love you, too."

130.

Adam takes Victoria to meet Sam.

(He's a little nervous at first.)

They walk up to Sam's crummy apartment building, and Adam looks at the place and thinks about Victoria's beautiful house and her perfect family and wonders what the hell he was thinking, bringing her here—

(Realizes there's no way he's ever bringing her to Remington Park.)

(Wonders what Victoria will think, when she sees Sam's cramped little living room and his shitty TV, the weird little gadgets and handrails and call buttons in the bathroom.)

(Wonders how long it'll take before she gets grossed out and runs.)

Victoria smiles at him. "You ready?"

Adam hesitates a moment longer. "Yeah," he says finally. "Let's do it."

131.

"Oh yeah," Sam tells Adam. "She's definitely out of your league."

Victoria giggles. They're in Sam's room, and the curtains are open and it's a beautiful day, and you can see the river through the trees and the other buildings outside.

"I'm so excited to finally meet you," Victoria says. "Adam talks about you, like, all the time."

Sam grins. "None of it's true," he says. "Absolutely not one word of it."

"I hear you guys are going to a hockey game," Victoria says.

"Red Wings and the Maple Leafs," Sam says. "Your boy-friend scored us some choice tickets."

"Yeah." Victoria plays with her necklace. "He's pretty good at the whole gift-giving thing."

"I can't wait," Sam says. "It's been a long time since I've seen a game live."

(*How long?* Adam wonders. *Before the accident?*)

"It'll be amazing," Victoria says. "You guys will have so much fun."

"As long as they win," Adam says.

They all kind of look at one another. Look around the apartment.

"So listen," Sam says, "I was going to offer you dinner, but I'm a terrible cook. You guys want to go for hamburgers or something?"

132.

They go out for hamburgers. Victoria doesn't seem to mind walking slow so Sam can keep up in his wheelchair.

   She doesn't seem to care when there's a snowdrift block-
ing the sidewalk and they have to take the long way around to the
burger shack.

   She doesn't complain when they have to wait an extra
ten minutes for the restaurant staff to move a couple tables around
so that Sam can wheel his way through.

   She talks to Sam, jokes with him, holds the door for him.

   She and Sam tease Adam mercilessly.

   Adam doesn't mind.

   Victoria's smiling.

   Sam's smiling.

   The burgers are delicious.

   It's a wonderful night.

133.

Adam and Victoria walk Sam back to his apartment. Victoria hugs Sam good night. Sam hugs her back. Then he looks at Adam.

"Don't look at me," Adam tells him. "I'm not hugging you."

They shake hands instead. It's awkward but it's also kind of nice. Adam and Victoria wait as Sam wheels himself into the apartment building and waves good-bye. Then they walk to the bus loop.

"Your brother is amazing," Victoria tells Adam. "He's a really cool guy."

"You like him?" Adam asks her. "You had a good time tonight?"

Victoria kisses him. "Of course," she says.

Adam feels his phone buzz in his pocket. It's a text from Sam.

(*She's a FOX, bro.*)

Adam laughs.

"Sam likes you, too," he says.

134.

Christmas break ends three days into January. The holiday is over. Adam's back to work.

And Tommy isn't happy.

135.

"I can't keep doing this, man," Tommy says as Adam hands over the profits from their latest booze run. "Forty bucks a week just isn't worth my time."

"Come on," Adam tells him. "We cleaned up at New Year's."

"I made a hundred bucks," Tommy says. "I can triple that on a Tuesday night moving pills. You want to make real money, you help me deal to these rich bitches."

Adam looks around the parking lot. Then he looks back at Tommy.

Nah, he thinks. *No pills.*

Adam has a better idea.

136.

Adam calls Brian. They shoot some more hoops.

"My cousin's still hooking you up?" Brian asks him. "Getting you all the booze you want?"

"Yeah, Tommy's cool." Adam shoots. Misses. "I think he's a little disappointed by the profits, though."

Brian catches the ball on the rebound. "I can see that," he says. "Forty bucks a week or something, right? Ain't paying his car note."

"I'm thinking I don't need him anyway," Adam says.

Brian shoots. Makes it. Adam passes the ball back.

"Of course you need him," Brian says. "You're not legal. Plus you don't have a car. How're you going to sell booze without him?"

"I'm working on it." Adam catches Brian's rebound. "How'd you like to make some money with me?"

"What, selling booze?" Brian shakes his head. "There's no profit in it, man. You said it yourself. Anyway, I'm not legal, either."

Adam dribbles the ball once. Then he holds it. "I'm not talking booze," he tells Brian. "I'm talking IDs."

137.

Adam's thought process:

      Tommy's unhappy. Tommy keeps pushing the pill angle. Adam doesn't want to sell drugs. But Tommy's probably not sticking around much longer at forty bucks a week.

      So.

      Tommy's out.

      Begs the question:

            Why doesn't Adam bail from the booze biz himself?

      Answer:

            Because there's fucking *cachet* in it.

            Because parties.

            Because popularity.

            Because duh.

      Adam's selling booze, with or without Tommy. Without Tommy is harder. Without Tommy requires:

      a)   a fake ID.

      b)   a car.

      Adam's thought process:

      Brian has a car.

      Brian probably knows someone with a fake ID hookup.

      Brian could probably use some extra cash.

      Ergo:

            Brian is the new Tommy.

         Brian can help Adam score the booze.

138.

But then Adam starts thinking about the other things he could do with a fake ID.

To wit:

- He could buy porn.
- He could buy cigarettes.
- He could get into clubs.

Adam doesn't smoke. He gets his porn online. But he sure as hell would love to get into Crash.

And then Adam thinks:

Wouldn't everybody?

139.

Brian takes Adam to meet this guy he knows, Bondy. Bondy works at a 7-Eleven a few blocks from Riverside High. Brian and Adam pick him up outside the store, drive him to this pretty little house in some suburb somewhere.

Bondy lets them in, offers them a drink, takes them downstairs to his workshop. Guy's got mad computer equipment, printers, camera gear, everything. Like he robbed a Best Buy or something.

"Holy shit," Adam says. "You're fully equipped."

Bondy nods. "Professional grade," he says. "We doing this or what?"

Adam looks around. The camera gear. "You gotta take every kid's picture here in this workshop?"

"Nah." Bondy shrugs. "They provide the picture. Passport picture's okay, but it's better if they bring in their old ID card, like from their learner's permit or something, and I can fool around with it. If they don't have one, though, it's cool. I can make it work."

"How long's the turnaround?" Adam asks him.

"Maybe a week? Maybe longer. Depends how busy things get."

"And this stuff is legit, right? You can get into Crash with this stuff?"

"You could cross the border," Bondy says. "Check it out."

He opens a drawer and pulls out a stack of licenses bound

by a rubber band. Hands one to Adam. Adam compares it with his own license.

"The magnetic strip is inoperative," Bondy says, "so you can't go to the casino or anywhere else they swipe it, but you want to get into a club downtown, you shouldn't have a problem."

"Fifty bucks," Adam says.

Bondy nods. "Fifty bucks. Cash in advance."

Adam hands him a hundred. "One for me and one for Brian," he says. "Let's see this stuff in action."

140.

Afterward, Brian and Adam drop Bondy back at the 7-Eleven. Then Brian drives Adam home.

"You must be cleaning up with chicks by now," Brian tells Adam as they drive. "With the booze and the homework and stuff. You sleep with that freshman yet?"

"Not yet." Adam reaches over, fiddles with the radio. Finds a rap station from Detroit. "She told me she's not ready."

"What about you?" Brian says. "Wait, are *you* still a virgin?"

Adam turns up the music. "Yeah," he says, staring out the window. "She's my first girlfriend."

"Shit, I'd go crazy," Brian says. "Think you can wait?"

"I think so," Adam tells him. "She's worth it."

"I hope so," Brian says. "For your balls' sake."

141.

Adam tests out his new ID on Friday.

It's the first week of school after break. Homework is steady but bearable. Victoria's at a movie with Steph.

What the hell, Adam figures. *I could use a night off.*

(Anyway, Crash is practically a business expense at this point.)

There's already a line out front when he rolls up. Pretty girls shivering in short dresses and guys with spiked hair and guido chains. Nobody Adam knows. No gods at the front of the line.

The bouncer's the same guy who turned Adam down a couple months back. This time, he just checks Adam's ID, checks Adam's face, steps aside.

Adam's in.

The club is foggy. Hot. Crowded. Adam pays the cover and walks into the mix. Nods his head to the music—

(some rowdy house/hip-hop mash-up)

—and pushes his way to the bar. Before he can get his drink, though, someone grabs his shoulder. "*Adam.*"

It's Janie Ng.

She hugs Adam. "So good to see you!"

"Hey, Janie," Adam says. "What's up?"

Janie says something, but it's too loud to hear. Adam just shrugs, and she gives up and drags him through the crowd to the back of the club, where

Paul Nolan and Sara Bryant and Alton Di Sousa are hanging out by a banquette. They're all hammered. They all smile when they see Adam. Smile wide.

(Except Rob Thigpen. Rob Thigpen doesn't smile at Adam, but whatever.

It's all good.

Because:

Paul Nolan slaps him five.

Sara Bryant gives him a hug.

Alton thrusts a drink in his hand.

Crash, baby.

Hell yeah.)

142.

Adam drinks the beer that Alton gives him.

He drinks the Bacardi and Coke that Jessie hands him.

He tries to buy a round. The gods aren't having it. Paul Nolan waves him off. "Don't even think about it, bro," he tells Adam. "You came through at the party. Tonight it's on us."

Adam protests.

(Weakly.)

Then he thinks, to hell with it.

He lets the gods buy him drinks.

He gets drunk, and then he gets drunker.

Crash, baby.

(And burn.)

143.

Dancing happens.

Jessie and Janie drag Adam to the dance floor. Paul Nolan and Sara Bryant start grinding. Alton picks up a college chick.

Adam's drunk.

He's a horrible dancer. Plus, he's distracted. He keeps looking over at Rob Thigpen, where he's standing at the bar with a couple of hockey buddies. He keeps having this thought, like he's realizing why he hates Rob Thigpen so much.

(Besides the fact that he's a dick.)

(And an asshole.)

(And he's probably trying to hook up with Adam's little sister.)

144.

Adam's remembering Sam's accident.

It was a hockey game, Riverside versus Nixon. Some douchebag from Nixon hit Sam into the boards from behind. Everyone said it was an accident.

(You know all this.)

Adam's remembering the accident. He was there, at the game. He's remembering the Nixon douchebag hitting Sam into the boards. The guy skating around while Sam lay on the ice. Watching as the paramedics carted Sam off on a stretcher.

The douchebag's name was Thigpen, Adam's pretty sure.

He's, like, 99 percent sure the guy was Rob Thigpen's brother.

145.

Adam's mind = blown.

He can *see* the name Thigpen on the back of the douche-bag's jersey. Can see the guy tapping his stick on the ice as the medics wheeled Sam away.

(The asshole didn't even get a penalty.)

Everything's suddenly clear to Adam. He suddenly sees the light. Of course Rob Thigpen's popular, if his brother was a hockey god. The Thigpen name would be royalty at Nixon. Rob wouldn't even have to try.

It would have been the same at Riverside, if Sam hadn't had his accident. If the Nixon douchebag hadn't paralyzed Sam. Sam would be royalty.

Adam would be royalty.

Adam has that Thigpen douchebag to thank that he's not.

146.

Adam stares at Rob Thigpen across the bar, until Rob Thigpen looks over at him. Rob curls his lip. Rob mouths something to his buddies.

Adam's suddenly mad.

He's suddenly headed over there to confront Rob Thigpen. Tell him what assholes he and his brother really are.

(He might even fight Rob Thigpen, maybe.)

Janie Ng intercepts him. Janie Ng saves the day.

She smiles at Adam. Leans in close and yells something Adam doesn't understand. Puts his hands on her hips and starts grinding—

(her ass)

—into the front of his Rag & Bone jeans.

Adam looks at Rob Thigpen again. Looks at Janie. Adam has a sudden flash of enlightenment:

No matter how much he hates Rob Thigpen for what his brother did to Sam—

(and for being an asshole),

no matter how much Adam wants to kick Rob Thigpen's ass—

(and he does),

there's no way Adam wins by fighting Rob Thigpen. There's no way he attains god status that way.

The minute Adam makes Rob Thigpen his enemy, it's all over.

The gods will side with Rob. They all love the bastard.
The goddesses, too.
And moments like tonight—
(with Janie Ng and the rest of them)
—will never happen again.
Rob's watching Adam. Watching Janie dance with him.
And Janie's all over Adam now. She takes his hands in her own
and runs them all over her body.
(She has a smoking-hot body.)
Adam dances with Janie. Adam can tell Rob is watching.
And suddenly, Adam knows how to beat him.
How to hurt him.
Just keep winning, baby. Win until you're a bigger god
than even Rob Thigpen. Win until you're big enough to tear him
to pieces.
And rub his face in it the whole fucking way.

147.

Janie turns around. Presses her body so close, Adam can feel her breath on his neck. She yells in his ear, "It's too hot in here."

Janie's right.

It's stifling hot.

So many people.

So much fog.

Adam takes Janie's hand, leads her to the bar. Tries to score a glass of water.

No dice.

The bartender laughs in his face. Someone gives Adam a beer instead. Adam leaves it behind. Finds Janie again. Janie pulls him toward the front door, the street. "I know a place."

Adam glances back as Janie leads him to the door. Finds Rob Thigpen in the crowd and gives him this wink and this smile, like,

I'm better than you, asshole.
And I'll make sure they all know it.

148.

It's chaos outside Crash. Snow's falling. Music's thumping. Drunk people everywhere. Janie leads Adam toward a pizza place down the block.

Then:

    Janie slips

        Loses her balance

            Screams a little bit

            Falls

                Adam catches her

            Holds her up

        Holds her tight

      Holds her close

    and that's when

Janie kisses him.

149.

At first, Adam thinks:

Holy shit.

And then, Adam thinks:

Eat it, Thigpen.

And somewhere, deep in the back of his mind, Adam thinks:

Victoria.

150.

"Let's go somewhere." Janie drags Adam back against a wall and starts kissing him again. "I know you want me."

Adam's too drunk to do much but let her kiss him. "Janie," he says.

"I *know* you want me." Janie giggles. "I can *feel* it."

She's not lying.

He can feel that she can feel it. And Adam's tempted. But he pushes Janie away. "Shit," he says. "Janie. I have a girlfriend."

Janie makes a face. "Who, that frigid little freshman?"

Adam shrugs.

Janie laughs. "I'll make you forget all about her, Adam," she says. "Come on." She looks up at him, and she's pretty and drunk and a goddess, and Adam thinks:

Damn it.

Damn it.

He walks Janie back toward Crash, where Rob Thigpen and Paul Nolan and Sara Bryant and Jessie McGill and Alton Di Sousa are on their way out. Jessie winks at Adam. "Thought we lost you guys."

"Just needed some air," Adam tells her.

"We're hitting the Pancake House," Paul Nolan says. "You guys coming?"

"There's, like, seven of us," Adam says. "We won't fit in a cab."

"So we'll take two," Alton says. "You coming or no?"

Adam looks around. He's wasted already. He probably should go home.

Get some sleep.

Work on homework assignments.

But Janie's hanging on Adam's arm. The kids in the Crash line are staring

like they're jealous of Adam,

like he's some kind of God

(and Rob Thigpen's watching him, too).

"Fuck it," Adam says. "Let's get pancakes."

151.

Needless to say, the weekend's a write-off.

Adam wakes up in Paul Nolan's basement late Saturday morning, fighting a—

(*killer*)

—hangover. Janie Ng's passed out beside him, in an old T-shirt and these little boy-shorts, and Adam's first thought is:

I'm still a virgin.

His next thought is:

I didn't cheat on Victoria.

(Well, not really.)

And his last thought is:

I'm going to throw up in Paul Nolan's basement.

Adam gets the hell out of there. Pukes in an alley. Staggers home to Remington Park, passes out in his room.

Sleeps—

(pretty much)

—until Monday.

152.

Sara Bryant's at Adam's locker first thing Monday morning. "Do you have my physics paper? It's due tomorrow."

Crap.

"I spent the weekend in bed," Adam tells her. "Worst. Hangover. Ever.

"I'm sorry," Adam tells her.

"I couldn't finish the paper," Adam tells her.

Sara stares at him. "What do you mean, you couldn't finish? It's. Due. Tomorrow."

"I didn't plan on getting so wasted on Friday," Adam tells her. "I'll get it done tonight. Sorry."

"You'd better," Sara says. "These are my fucking *grades*, Adam. Where are your priorities?"

Sara swears. *"Jesus."*

153.

Adam goes home Monday night. First thing he does is finish Sara Bryant's chem assignment.

("Where are your priorities?")

Then he goes on Facebook and updates Pizza Man Enterprises. Sends a PM to every one of his two hundred Likes. Offers club access.

Offers booze.

DIY.

Fake IDs, a hundred bucks a pop. Good as government.

Satisfaction guaranteed.

Five kids write back within the hour. By Tuesday morning Adam's taken his first ten orders.

A hundred bucks each.

A thousand bucks gross.

Five hundred bucks profit.

154.

It's not enough.

        Because—

                (after everything)

       —he's still just a hustler.

          (He's not quite a god.)

            Rob Thigpen—

                    (that asshole)

             —is still cooler.

                And that's just not allowed.

155.

Adam and Brian pick up the first batch of IDs. Brian's quiet as he drives. "What's up with you?" Adam says finally. "You're weirding me out."

Brian doesn't say anything for a mile or two. Then he shrugs. "I'm cool."

"Come on," Adam says.

"Shit." Brian sighs. "This ID thing, man. You sold a thousand dollars' worth of cards overnight."

Adam grins at him. "Damn right, *we* did. What's the problem?"

Brian shakes his head. "I just wasn't expecting this," he says. "I figured you'd pop off an ID a week, get us some weed money, that kind of thing.

"*This* stuff," Brian says. "This is big business."

"Yeah?" Adam says. "So what's the problem?"

"I just don't get your angle," Brian says. "You're already in with the popular kids, right? You have this sexy girlfriend. Why bother going crazy at this point?"

Adam looks across the car at him.

Adam thinks:

Tony Montana, man.

The world is yours.

"I know what I'm doing," Adam says. "Just roll with it."

156.

The ID thing takes off. Bondy's good for ten cards a week. Brian stops worrying when Adam pays him his cut.

(Money does that.)

And meanwhile, at Nixon:

Some pretty blond sophomore stops Adam in the hall one day. Looks up at him with these big blue eyes. "You're Adam, right? Can we talk?"

Audrey Klein. Adam's pretty sure he went to grade school with her. He's positive she's never said a word to him before in her life.

Until now.

"Yeah," he tells Audrey. "What's up?"

She pulls him aside. "My brother, you know, Simon?" she says. "You did a couple assignments for him before Christmas. He said it was money well spent."

Adam nods. Adam knows Simon. Starting goalie for the Nixon varsity soccer team. Not exactly a god, but close enough to matter.

Another satisfied customer.

"So . . ." Audrey blushes a little. Bites her lip. "I was wondering if you might be able to help me with my social studies project?"

Bingo.

Adam savors the moment a little bit.

The look in Audrey's eyes.

The envious glances from the guys walking past in the hallway.

"I charge ten bucks a page," he tells Audrey. "Twenty-dollar bonus for an A."

Her face falls. "That much?"

Adam shrugs. "I hear it's money well spent."

157.

"Who was that?" Victoria asks Adam as Audrey Klein walks off.

"Audrey Klein," Adam tells her.

"I know who she is," Victoria says. "What did she want?"

Adam shrugs. "She just had some homework questions. Nothing serious."

"She's a sophomore, Adam."

"Yeah." Adam shrugs again. "Tutoring. She wanted social studies help."

"Tutoring." Victoria watches Audrey walk away. "You sure do a lot of tutoring, don't you?"

"Wait," Adam says. "You're not jealous, are you?"

Victoria blushes.

"What," he says. "Of me and Audrey?"

She looks down at the ground. "Of you and anyone, Adam. You hang out with all these pretty girls, and I . . ."

Adam waits. "Yeah?"

"I'm just afraid," she says. "You know, since we're not . . . I just don't want . . ."

Adam thinks about Janie Ng outside Crash. About how he turned down a golden chance to sleep with a goddess.

He kisses Victoria. "Hey," he says. "You have nothing to worry about."

158.

And she doesn't.

    Not really.

    I mean, Adam thinks, *it would be nice to not be a virgin anymore*. It would be nice if everyone at Nixon knew he'd slept with a goddess.

    It would confer upon Adam instant god status. It would put Adam on par with Rob Thigpen.

    (Where he's supposed to be.)

    (Probably.)

    But Adam loves Victoria.

    And Victoria loves Adam.

    And that's all that really matters.

Right?

159.

Even if Victoria has nothing to worry about, Adam does.

Because Audrey Klein tells her friends about Adam. Soon there's a horde of pretty sophomores crowding Adam's locker after school. And it isn't long before their boyfriends come sniffing around too.

Jason Poulin.

Max Tanner.

Gordie Robson.

GITs. Gods in Training.

They don't mean much to Adam, but he can't turn them down. Money is money. Power is power. Prestige is everything.

And if he's not sleeping with goddesses, he's going to need to bust his ass to build his *Scarface* empire instead.

160.

So Adam decides he needs another new employee. Two, maybe.

First thing, he figures he'll give Darren another shot. Catches up to him after math class.

"Hey, man," Adam says. "What are you doing this weekend?"

Darren shrugs. "Was thinking about seeing the new Iron Man movie. You?"

"Homework," Adam tells him. "Listen, what are your grades like?"

"I dunno, B's?" Darren says. "I do okay. I mean, whatever, right? We're juniors. I don't want to spend my whole life doing homework."

"Yeah," Adam says. "I guess. I mean, what else do you do?"

"What does anybody do? Hang out with friends, go to hockey games, watch movies, play Xbox, try to pick up girls. I'd rather do that than worry about my grades, I guess."

"What about being popular?"

Darren frowns. "What, like with Paul Nolan and them?"

Adam nods. "Exactly."

"I mean, whatever," Darren says. "It's nice to be popular, but I have enough friends."

Darren shoulders his backpack. "Listen, I gotta run. If you want to see Iron Man this weekend, there's a bunch of us going. Might be a good break from homework or whatever."

161.

Iron Man.

    Fat chance.

    Darren's a no-go. Fortunately, Adam has a few other candidates in mind.

    Next stop: Deborah Menard.

162.

Deborah Menard:

Bookworm.

Spends hours in the library, her nose in a book. Never speaks to anyone, just reads. Sometimes it's European history. Sometimes it's gardening manuals. Adam figures, anyone who reads that much *has* to be smart, right?

He finds Deborah in the back of the library at lunchtime. She jumps when he says her name. "Jesus," he says. "Sorry. Didn't mean to scare you. What are you reading?"

Deborah blushes a little. *"On the Origin of Species,"* she says. "Charles Darwin."

(*Bingo*, Adam thinks.)

"No kidding," he says. "You into that stuff?"

"Evolution?" She fidgets. "I mean, I guess."

Adam looks around. Nobody nearby. "Listen, can you keep a secret?"

Deborah's eyes go wide. "Oh my god," she says. "You're the guy who does homework for money, right?"

Adam grins. "Uh, yeah. That's actually what I want to talk to you about."

Deborah gives him a look. "I don't need my homework done for me, thanks. I can handle that myself."

Adam grins bigger. "I'm not trying to angle for your business, Deborah," he says. "I'm looking for your help."

"I don't get it," Deborah says.

"I'm overloaded," Adam tells her. "I need someone to work for me."

Deborah laughs. "What, like, you want to pay me to do someone else's homework? Why wouldn't I just work something out with them personally?"

"Because I have the customer base—the in with the right people," Adam says. "They know me. I guarantee good work."

"Yeah, but you wouldn't be actually *doing* the work," Deborah says. "I would."

"I'd check it over. Make sure it's up to par. Quality control. I'd get you the contacts with the popular kids. I'd handle the business side."

Deborah laughs again. "You sound like a pimp." She opens her book. "Look, I'm sure it's a great little scheme, but I'm really not interested."

Adam stares at her. *You have no friends*, he wants to tell her. *You spend your whole life in the library, reading books. You don't go to parties. You eat lunch alone.*

You're not *interested*?

Some people just need to reexamine their priorities.

163.

Adam finds another candidate.

George Dubois. He's like the male version of Deborah Menard, with minor and insignificant variations.

Spends every lunch hour in the computer lab, alone. Eats alone. Sits alone. Walks home alone.

George doesn't have many friends. Plus he won the academic award for highest average last year, so he's gotta be smart.

George Dubois is the perfect candidate.

Except:

George Dubois's name sounds familiar. As Adam approaches the kid, he figures out why.

George Dubois's mom is Bonnie Dubois.

Bonnie Dubois is the Nixon guidance counselor.

(*Abort! Abort!*)

George Dubois is a no-go.

164.

Fortunately, there are other smart, desperate kids at Nixon. And after a week of looking, Adam finds two of them.

First up: Devon Parent. Your average social outcast with a high IQ. And a *crazy*-big crush on Leanne Grayson.

Adam flags down Devon after English class. "Devon," he says. "Can we talk?"

Devon looks back at him, shrugs. Noncommittal. At that moment, Leanne Grayson walks past. "Hey, Leanne," Adam says. "How's it going?"

Leanne smiles at Adam. Smiles big. "What's up, Adam?"

Leanne *breezes* down the hall. Devon watches her go. "Want to know my secret?" Adam asks him.

Devon's still focused on Leanne. "What?"

"You want to get in tight with Leanne Grayson?"

"I guess," Devon says.

"Let me put it another way," Adam says. "You want to make some money?"

Devon shakes his head. "I don't do drugs, man."

Adam grins at Devon. "It's not drugs. It's homework. I want to pay you to do Leanne's homework. Are you in?"

165.

Devon's in. Devon's way in. Devon listens to the spiel and he's nodding before Adam even gets to the money part. Devon shakes Adam's hand and promises to meet him after school. Devon watches Adam walk away like he's some kind of . . .

god.

So that's one down. Next up: Lisa Choi.

166.

Lisa Choi is:

-Alternate captain of the Academic Challenge team.

(Wayne's teammate.)

- Famous around school for melting down in math class after Sara Bryant called her out for owning a counterfeit Coach bag.

(Turned bright red and ran out of the classroom.)

(Was reported crying in the girls' bathroom for hours afterward.)

Lisa Choi is:

A perfect candidate.

167.

Adam gets Wayne to introduce him to Lisa. Lisa scowls at Wayne when they chase her down. "Can I help you?"

Wayne kind of blushes. "Uh, yeah," he says. Stammers a little. "Uh, hey, Lisa."

"Lisa," Adam says, stepping in, "I'm Adam."

Lisa looks Adam up and down. "Forget it," she says. "Wayne, don't ever try to set me up with your friends again."

Adam laughs. "I don't want to go out with you. I want to make you an offer."

"If it has anything to do with sex, you can die in a grease fire," Lisa tells him.

"It's not sex, Lisa," Adam tells her. "It's homework."

Lisa relaxes a little. "You need a tutor or something?"

"Not me," Adam says. "But I know some other kids who need help."

He pitches the scheme. Lisa listens. Thinks about it. Then she looks at Wayne. "You're in on this?"

Wayne nods. "Uh-huh. It's great. I—"

"How much do you make?"

"Lots," Wayne says.

"Enough for a real Coach bag," Adam tells her.

Lisa goes red. "Shut up."

The bell rings. "Locker two fourteen," Adam says. "You can pick up your assignments after school."

168.

Lisa and Devon turn in their first assignments a few days later.
Lisa writes too much—
      (probably trying to pad her page count for more money)
      —and Devon needs a little work on his grammar, but
otherwise,
         everything
             is
               gravy.
And that's good, because Adam is swamped with work.
Pizza Man Enterprises has five hundred and twenty-three likes on
Facebook.

Bondy is maxed to capacity, printing ten fake IDs a week,
and there's a three-week waiting list. Already, the guy's complain-
ing about his dwindling social life.

"You want a social life?" Adam asks him. "That's cool. I'll
find somebody else to make my IDs. You can go back to 7-Eleven,
pick up a couple more shifts."

Bondy looks at Brian. Brian just shrugs. Brian's pulling
his own profits delivering booze to kids who haven't scored IDs
yet. He gets invited to a lot of parties.

(So does Adam, but Adam doesn't have time to party.)

Brian's started dating this Nixon chick he met at one of
those parties, a punk-rock sophomore named Amanda Rimes who
wears Ramones T-shirts and fishnet stockings. Amanda's cute.

Amanda *loves* Brian. Brian doesn't give a damn about Bondy's social life.

Neither does Adam.

"You guys are real assholes, you know that?" Bondy says, sighing.

Adam peels off a stack of hundreds. Five of them, minty-fresh. "Ten more," Adam tells him. "See you next week."

169.

"I'm so looking forward to this hockey game," Sam tells Adam.

He's admiring the tickets again while Adam does a little homework on his couch—

(Another English essay for Jessie McGill.)

—"March is too damn far away," Sam says. "I mean, time just seems to be *dragging*, man. Don't you think?"

Adam looks up from his essay. "Yeah?" he says. "Yeah."

Sam looks over at him, then back at the tickets. "I wish I had a jersey or something," he says. "It would be sick to roll in there all pimped out. Show them we're true fans, you know?"

Adam closes his eyes. Tries to concentrate. He knows he should be paying attention, but this freaking essay's due tomorrow.

"Adam?"

Adam looks up again. "Yeah," he says. "You want a jersey. I'll see what I can do."

170.

Locker 214 is getting crowded. Chaos ensues every day after school.

>Wayne.

>Lisa.

>Devon.

>Alton Di Sousa.

>Audrey Klein.

>Audrey Klein's douche boyfriend.

>Sara Bryant.

>Some random sophomore looking for a fake ID.

>Etc.

>Etc.

>Etc.

>It's too much.

>>Too suspicious.

>>>It's time to move Pizza Man Enterprises off-property.

>There's a little restaurant across the street from the school, Cardigan's. It's a mob scene during lunchtime and a dead zone any other time.

>Adam takes it over.

>Posts up in the corner booth with a milkshake after school and presides over his little empire, Wayne and Lisa and Devon beside him. Students roll in, drop off their homework, pick

up their homework, pay for fake IDs. The waitress gives Adam dirty looks, but what the hell, right? It's not like Adam doesn't tip.

Some of the kids stick around, buy hamburgers. There's no one else in the place, anyway.

171.

Business booms. All through January and into February. And then:

      Business stops.

      Business hits the pause button.

      Business takes a commercial break.

          Because:

               exams happen.

172.

It's the end of the first term. Teachers hand back the last of the projects and focus on review for the last couple weeks.

ID sales dry up. Booze, too. No one's looking to party. Adam pays Bondy a hundred dollars, bonus, tells him take it easy for a while.

Bondy looks at the money. Smiles. "I take it back, man," he says. "I like you just fine."

So, okay. A little relaxation, right? A little downtime? Adam's been working so hard, he figures he could use a break. Hang out with Victoria a little. Catch up on sleep. Be a normal kid for once.

Wrong.

Adam catches up on his sleep. Adam hangs with Victoria. Adam does the normal-kid thing.

Adam gets antsy.

No homework to do, no parties to supply equals no way to increase his social standing. Equals no way to win.

Adam's momentum is building. He's trending all over Nixon. He's so damn close to winning, and now he has to press pause.

So he searches for a way to keep himself in the game.

Stay relevant.

Win.

He racks his brain and comes up with nothing, until—

(a week before exams start)

—he figures it out.

173.

Physics class.

Powers—

(remember him?)

—is promising his exam will Kick. Your. Ass.

Everyone's terrified.

Even Sara Bryant.

"I can't afford to flunk this exam," she tells Adam. "My dad's going to cut off my credit card. I'm so fucked, Adam."

Adam looks at her. "Maybe I can un-fuck you."

Sara makes a face.

"You know what I mean," Adam says. "Maybe I can make this test easier."

"How?" Sara says. "It's not like you can write the thing for me."

"No," Adam says, "but maybe I can work a little Pizza Man magic."

174.

"A hundred bucks to anyone who can get me Mr. Powers's physics exam," Adam tells his team.

(His team being:

Wayne,

Devon,

Lisa.)

His team stares at him. "Are you serious?"

Adam pulls a hundred-dollar bill from his wallet. "Plus half of whatever we can get for it on the open market," he tells them. "Who's in?"

"You're out of your mind," Lisa says.

"So you're not interested?" Adam says.

"I didn't say that," Lisa says. "I want two hundred bucks."

"Two hundred's more like it," Wayne says. "This is risky."

"Two hundred bucks," Adam tells them. "And I need it this week."

175.

A couple nights later, Wayne calls. "I have an idea."

"What about Lisa and Devon?" Adam asks.

"They're out," Wayne says. "They think it's impossible. I think they're wrong."

"So do it," Adam tells him. "Test out your theory."

"I need help," Wayne says. "If I'm right about this, you won't just get the physics exam. You'll get *every* exam in the school."

"Holy shit," Adam says. "Really?"

"Really," Wayne says. He explains his idea. It's decent. It's insane. It's risky as hell, but it's definitely workable.

And it will make the Pizza Man a legend at Nixon if Adam can pull it off.

A *god*.

Adam won't ever have to hustle again. No more home-work, no booze, no fake IDs. Just coasting on that Pizza Man reputation. That Hall of Fame status.

"I'll help you," he tells Wayne. "But we'd better do it quick."

176.

Later that night, Adam meets Wayne in the empty parking lot outside Nixon. Wayne shows up in all black, like a cat burglar. "That's not suspicious at all," Adam tells him.

"I don't want to get seen," Wayne says, pulling a dark ski mask over his face. He hands another to Adam.

Adam points to the school. Every light in the building is burning. "You should have worn white," Adam says.

There was a basketball game in the gym earlier. The gym doors are still unlocked. Adam and Wayne slip inside.

The gym is way dark. It's like walking in space. They cling to the walls until they reach the far side, the door into the school. Inch it open and peer out.

The hallway is lit up bright, but it's empty. Somewhere in the distance, a radio is playing classic rock. Adam looks at Wayne. "Where now?"

"Janitor's office," Wayne says. In the light he looks pale, terrified. Like he's going to wet himself, or have second thoughts, or both. Adam figures he can't blame him. His heart's pounding, too.

Adam stands watch while Wayne ducks into the janitor's office. Pictures the janitor coming around the corner, finding them both. Freaks himself right out.

After an eternity, Wayne comes out with a key ring. Grins at Adam. "Knew it was in here."

Adam looks at him.

Wayne shrugs. "I saw that old janitor, Hawksley, doing something in here when I was walking past. He had a spare key ring on the wall."

"Okay," Adam says. "So what now?"

Wayne grins. "I've been shadowing Powers," he says. "Trying to figure out where he's stashing the exam. Finally figured it out."

"Yeah," Adam says. "Go on."

"I tailed him to the administrative office," Wayne says. "Turns out he locks up the exams in a little side room by the secretaries. They *all* stash exams there, every teacher in the school."

Adam looks at him. Looks down the empty hall toward the administrative office. Imagines walking out with every exam in the school. If he can somehow get them photocopied, he'll have it fucking made.

"Okay," he tells Wayne. "Get us into the office."

177.

(In the back of his mind, Adam's already thinking this is a bullshit idea.

He's already regretting even bringing Wayne here.

There are two, maybe three janitors in the building. Any one of them could make Adam and Wayne at any moment.

There's a stack of exams in the administrative office, but even if Adam takes them, the teachers are going to notice, right?

I mean, nobody's going to *not* notice a bunch of missing exams.

So.

It's a stupid plan to begin with.

The whole idea is stupid.

Adam knows he should just turn around and walk out, abort the whole thing. Let Sara Bryant fail her exam.

Let Sara Bryant's dad cut up her credit card.

Hell, it's not Adam's concern.

Adam knows this.

But.

What if he *can* photocopy that physics exam somehow? Would be the biggest win of his life. The biggest win in school history.

Would be god mode times infinity.

So Adam follows Wayne down the hall to the administrative office. Adam knows it's a bad idea.

Adam follows through with it anyway.)

178.

Adam and Wayne crouch in the hall across from the office. There's a hallway running perpendicular to the hall they just snuck down. There's a janitor at the far end of that hallway, whistling—
 (off-key)
—and working a mop. Adam and Wayne watch him for a minute. Then Adam looks at Wayne. "Now or never, man."

Wayne looks at Adam like a raccoon looks at a car on the interstate.

"Forget it," Adam says. "Give me the keys."

Adam takes the keys. Bolts across to the office doors and starts trying keys in the lock. The ring has about a million keys on it. Adam keeps fumbling. Finally, something fits.

Adam glances back at Wayne. Wayne nods. Adam nods. Adam turns the door handle and pushes it inward.

Immediately, something beeps inside—
 (*shit*)
—and Adam looks up and sees a little flashing red light in the ceiling as whatever it was that beeped . . .
 beeps again.
 (*Shit.*)
Across the hall, Wayne is gesturing. Urgently. Like, *Get the hell out of there* frantic. Adam ducks inside the dark office and closes the door, quick. The beeping continues. It's getting louder.

(*SHIT.*)

The office is dark. Adam feels his way around the secretaries' desks to the little room where the exams are supposed to be. Jimmies the door and ducks in just as the office lights come on.

"Hello?"

Hawksley, the janitor. Adam waits in the room—

(it's still dark, thank god)

—while Hawksley fiddles with the alarm. It stops beeping. The office is silent. Adam doesn't move. Doesn't breathe.

"Hello?" Hawksley starts around the secretaries' desks. He's coming toward Adam's little room. Adam backs into the darkness. Navigates by touch and sheer panic alone. Finds a doorknob. Turns it, slips through the doorway and back into the light. Back into Wayne.

"Holy crap." Wayne's hyperventilating. "Come on, man, let's go."

They're standing in the main hallway. Adam's come out a back entrance. Down the hall is the gym and the school doors and freedom.

Adam glances back into the office. Hawksley's not in the little room yet.

And they've come this far.

"Wait." Adam pulls away from Wayne and ducks back into the little room. The light from the hallway spills in, and Adam can see filing cabinets, tables, stacks of paper. He rifles through, desperate.

(*Come on.*)

Hawksley pushes open the door. Sees Adam. "What the hell?"

Adam finds a file folder. *Mr. Powers*, it reads. *Final Exams—First Semester.*

Adam reaches in. Grabs an exam off the top of the stack and books it for the hallway. For Wayne. For the exit.

They *run*.

Hawksley calls out behind them. They ignore him. Bolt down the hallway and burst out through a fire door and into the parking lot, the darkness. Keep running, until they're off school property by a solid five blocks, ducked into an alley, hands on their knees, panting for breath.

"Did he see us?" Adam says.

"How should I know?" Wayne says. "You're the one who had to go back there."

"I couldn't leave without at least trying," Adam tells him. He brandishes the exam paper. "We're going to be *gods*."

Wayne looks up. Looks at the paper. Grins, wide, like in that instant he sees himself in the future. God status attained. Popularity. Girls. Party invites.

Everything.

Then Wayne's smile fades. He squints at the exam paper. "Oh crap."

Adam flips the page over. Sees why Wayne stopped smiling. *Final Exam*, the paper reads. *Mr. Powers, Applied Science, Grade 10.*

Wayne looks at Adam. "So, um," he says, "do I still get the two hundred bucks?"

179.

Nixon is chaos. Mr. Powers looks exhausted. Wayne looks like he's chained to a time bomb. There are cops in the vice principal's office. It's Nixon on lockdown.

The vice principal makes an announcement. "As you may have heard, we had an incident at Nixon last night. A student—or group of students—broke into the administrative office and stole one of next week's exams."

He pauses, and you can hear cheering and applause from every classroom.

"This may sound like a joke," the VP says, "but the perpetrators will be tracked down. Justice will be served. Moreover, the exams they've stolen will be redesigned. They've jeopardized their academic careers for nothing."

The VP urges anyone with information to step forward. Encourages the perpetrators—

(Adam and Wayne)

—to make it easy on themselves. Then he's gone. There's a moment of silence. Then more cheers.

"Hot damn," someone says. "The balls on those kids."

"Fucking celebrities," Paul Nolan says.

"Superstars."

"*Gods.*"

Sara Bryant grins at Adam. "How much would we have to pay you to swipe the physics exam, Pizza Man?"

Adam looks at her. Looks around the classroom. Knows every kid in the school would worship the ground he walks on if he copped to the break-in.

Knows it's an automatic, first-ballot induction to the Badass Hall of Fame.

Adam wants to tell Sara how close he came. Wants to show the whole school just how badass the Pizza Man really is. But he knows he'd be expelled if word got around. He doesn't quite have the balls to do it.

He just grins at Sara instead. "More than you've got, Sara," he says. "*Way* more."

180.

"Can you believe it?" Victoria asks Adam. "Who would try something that stupid?"

Adam shrugs. "I dunno, I think it's kinda cool."

"Kinda cool?" Victoria stares at him. "Adam, it's cheating. It doesn't accomplish anything."

"Yeah, but it's badass," Adam says. "You have to admit, it's, like, *legendary*."

"What does that even mean?" Victoria shakes her head. "It's stupid. Those kids will spend their whole lives regretting it if they get caught."

"Or maybe they'll be gods," Adam says.

"To a bunch of high school kids?" Victoria says. "If that's what you want out of your life, sure, I guess it's all worth it. You can be a high school legend who has to pump gas because no university will take your cheating ass, but at least you're *legendary*, right?"

"Anyway," Adam says, "I doubt they'll even get caught. I heard the janitor didn't even see their faces."

181.

"What do you want to be when you grow up, anyway?" Victoria asks Adam.

They're sprawled out in her living room now, pretending to study.

(Her parents are on the morning shift, and it's afternoon now.

Her dad's watching TV and

her mom's in the kitchen, and

all Adam can think about is how sexy Victoria looks in that tight shirt she's wearing.

How much he wants to . . .

you know.)

"Have you started looking at colleges yet?" Victoria says. "I want to go to Stanford, but my dad wants me to stay close to home. He says it's expensive, but I can probably get a scholarship or something, right?"

Adam looks at her. Adam shrugs. "I mean, I guess so," he says.

(It's not like Adam's ever really thought about college before. It's not like he ever had the grades, or the money, or the motivation.

Thanks to this homework thing, though, Adam has the grades.

(#FringeBenefitNumberOne)

He has a steady source of income.

(#FringeBenefitNumberTwo)

And hell, if college is anything like high school, maybe he can be a god there, too.

So maybe there's something to this college idea.)

182.

"Adam?"

Adam blinks. Snaps back to reality. "Sorry?"

"What are you going to take in college?" Victoria says. "I think I want to study marine biology."

"I don't know," Adam tells her. "Something that makes a lot of money."

"Money?" Victoria frowns. "Money isn't everything, Adam. You should do what you like."

Easy for you to say, Adam thinks. *Your dad didn't get laid off.* He shrugs. "I just want to be rich," he says. "So I won't be a loser."

"You're not a loser." Victoria sits down beside him. Gives him a look. "You work so hard all the time, like you're constantly trying to prove you're somebody else."

She kisses him. "The people who really matter don't care how much money you have, Adam, or whether or not you have a million Facebook friends or if you're a nerd. They just care that you're a decent guy. That's all I care about."

"Yeah," Adam says. "I guess so."

He kisses her back. He lets her believe what she wants to believe. Deep down, though, he knows Victoria wouldn't be so sure of herself if *she'd* ever been poor. If *she'd* ever not been popular.

If she'd ever been called . . .

a loser.

183.

Adam dreams about Rob Thigpen. Dreams about Sam.

About the accident.

A freak play in the Nixon end. Sam's going for the puck. Some big Nixon douchebag nails him from behind, hard.

Sam hits the boards weird.

Sam never walks again.

(And Adam Higgs is consigned to loserdom.)

Adam wakes up hating Rob Thigpen.

(Hating all Thigpens.)

He's too busy to make Rob Thigpen pay for it right now. Too focused on becoming a god.

Someday, though, Adam thinks.

Someday, Rob.

184.

Exams happen. Wayne still wanders the halls like a fugitive. Adam lies awake nights and prays Hawksley doesn't make them.

Hawksley doesn't. The chaos dies down. Exams begin and the whole ordeal is forgotten.

And the exams themselves?

Well.

It turns out writing an essay on *The Grapes of Wrath* five different ways is a pretty damn good way to learn *The Grapes of Wrath*. Adam knows the material. Every class. Knows it cold.

(#FringeBenefitNumberThree)

The gods, on the other hand?

No bueno.

Goes without saying. They spent half the term paying Adam to handle their courseload. How in the hell were they supposed to learn the material?

A couple weeks' cramming can only do so much, man.

Still.

If you think that means Nixon's A-list isn't lining up to hire Adam back, first day of second semester, pal, you have another think coming.

185.

"Holy crap, I bombed that physics exam," Sara Bryant tells Adam in economics, first day of classes.

(Adam switched out from art to econ before the semester. Figured he likes making money more than he likes painting sucky pictures, so . . .)

"Like, *bombed* it," Sara says. "Afghanistan style. I thought my dad was going to ground me for life."

"Crap," Adam says. "Listen, if you think you're better off without me this semester, I totally—"

"Are you kidding?" Sara stares at him. "Pizza Man, I *need* you, buddy. I need A-plusses this term, nothing lower."

Every class. Every god. It's the same story. A-plusses. Desperate times.

Pizza Man, we need you.

186.

Adam isn't so sure about the A-plus idea. Every god in the school suddenly starts rolling high nineties? Somebody's bound to get wise.

"So disguise it," Sara Bryant tells him. "Make it untrace-able. Jesus, Adam, what do we pay you for?"

"You gotta do this, man," Paul Nolan says. "We need you."

"And you know we pay better than any goddamn pizza job," Rob Thigpen tells him.

"You don't want to go back to Pizza Hut, do you?" Sara pats his arm. "Do the work. A-plusses. You name your price."

187.

So now Adam has that to worry about.

He doubles the page rate for each A-plus assignment, plus a fifty-dollar bonus.

(Might as well make it pay, right?)

Restricts VIP access to bona fide gods. Paul Nolan. Sara Bryant. Jessie McGill. Leanne Grayson.

(Damn it, and Rob Thigpen, though Adam charges that chump a 50 percent markup. It makes him feel marginally better.)

Janie Ng? Funny story.

Adam explains the situation to Janie. Special offer. Guaranteed grades. Top of the class. Janie shakes her head. "Thanks, Adam, but I'm cool."

Adam frowns. "You don't want A-plusses?"

"I pull A-plusses already." Janie grins at him. "I rocked those exams. I'm pretty much a huge nerd at this point."

"So why bother with me, then?" Adam asks her. "If you're doing so well on your own?"

Janie shrugs. "Sometimes I just need a break," she says. "My parents are insane about grades."

Then Janie cocks her head. "And maybe I kind of like having an excuse to hang out with you."

"Oh yeah?" Adam says.

Janie winks at him, sly. "Thanks for the offer, but if you ever want to come over and study sometime—"

"Yeah," Adam tells her. "I'll let you know."

188.

A couple weeks into the spring semester, and Adam's walking along that same long hallway he escaped down with Wayne, the night of the botched exam raid.

(Just being there gives him PTSD.)

(Seeing that janitor, Hawksley, makes him sweat.)

Anyway, Adam's walking down that hall. Thinking about that night—

—when the vice principal steps out of his office and calls Adam's name.

Gulp.

He's a big guy, Mr. Acton. Played tight end on the Nixon football team back in the day. Acton handles discipline at Nixon. You don't mess with him.

He's

        one

               scary

                      dude.

So, Adam's terrified. Adam's thinking, *This is it.* Adam's thinking, *I'm screwed.*

Acton looks him over. "You're new here," he says. "You came from where, Riverside?"

"Yes, sir," Adam says.

Acton nods. "How do you feel you're adapting to the Nixon mind-set?"

Adam shrugs. Adam has no clue what he means about the Nixon mind-set, unless "the Nixon mind-set" means sucking up to rich kids who live their lives like royalty, in which case, Adam's all about it.

But Adam doesn't think that's what the VP means. "I don't know," he says. "I guess . . . good?"

"I was in touch with Mr. Nelson, back at Riverside," Acton says. "He was surprised I hadn't met you yet. I hear you two were on familiar terms."

Adam nods. Adam remembers Mr. Nelson. Mr. Nelson caught him smoking up in the park a couple of times. Busted his ass for it.

Adam never liked Mr. Nelson. The feeling was mutual.

Acton studies Adam. "So what happened?" he says.

Adam blinks. "Sir?"

"By Mr. Nelson's account, you were a problem child at Riverside," Acton says. "Here, you're top of your classes. What happened?"

Adam shrugs. "I don't really know, sir."

"Come on," Acton says. "You must have some idea. What caused this big change?"

"I don't know, sir," Adam says. "I guess I just bought into the Nixon mind-set."

189.

"Have you given any thought to what you're going to do with yourself once you graduate?" Acton asks Adam.

Adam shrugs. "I was thinking about college, maybe," he says.

"Any particular field of study?"

Adam shakes his head. "No, sir."

"Hmm." The vice principal purses his lips. "I'd like you to talk to Mrs. Dubois," he says. "She's the guidance counselor here. Have you met her?"

"No, sir," Adam says.

"I'm going to make you an appointment." Acton looks at him again. "You have every reason to be proud of your performance last term, Adam. I'd like to make sure we keep moving in this direction."

"Yes, sir," Adam says. "Thank you, sir."

"No need to thank me," Acton tells him. "Just keep up the good work."

190.

So, that's a new one.

Adam figures he should be scared of the VP. Figures he should be hunched over in a bathroom stall, breathing through a paper bag right now.

Figures he should be terrified at how close he came to discovery.

But Adam . . .

doesn't really care.

Adam's proud of himself.

Adam's an honor-roll student.

The teachers like him.

Hell, *Mr. Acton* likes him.

Paul Nolan shakes his hand. Leanne Grayson hugs him on the regular. The popular kids swarm his locker, and everyone else at Nixon looks at him like he's a god.

Adam realizes he's so much more than just Adam anymore.

He's the Pizza Man now.

And life is pretty damn good.

191.

One afternoon in March, about a month into the new term.

Adam's holding court at Cardigan's, across the street from Nixon. Handing back math papers, geography assignments, chemistry labs. Selling IDs to a couple of runty sophomores. Gradually the place clears out. Adam pays off Wayne and Devon and Lisa. Devon and Lisa drift away.

Wayne sticks around.

He's kind of fidgeting. Can't look Adam in the eye.

"Hey, man," Adam says, thinking, *This is about the exam stuff again.* "How are you holding up?"

Wayne nods. "I'm okay," he says. "I'm fine." He looks around, fidgets some more, like he has to go to the bathroom or something. "I, uh . . ."

Adam looks at him. "What's up, Wayne?"

Wayne doesn't say anything. Wayne's creeping Adam out. Wayne's making Adam think maybe he's about to crack.

Like,

> maybe Adam should go home and delete a
> bunch of homework files off his computer,
>
> > *stat.*

But then Wayne straightens. "Are you, uh, going to the spring formal?"

Adam blinks. "Are you asking me out, dude?"

"No." Wayne blushes. "No, man. No."

"It's cool if you are," Adam tells him. "It's just, I have a girlfriend and stuff."

"Jesus, man," Wayne says. "That's not it at all." He laughs. "It's like, you're tight with the popular girls, right?"

Adam shrugs. "I mean, yeah."

"Exactly," Wayne says. "Do you think you could, you know?"

"No, Wayne." Adam checks his watch. "I *don't* know."

Wayne's bright red. Out it comes. "Do you think you could get me a date for the formal?"

192.

Adam nearly laughs in Wayne's face.

Holds it in.

Barely.

"You want me to get you a date?" he asks Wayne. "You think I'm the love doctor or something?"

Wayne shifts his weight. "No, I just—" he says. "Forget it. I never went to formal before. I just thought maybe you could help."

"Why formal?" Adam says. "Why not prom?"

Wayne grins. "Well, I just figure if formal works out, maybe I can take care of prom myself."

Hmm, Adam thinks.

Interesting, Adam thinks.

Hilarious?

Sad?

All of the above.

"I could pay you," Wayne says. "If you want."

Adam thinks about it. Thinks: *I always liked a challenge.* Thinks: *Let's see how much pull I have with these popular girls.*

Thinks: *Let's see how close I am to god status.*

Adam shakes his head. "Put your wallet away, Wayne," he says. "I'll do it for free."

193.

Adam tries Janie Ng first. Figures, Janie likes him. Maybe she'll do him a favor.

He finds her in the hall the next day between classes. "Are you going to formal, Janie?"

Janie's eyes kind of light up. "If the right guy comes along," she says. "You?"

"Still deciding," Adam says. "Waiting for the right guy, huh?"

"Uh-huh. Know anyone who might be interested?"

"I might," Adam says. "You know Wayne Tristovsky?"

Janie's smile disappears. "Wait, what? You want to hook me up with Wayne Tristovsky?"

"For me, Janie," Adam says. "As a favor. I'll discount your next paper or something."

Janie shakes her head. "I don't think so, Adam. Not even if *you* paid *me*."

194.

Leanne Grayson laughs in Adam's face. "I'm sure I could find someone better, Adam."

"I'm sure you could, too," Adam tells her, "but I'd be *so* grateful, Leanne."

"Sorry," she says. "Who are you taking?"

Adam shrugs. "Victoria, I guess."

Leanne winks at Adam. "Well, if she's busy or something . . ."

"Thanks," Adam tells her. "I'll keep that in mind."

195.

"Why are you so concerned about who your friend takes to formal, anyway?" Sam asks Adam, his voice tinny through the receiver.

"I just—" Adam wedges the phone against his ear. Studies his econ textbook. "Wayne's a lonely guy, you know? And I guess he wants to go to formal pretty bad."

Sam's watching hockey in the background. They were supposed to watch together. Adam's calling to tell Sam he can't make it.

(Homework.)

"You're a good friend," Sam says.

Adam thinks about Wayne. Poor, pathetic Wayne.

"Yeah," he says. "I guess I am."

196.

"What about you?" Sam says. "Are you taking Victoria?"

"To formal?" Adam flips a page in the textbook. Highlights a key concept—

(*market saturation*).

"I guess I hadn't thought about it," he says.

"You should take her," Sam says.

"She hasn't said anything about it," Adam says. "I don't even know if she wants to go."

"She wants to go." Something's happening in the hockey game in the background. People are cheering. "A girl like Victoria?" Sam says. "She's just waiting for you to ask."

197.

"The formal?" Victoria says. "Really?"

"The formal," Adam says. "You know, dresses, dinner, dancing. The formal."

Victoria giggles. "I know what it is," she says. "I just never would have thought it was your style."

"Is it *your* style?" Adam asks her.

"Maybe," she says. "Are you asking me on a date?"

Adam grins at her. "Depends who else I can find between now and then."

"You loser." Victoria punches him. "Maybe I'll just find someone else, then. Maybe Chad will take me."

"Or maybe we should just go together and save ourselves the trouble of finding other people," Adam says.

Victoria rolls her eyes. "*Such* a romantic."

"I'll pick you up at eight," Adam tells her. "In a month or so."

198.

Sam was right. Obviously.

Victoria's thrilled about formal.

(Hey, she's a freshman girl. She goes gaga over formals. Dresses, expensive hairdos, romance.

It's like popular girl catnip.

Plus, she gets quality time with Adam, which doesn't always happen when business is booming.)

(And business is booming.)

Wayne and Lisa and Devon are kicking homework ass. The gods are thrilled with their new A-plus standard. Pizza Man Enterprises has seven hundred Likes on Facebook. Adam himself has a thousand Twitter followers.

(#success)

(#godmode)

(#PizzaMan)

(#winning)

Brian's shipping IDs as fast as Bondy can make them. And Adam's taking a cut of the whole

fucking

pie.

Life is good.

Life is *very* good.

And then they catch the kid who swiped Mr. Powers's Applied Science exam.

199.

The kid is a sophomore—a stoner named Ryan Grant. He wears weird punk-rock T-shirts and always reeks of weed. And Mr. Acton makes him for the exam fiasco.

"Hawksley identified him," Darren tells Adam. "The old janitor, you know him? I guess he saw this Ryan guy in the hall yesterday and it triggered something."

"Crazy," Adam says. "What's the kid saying?"

Darren shrugs. "I heard him pitching a fit in the office when I walked past," he says, "but you have to figure he'd deny everything anyway, right?"

"Right," Adam says.

"I mean, it's cut-and-dried. Hawksley saw him. And he's in the Applied Science class to begin with."

"Sure," Adam says.

"Of course he did it," Darren says. "Ryan Grant is a loser."

200.

Adam has his meeting with Mrs. Dubois—
    (the guidance counselor)
    —that afternoon. She's good-looking, for an older woman. She makes Adam call her Bonnie. She asks Adam a bunch of questions about what he wants to do after high school, gives him a career guide, and tells him to come back when he picks out something that interests him.
    Adam takes the handbook. Thanks Mrs. Dubois—
    "Bonnie, *please*."
    —and stands to leave. Then he stops.
    "Bonnie," he says, "what's going to happen to that kid who stole the exam last semester?"
    Bonnie's face clouds. "Expelled," she says. "Maryvale Tech."
    Whoa, Adam thinks.
        (Maryvale Tech is where they send all the problem kids. The supreme screwups. It's basically a holding pen where they keep you until you do something bad enough to land you in juvie. Or full-on prison. And pretty much everyone at Maryvale winds up in prison eventually.
        It's just how it is.)
    "There's a chance he could apply to come back here in the fall, if his parents are interested," Bonnie tells Adam. "But I

don't think that'll happen, in this case."

"Wow," Adam says. "So that's it, then."

"Yeah." She smiles and shakes her head. "Some kids you just can't help, I guess."

201.

Ryan Grant.

Maryvale Tech.

Heavy shit.

"Good riddance," Audrey Klein says when Adam hands back her history assignment. "He was a burnout anyway."

"Yeah," Adam says. "What if he was innocent, though?"

Audrey thinks about it for, like, half a second. "Who cares?" she says. "He was a loser. It's not like he was doing anything with his life."

Adam thinks: *Maybe Audrey has a point.*

Adam thinks: *Maybe Ryan Grant didn't even like Nixon.*

Adam thinks: *He'll fit in better at Maryvale, anyway.*

But still, Adam thinks. *Heavy shit.*

202.

Wayne's thinking the same. "What should we do?" he asks Adam.

Adam looks at Wayne. Adam shrugs. Adam's feeling guilty.

But Adam can't tell Wayne that.

"What should we *do*?" Adam says. "We should keep our mouths shut, Wayne."

Wayne blinks. "And just let him take the fall? They're expelling him."

"They're sending him to Maryvale," Adam says. "It's not so bad. Maybe he'll fit in better there."

"Are you kidding?" Wayne says. "I heard some kid got stabbed there last month."

Adam knows this. Adam heard the same thing. "What do you want to do?" Adam says. "You want to walk into Mr. Acton's office and tell him *we* stole the exam? You want to book a ticket to Maryvale ourselves?"

Wayne shudders. "No."

"I feel shitty about what happened," Adam tells him. "But it's not like he was doing much at Nixon anyway. Those kids will worship him for stealing that exam. They'll make him a god."

Wayne thinks about it. Wayne nods. "I mean, I guess you're right."

"I know I'm right," Adam says, and wonders if he means it.

203.

"Anyway," Wayne says. "You find me a date to formal yet?"

Adam hesitates. "I'm working on it," Adam tells him. What Adam doesn't tell him is: *I'm striking out.*

(With every girl who Adam thinks would be remotely interested in doing him a favor.)

"Who'd you talk to?" Wayne asks him. "You ask Sara Bryant yet?"

Adam sighs. "Wayne, you're not going to formal with Sara Bryant. Sara Bryant hates the ground we walk on. She—"

Just then, Sara Bryant walks by. "Are you talking about me, Adam?"

"Hey, Sara," Adam says. "Just figuring out who's doing your next assignment. Nothing major."

Sara frowns. "I didn't give you my next assignment yet." She narrows her eyes at Adam. "What are you *really* talking about? Are you gossiping?"

Adam looks away. He still can't look Sara (*freaking*) Bryant in the eye when she's in full-on Beast Mode. "Wayne was just wondering who you're taking to formal," he says.

Beside Adam, Wayne sucks his teeth. Sara blinks. "Who's Wayne?"

Adam points to Wayne. Wayne kind of shrugs. "He doesn't have a date," Adam tells her.

Sara cocks her head. "And?"

"And," Adam sighs, "he was wondering if you're available."

Sara stares at Adam. Adam shakes his head, thinking, *How the hell did I get mixed up in this?* Thinking, *My rep is shot the minute this gets out.*

Sara looks Wayne up and down. "This is Wayne?" she says. "Does he speak?"

"Y-yes," Wayne says. "I can speak."

Sara keeps studying him. "I think formal is a waste of time," she says.

"Oh, okay," Adam says. "Well thanks anyway."

"Hold on!" Sara glares at him. "What I was going to say, *Pizza Man*, is that I think formal is a waste of time, *but* Wayne here is kind of cute. In an anti-establishment, counterprogramming kind of way, obviously."

"Obviously," Adam says.

"It might be interesting to take him to formal," she says. "Just to say 'Fuck the popular kids. Fuck the cliques,' you know what I'm saying?"

"Sure," Adam says. He thinks, *What the hell is happening?*

Sara looks at Wayne again. Looks at him a long time. "I'll think about it, Wayne," she says. "I'll tell Adam what I decide."

Wayne nods. "Okay."

"Okay," Adam says.

"Okay," Sara says. "I'm leaving."

Then she *breezes* down the hall and is gone.

204.

Adam and Wayne look at each other. "What the hell just happened?" Wayne asks Adam.

Adam shrugs. "She thinks you're cute," he says. "In an anti-establishment way, of course."

"'Fuck the cliques'?" Wayne says. "I don't even know what that means."

"Who cares?" Adam tells him. "Play your cards right and maybe you'll get to 'fuck a popular kid' yourself."

205.

Adam buys two tickets to the spring formal the day they go on sale.
Two tickets. Seventy bucks.

A hell of a price to pay for a crappy dinner and some dancing, but Adam figures he can make up the difference in booze sales.
(Technically, it's a dry event. What that means is that
everyone and their sister is going to pre-drink before-
hand. And post-drink at after-parties. What that means
is that flask sales are going to skyrocket.)

And anyway, Adam figures, maybe formal will finally con-
vince Victoria Lemieux to sleep with me.
(Doubtful, but who knows?)
(Stranger things have happened.)

Adam takes Victoria to the mall to pick out a dress. They
hit about a hundred little boutique stores and she tries on ten
dresses in each store. It's a long day. Adam doesn't mind at all. He
thinks Victoria looks hot in every one of them.
(And she does.)

Finally, she narrows it down to two dresses. One is tight
and black. The other is short and red. Victoria comes out blushing. "You think it's too flashy for me?"

"Hell no," Adam says.

Victoria looks at the price tag. "It's expensive, though."

"Don't even sweat it." Adam tries not to drool as he looks
at her legs. "It's worth every penny."

206.

The next day, Adam goes back to the mall to pick out a suit. "Money's no object," he tells the sales guy. "I want to look good next to my girl."

The guy sees dollar signs. Hooks Adam up with a slick pinstripe suit, a pimpin' tie. It's not cheap but it's worth it. Victoria's hot. Adam's suit is so money.

The formal's going to be awesome.

207.

Adam stops by the sporting goods store while he's at the mall. Picks up a Red Wings jersey, one of the official ones, the home red with the white trim.

      Has it customized with Sam's name and his old jersey number—

           (19)

           (after Steve Yzerman, the guy who was captain of

           the Red Wings back when Sam was still walking)

      —pays a shitload of money for it, but the jersey looks pimp.

Sam's going to love it.

208.

Adam takes the bus downtown.

(Thinks, *How many homework assignments would a used Porsche cost?*)

(#TonyMontana)

(#PizzaMan)

Sam's watching a sports talk show on TV in his living room when Adam shows up.

"I can't stay," Adam tells him. "So much freaking homework. I just wanted to give you this."

He gives Sam the jersey. "Holy shit," Sam says, grinning. "You even got my number on it."

"Swag, right?" Adam says.

"*So* cool," Sam says. "Here, help me try it on."

Adam looks back at the door. "I can't stay," he says. "Homework and stuff."

Sam frowns. "Oh. Shitty."

"I'll come back, though," Adam tells him. "I'll come back again soon."

209.

"You bought him a jersey?" Victoria says. She's holding on to Adam's arm as they walk out of Nixon. "That's so sweet, Adam."

"Got it customized and everything," Adam tells her. "His last name, his old jersey number. Just like the real thing."

Victoria smiles at him. "He must have loved it."

Adam thinks about Sam, about his messy apartment, that boring talk-radio show on TV. Feels a little guilty about leaving so quick.

"Yeah," he says. "He sure did."

Victoria looks at him. "How's he doing, anyway?" she says. "You haven't talked about him very much."

Adam shrugs. "I haven't seen him lately," he says. "Homework and stuff."

"Is it my fault?" Victoria says. "Am I taking up too much of your time?"

"No," Adam says. "Of course not."

"We could go see him together if you want," she says. "It might be fun."

"Yeah," Adam says. Then he thinks about the bus ride downtown. How embarrassing it is to take your girlfriend on a date with transit tokens, how much better it would be if he could drive Victoria to visit Sam.

How much better life would be with a sweet car.

(How much more Tony Montana.)

Then he thinks about how many fake IDs he'd need to sell to afford even a basic ride. How many econ assignments.

(Tons.)

"Sam would like it," Victoria is saying. "You said he liked me, right? We should definitely see him."

Adam thinks about all the places he could go if he had a car.

"Yeah," he tells Victoria. "Maybe sometime."

210.

"Sometime" never happens, though.

Because a couple weeks before formal, disaster strikes.

211.

School's out. Adam's leaving Cardigan's with Wayne and Lisa and Devon.

Handing back assignments.

Handling business.

Then someone calls his name from across the street. "*Adam.*" It's Victoria. She hurries over.

"Hey." Adam kisses her. "You know Wayne, Lisa, Devon, right?"

Victoria cocks her head. "I don't think we've actually met." She smiles at the team. "Nice to meet you guys."

"There you go," Adam says. "You wanna get out of here?"

"Uh-huh." She takes Adam's arm and they start to walk away.

Then Wayne goes: "Hey, Adam, you forgot to pay us."

Shit, Adam thinks.

Wayne, Adam thinks.

You're an idiot, Adam thinks.

Adam smiles at Victoria. "Sorry, one sec." Walks back to Wayne and Lisa and Devon, pulls out his wallet.

"What are you paying them for?" Victoria says.

"Tutoring," Adam says. "Nothing. Never mind."

"That's a lot of money," Victoria says. "All that from tutoring? And why are *you* paying *them*? I don't get it."

"It's tricky," Adam says. "It's a complicated arrangement. I have to—"

Victoria's eyes are wide. "Oh my god," she says slowly.

Adam looks at her. "What?"

"It's true, isn't it?"

"What's true?" Adam says. "No, of course not."

"I thought it was a joke," Victoria says. "That Pizza Man rumor. I didn't think it was real, but it's real. Isn't it, Adam?"

Adam feels his stomach starting to implode. "What are you talking about?"

"I heard people talking," Victoria says. "Some stupid little scheme. They said you do homework for all the popular kids, you and your little gang here. I thought it was all made up, but it isn't, is it?"

Adam reaches for her arm. Victoria shakes him off.

"Come *on*," he says. "Victoria. It's no big deal."

Victoria looks around. At Nixon. At Cardigan's. At Wayne and Lisa and Devon. "How long have you been doing this?" she says.

"Not long." Adam shrugs. "Since October, I guess."

She steps back like she's been slapped. "So pretty much always, then. The whole time we've been together. You've been lying to me this whole time."

"I wasn't lying," Adam tells her. "It's a tutoring thing. I told you that."

"It's *not* tutoring." There are tears in her eyes. "It's *cheating*, Adam. You're screwing up your whole life. Why?"

Adam shrugs again. "It beats working at Pizza Hut."

212.

"So it's the money," Victoria says. "That's why you're doing this."

They're down the block now. Wayne and Lisa and Devon have wandered away—

(mercifully)

—giving Adam and Victoria some space.

Adam shrugs. "The money's good. Yeah, there's that."

"There's something else?" Victoria says.

Adam looks at his feet. Adam tries to explain. Adam can't. "You don't get it," Adam says. "Everything's so easy for you."

Victoria stiffens. "Pardon?"

"You're popular," Adam says. "You're good-looking. Your dad still has his job. You've never had to work for anything in your life. You just don't understand."

"What don't I understand, Adam?" Victoria says. "What are you missing from your life? You have a girlfriend who loves you. You have actual friends, not those people you pay to hang around and do homework. You could do anything you want in the world if you put your mind to it. What are you missing?"

"I'm a nobody," Adam tells her. "I'm still just a loser."

Victoria stares at him.

"I want to be a god," Adam says. "I want to be bigger than Rob Thigpen, that piece of shit. I want to be bigger than all of them. I want to *win*."

"*Why?*" Victoria's voice wavers. She shakes her head,

blinks back tears. "What the hell does it matter what those assholes think about you? You're a hundred times better than any one of them."

"I told you. You don't get it," Adam tells her.

Victoria doesn't say anything. Just stares at Adam. Traffic whizzes past and around them. A couple students walk by.

"I can't be a part of this, Adam," Victoria says finally. "I can't go out with a cheater. If you want me to stick around, you have to end this whole scheme."

Adam closes his eyes. "Don't do this," he tells her. "Don't make me choose."

(*Dump her.*)

(*Let her walk.*)

(*There will be nothing holding you back once she's gone.*)

"I'm not doing anything." Victoria starts walking. Away from Nixon. Away from Remington Park. Toward Walkerville, toward home. "I'm just telling you where I stand," she says. "The rest is up to you."

213.

Adam calls up Brian. Takes a bus out to Riverside. Meets Brian in the park and gets high. "Girls, man," Brian says. "So unpredictable."

Adam hasn't smoked up in a while.

(He's been too busy.)

He's flying off a couple of hits.

"Everything's so easy for her," he says. "All she has to do is show up and smile and the whole stupid school drops to its knees."

"You don't think it's tough for her, though?" Brian says. "Being a smart chick in that body? You think anyone takes her seriously?"

Adam takes another drag. "Whatever," he says. "She's popular. Everybody likes her. What does the rest of it matter?"

"I don't know, man." Brian takes the jay. "You don't think she could be right?"

"About the homework stuff?"

"About everything," Brian says. "What does it really matter if you fit in with those stuck-up bitches? You're getting honor-roll grades. And she's a great girl. Why do you care so much about the rest of those douchebags?"

"I just do," Adam tells him. "I deserve this, okay? This is my *right*. If Sam hadn't had his accident, I'd be a god already; I'm just taking what should already be mine."

Brian takes another long drag. "Whatever," he says. "I guess you know what you want. I'd just think twice before I gave her up, man."

214.

Adam thinks twice.

(And probably more.)

Adam already knows what he wants.

Adam wants Victoria kissing him by her locker.

He wants her holding his hand while they walk home from school.

He wants her teasing him in front of Sam and making Sam laugh while they drink soda and eat burgers and watch the Red Wings play.

He wants Victoria Lemieux.

He wants to love her.

(Maybe he really *does* love her.)

(Maybe.)

215.

But Adam also wants to win.

He wants to drive into the school parking lot in a Porsche with a goddess on his arm.

He wants to get laid.

He wants the whole fucking world to know him.

To love him.

To see him like he's a god.

The way they should have seen Sam—would have seen him—if not for that game against Nixon.

Adam wants to take over.

(Adam is taking over.)

Adam wants

wants

wants

needs . . .

to win.

216.

Victoria avoids Adam the next day at school. Every time he passes her in the hall, tries to talk to her, she looks away.

(Her eyes are red. She looks tired.)

(She's been crying all night, probably.)

Finally, Adam catches up to her as she's walking past Cardigan's after school. "Can we talk?" he asks her.

Victoria looks at him. Looks back at Cardigan's, where Wayne and Lisa and Devon are trying not to look like Adam just gave them their latest assignments

trying not to look like Adam just paid them off.

trying not to look interested.

and failing.

"No," Victoria says. She keeps walking.

Adam hurries to keep up. "Victoria," he says. "I'm sorry. I swear."

"Not sorry enough," she says. "If you were really sorry, you would have told everyone at Cardigan's to leave you alone, that you were through with that stupid scheme. But you didn't, did you?"

Adam shakes his head. "I just need to make it to the summer," he tells her. "Then it's over, I swear. Just give me this semester to make it work."

"Listen to yourself," Victoria says. "You sound like an addict."

"I can't just walk away," Adam says. "People need me."

"To do their fucking *homework*," Victoria says. "I do my own homework, Adam. What makes them so special?"

"They're the gods," Adam says. "They can make or break me."

"Bullshit," Victoria says. "*You* make or break you."

"Just one more semester," Adam says.

Victoria shakes her head. "No. I can't do it," she says. "I'm sorry."

She keeps walking. Doesn't look back at Adam. Just walks away. Cold. It triggers something, and Adam disappears.

Enter Pizza Man.

"Fine," he calls after Victoria. "Whatever. I don't need you, anyway."

Victoria flinches, but she doesn't answer. Doesn't even turn around. Suddenly, Adam wants to hurt her. Wants her to know that he's mad.

"I can have any girl in the school," he tells her. "And they'll all *sleep with me* if I want them to. What do I need you for?"

Victoria stops walking. Stands there a moment, and her shoulders hunch and he can tell that she's crying.

"I'm sorry," Adam tells her. "Damn it, I'm sorry."

(And Adam is sorry.

He's

so

fucking

sorry.)

But Victoria isn't having it. "Fuck you, Adam," she says. "You're a real fucking asshole."

She starts walking again.

She walks away, and this time, Adam lets her. Because he knows she's right. He is a real fucking asshole.

And Victoria's gone.

217.

Adam goes home.

Adam regresses.

Reattains Loser Mode.

Adam locks himself in his room and turns on angry music and just kind of lies there. He tries calling Victoria but she won't answer her phone.

He leaves a couple dumb messages but she doesn't call back.

Finally he gives up.

He just lies there some more.

218.

Steph comes in.

"Heard about you and Victoria," she says.

Adam looks at her. "Guess you got your wish."

Steph makes a face. "You don't have to be such a dick, Adam. So what if you can sleep with any girl in the school. Did you really have to tell her that?"

(So he wasn't wrong. He *can* sleep with anyone. Even Steph knows.)

"I was pissed off, okay?" Adam says. "She was dumping me."

"Maybe if you weren't such a lunatic she wouldn't have to dump you."

"Whatever," Adam says. "It's not like you wanted us to be together anyway."

Steph shakes her head. "I don't like seeing my friends get hurt, Adam."

Adam stares up at the ceiling. "What did you say, anyway?" he says. "When she told you what happened."

Steph sighs. "I told her the truth," she says. "I told her you cared more about being popular than you ever would about her."

"That's not true," Adam says. "I love her."

"Then give up the stupid homework scheme, you douchebag," Steph says.

She stares at Adam. Adam says nothing.
(*Not a fucking chance.*)
Steph nods. "That's what I thought."

219.

Wednesday morning, Victoria's at Adam's locker with a big shopping bag. "Here," she says. Shoves the bag at him. "Just take it."

Adam looks at her. She looks away. Bites her lip like she's trying not to cry. Adam looks in the bag. Red fabric.

The dress.

The short, tight red number that made her legs look so long. That made her body look *right*. That she and Adam both *loved*.

"You paid for it," Victoria says. "You might as well have it."

"I can't take this," Adam tells her. "What the hell am I supposed to do with it?"

"I don't know," Victoria says. "Maybe you could give it to whatever hot chick you decide to sleep with first, Adam.

"I don't really care," Victoria says.

"I just don't want it," Victoria says.

"Bye," Victoria says.

220.

Rob Thigpen's coming down the hall as Victoria walks away from Adam. He's wearing that cocky smirk of his—

(he looks like he should be playing lacrosse, or rowing, or something)

—and Adam flashes back to that night at Janie's party. To Rob Thigpen in the corner, watching Victoria dance with Adam.

He flashes back to the night at Crash with Janie Ng.

He suddenly knows what's going on.

221.

"You told her," Adam says as Rob walks past his locker. "You told Victoria about me, didn't you?"

Rob stops walking. Looks at Adam. Looks at the bag in his hands.

(Doesn't stop smirking.)

"I don't know what you're talking about, bro," he says. "Sorry if I did you wrong somehow, though."

He starts walking again. Walks away from Adam. Adam watches him go.

"You'll get yours," he says.

(Mostly under his breath.)

"When I take over this school," Adam says, "you'll get yours."

222.

Janie Ng walks up. "What's in the bag, Adam?"

"Nothing," Adam tells her. "Just the end of my fucking relationship."

He opens the bag and shows Janie. Janie looks in and frowns. "I don't get it."

"I bought this dress for Victoria," Adam says. "For formal. Except we're not going together anymore."

"Oh no," Janie says. "What happened?"

"Just stuff." Adam shrugs. "Irreconcilable differences. Anyway, whatever. I'll get your math paper back tomorrow."

"Don't worry about it," Janie says. "I'm sure you have other things on your mind."

Adam shakes her off. "I'll be fine. Business as usual."

Janie makes a sympathetic face. "Well, if you ever need anyone to talk to—"

"I'll come and find you," Adam tells her.

223.

Cardigan's, after school.

"We're really sorry, Adam," Devon says. "We thought Victoria knew."

"How could she not?" Lisa says. "How'd you keep it a secret for so long?"

"Are you going to be okay?" Wayne says.

Adam shakes his head. Shakes them off. "Forget it," he tells them. "It's business as usual. We're going to take over this school, understand?"

Adam looks at his team. They glance at one another. Devon looks at the ground. Lisa just smirks. Finally, Wayne shakes his head.

"Are you sure you don't need a little more time?" he asks. "We all know how much you liked Victoria. It's cool if you want to take a break or something."

"Were you listening?" Adam asks him. "I'm not taking a break. I worked too long and too hard to get to this point. I'm not bailing now, okay?"

"Okay," Wayne says. "No problem. We keep going."

"Forget about Victoria," Adam says. "Nothing's changed."

224.

Onward and upward.

The next day, Adam tracks down Janie Ng. "Still need a date for formal?"

Janie blinks. "Wait, what?"

"Formal," Adam says. "Who are you going with?"

Janie hesitates. Janie blushes. "Well, Simon Klein asked me, but . . ."

"Ditch him," Adam tells her. "Go with me. I already have the tickets. I'm renting a limo. I'm better than Simon Klein. Go with me."

Janie thinks about it for, like, half a second. Then she grins. "Sold," she says.

225.

Adam's date? Locked down.

Victoria? Replaced.

The formal? A week away.

It gets hectic.

Adam and Brian coordinate booze drop-offs and last-minute fake-ID hookups. Just as Adam predicted, fewer and fewer people are buying booze now, but the ID sales are making up for it. Of course:

There's a logical endgame in sight, Adam knows. Soon every kid who wants a fake ID will have one, and nobody will need Adam and Brian—

(and Bondy)

—anymore.

And what then? Adam thinks. *What's my next move?*

He doesn't know.

He's thinking about it.

He'll come up with something.

In the meantime, he sells IDs and a little bit of booze. Polishes off a few homework assignments and brings Victoria's dress back to the mall. Gets a refund from the same salesgirl who sold him the dress.

"Oh no," the salesgirl says. "What happened? Your girlfriend looked so pretty in that dress."

"She died in a car wreck," Adam tells her. "It's all very sad."

226.

"Philosophical differences," Adam tells Sam. "Nothing I could do."

"Shit," Sam says. "That's awful, man. You guys were supposed to go to that formal thing too, right?"

"Yeah," Adam says, "but it's cool, though. I'm taking this hotter girl instead."

He shows Sam a picture of Janie Ng from Facebook. She's in Mexico on vacation or something, and she's in a little two-piece swimsuit, and she could actually—

(*actually*)

—be a model.

Sam studies the picture. Hands Adam his phone back.

"Right?" Adam says. "Smoking hot."

Sam shrugs. "She's hot, sure," he says, "but I thought you were into Victoria. Are you sure you're all right?"

Adam looks down at his phone. At the picture of Janie.

"I'm great," he tells Sam. "I'm just great."

227.

Brian's cousin Tommy—

("When you gonna hook me up with those hot high school honeys, man?")

—sets Adam and Brian up with a limo. He knows a guy who knows a guy.

(You know how it goes.)

Brian and Amanda swing through Remington Park to pick Adam up. Brian's rocking a vintage suit he picked up at some thrift store. Amanda's in a fifties prom dress and fishnets. Punk rock.

They look *good*.

Almost as good as Adam and Janie. Adam's suit is so money, and Janie's in this little black cocktail dress, fits her like paint. She looks stunning.

(*Better than Victoria*, Adam thinks.)

(*Almost as good*, Adam thinks.)

(*Shit*, Adam thinks.)

Brian hands him a flask. Adam drinks. Whiskey. Calms the nerves. Loosens him up. Makes him forget—

(mostly)

—about—

(Victoria).

Shut up, Adam thinks. *You're in a stretch limo with a goddess. Everyone in the school knows your name. This is your big night. Take it over.*

The limo pulls up to the convention center downtown. Brian reaches for the door. Grins at Adam. "You ready?"

This is it, Adam thinks. *Be a god.*

He hesitates—

(just a moment)

—then he follows Brian and Amanda and Janie out into the night.

228.

The formal's in a grand ballroom overlooking the river. When the sun sets, the windows fill with the lights of the city skyscrapers and their reflections on the water. The whole room is lit up with candles.

Even in the dim light, though, Adam notices when Wayne Tristovsky walks in. How could he not?

The kid's in a white suit. Sara *freaking* Bryant's on his arm. He looks like he's king of the universe. He's grinning and kinda blushing like a lottery winner.

(Meanwhile, Sara's got this smirk on her face like she's the funniest person in the world for bringing Wayne to the formal.

Oh shit, Adam thinks. Carrie *moment.*

(Google it.))

229.

Dinner is served.

Adam and Janie are at a table with Rob Thigpen and Jessie McGill and Alton Di Sousa and his date—

(some sophomore in heavy makeup and a low-cut dress).

"So, Pizza Man," Rob says, when everyone is seated and choking down their bland chicken cutlets. "You broke up with Victoria?"

Adam's buzzing. He doesn't feel like Adam anymore. He doesn't feel anxious. He feels like Pizza Man, and Pizza Man doesn't give a shit about Rob fucking Thigpen.

"Yeah," he says. "We agreed we should go our separate ways."

"I heard she found out about your little moneymaking scheme and had a fit," Rob says. "You must really like doing home-work."

Adam looks around the room. Looks for Brian and his flask. The bastard is AWOL. Fuck it.

"I guess I do, Rob," Adam says. "*Anyway.* Where the hell is the booze?"

Everyone laughs. Paul Nolan slaps Adam on the back. "Don't worry about it, man," he says, leaning in close. "Forget Victoria. I have a feeling you could get to know Janie *real* well tonight."

Adam glances at Janie. Janie gives him this confused look, like,

What the heck did Paul just say to you?

Adam smiles and shrugs. Admires the way Janie's dress clings to her body. Thinks, *You know, Paul, you might be onto something.*

230.

Dessert happens. Then someone shines a spotlight on the DJ, who wakes up and starts spinning, like, Skrillex or something. Janie grins at Adam. "Wanna dance?"

Adam thinks about what Paul Nolan said. Thinks about grinding with Janie at Crash. Thinks about not being a virgin tomorrow.

(*You're going to be a god.*)

"Hell yes," Adam says.

231.

Everyone's drunk. Everyone's dancing dirty. Paul Nolan is passing around a flask of something noxious. Adam nearly dies when he drinks it.

"Bacardi One-fifty-one," Paul says, laughing. "Guaranteed to straight-up destroy you."

Adam's too busy coughing to pay attention. By the time he gets his breath back he's

really

goddamn

drunk.

"I gotta take a break," he tells Janie. "You wanna sit down?"

Janie shakes her head. "I'm gonna keep dancing."

"Okay," Adam says. "I'll be right back."

Before he can go anywhere, Janie pulls him close and kind of melts into his arms. Adam holds on to her. The room's kinda spinning at this point, and he figures he could use the support. Things are

b   l   u   r   r   y

and for a minute, Adam can almost imagine that Janie's Victoria, and they're at a party or something, and he all of a sudden relaxes, holds on to Victoria

(Janie)

like she's the ship's mast in a storm, the only thing

keeping him upright. And then he opens his eyes and—

fuck

—it's not Victoria, it's Janie, and she's looking at him like she wants to be kissed.

And Adam's too drunk to do anything but kiss her, at this point.

232.

Adam breaks off the kiss. Staggers to the bathroom and pukes. Gets that 151 out of his system and splashes some water on his face and stares at himself in the mirror for a while.

This is your night, he thinks.

You're a god, he thinks.

What the hell are you doing? he thinks.

He gets out of the bathroom. Away from the mirror. Wanders outside to the balcony overlooking the river. There's a ship coming, a freighter. Adam watches it slide past. Slow.

Then the door opens behind him and Wayne comes out, smiling like the lightning bolt of sex just smacked him in the face. "Adam," he says. "*Thank you,* man."

Adam's still watching the freighter. "Yeah," he says. "No problem. For what?"

"For setting me up with Sara, bro. She's awesome. We have so much in common."

Adam looks at Wayne. Thinks, about the only thing they have in common is they both think Sara Bryant's the greatest creature to ever walk the earth.

"You're a great friend, man." Wayne slaps Adam on the back. "Thanks again."

Adam nods. Watches Wayne stagger back to the party. Thinks, *No problem, Wayne, but . . .*

you're not my friend.

233.

Janie's dancing with Leanne Grayson when Adam finds her again. Dancing close.

Very close.

Janie smiles huge when she sees Adam. *"Adam!"* She opens her arms, wide. Hugs him, her body pressed tight against him, top to bottom.

"Leanne's date is *drunk*," Janie says.

Adam looks around. "Aren't we all?"

"Like, *really* drunk," Leanne says. "He puked in the bathroom. Mrs. Stewart threw him out."

"Oh, crap," Adam says. "That sucks."

"He was boring anyway," Leanne says.

"I told Leanne she could dance with us," Janie tells Adam. "Do you mind?"

"Not really," Adam says. "I'm pretty drunk myself."

"I have just the thing," Janie says. She reaches into her purse and slips something into her mouth. Then she kisses Adam and he feels her push it into his mouth with her tongue. A pill.

Shit, Adam thinks. *What am I supposed to do with this?*

Janie's grinning at him.

Adam rolls the pill around with his tongue. Thinks about spitting it out.

Then he thinks, *What the hell.*

He swallows the pill. Janie grins wider. "Wait till that

kicks in," she tells him. "You'll be out of your fucking *mind*."

"Fuck," Adam says. His mind's already blown. He's barely keeping himself

upright.

But Janie and Leanne are dancing again—

(*dirty* dancing)

—and every guy in the room is staring at Adam like he's

a god.

(Even Rob Thigpen's staring.)

Keep it together, Adam thinks.

Don't pass out.

Don't puke.

Don't fuck this up.

(Don't you dare.)

234.

Adam's pressed up behind Janie. Leanne's pressed up in front of her. They're all dancing.

Janie twists her head back and kisses Adam. "Did you hear about the after-party? Super 8 on Huron Line."

Adam shrugs.

"We want to go," Janie says.

Adam looks at Janie. Looks at Leanne. Looks at Rob Thigpen and Paul Nolan and Jessie McGill and Alton Di Sousa and Wayne Tristovsky and Sara *freaking* Bryant, and—

(all he wants is to be home with Victoria)

(*shut up*).

"Cool," Adam says. "Let's do it."

Janie kisses Adam again. Reaches into his hair, pulls him closer, bites his earlobe. "You're going to have the best night of your life," she says.

235.

The limo's waiting outside.

    (#rockstars)

    Brian and Amanda are sharing a cigarette at the curb. Their eyes go wide when they see Adam come out with Janie and Leanne on his arms.

    "After-party," Adam tells them. "Super 8 on Huron Line. Gonna be legendary."

    Brian and Amanda swap glances. "Not really our scene, man."

    "Cool." Adam gestures to the limo. "You mind dropping me off?"

236.

The Super 8's on the highway on the outskirts of town. A lonely-trucker motel. Nobody around. Perfect place for a party.

The limo pulls up to the lobby. Leanne climbs out. Janie climbs out. Brian nods at Adam. Gestures to the girls. "You know what you're doing, man?"

Adam grins at him. "Hell no," he says.

Brian grins back. "Pimp."

Even Amanda looks impressed. "You're the man, Adam."

"I'm just trying to stay conscious," Adam tells them.

237.

There are about fifteen, twenty people crammed into one shitty motel room.

Gods

Goddesses

The cream of the crop

Upper echelon

Elite

Paul Nolan and Jessie McGill. Alton and his date. Sara and—

(yeah, even)

—Wayne Tristovsky.

Bacardi. Smirnoff. Jack Daniels. Budweiser.

Pot

Pills

(*Party.*)

Adam's head is spinning. The pill has kicked in and he loves everybody. This is it. The highlight of his junior year.

(The highlight of his *life*.)

This is what it all comes down to. All the long hours slaving over shitty homework assignments. All the sleepless nights. All the money on booze, on clothes, on shoes, haircuts, cologne. The ID scheme. The booze scheme. The exam fiasco. *Pizza Man.*

(Even losing Victoria.)

It's all led up to tonight.

The formal.

Janie Ng (*goddess*).

Leanne Grayson (*goddess*).

Adam's high. Adam's drunk. Adam's wasted.

Adam's *winning.*

He stands at the doorway a moment. Surveys the motel room. Takes it all in. Then Janie and Leanne take his hands and lead him into the party.

238.

Paul and Jessie are smoking a joint on the bed. *"Adam,"* she says. "You made it!"

Adam looks at her. "Fucking A," he says. "Can't have a party without the Pizza Man."

Jessie laughs. Jessie blinks. Then Jessie turns green. "Shit," she says. "I think I'm going to puke."

She runs to the bathroom. Paul grins at Adam. "She's wasted," he says.

"I puked at the formal," Adam tells him. "I felt better."

"That's how it works." Paul motions to where Janie and Leanne are mixing rum and Cokes in red plastic cups. "Looks like you're getting lucky tonight, huh?"

"I hope so," Adam says. He looks around the motel room. "If I can find a bed."

"We have a bed," Sara Bryant says from across the room. She's all over Wayne. "We got a private room for the night."

Adam looks at Wayne. Wayne's still wearing that same dumb *I just won the nerd lottery* look on his face. He grins at Adam.

Sara leers at Adam. "You want to join us, Pizza Man?"

"Hell no," Adam says. "Nobody needs to see that shit."

"Whatever," Sara says. She goes back to making out with Wayne.

Adam feels Paul nudge him. "Hey." Paul hands Adam a key card. "Got this for me and Jessie tonight, but, you know—"

He gestures toward the bathroom. "I think I might just take her home."

Adam looks at the key. Looks at Paul. "Seriously?"

Paul grins at him. "Have fun."

239.

Janie and Leanne stumble over. They have red plastic cups and Leanne's having trouble standing. She smiles at Adam, unfocused. "We brought you a drink."

Adam looks in the cup. Smells the rum. Wants to puke again, but knows everyone's watching. So he drinks it, as slow as he can. People cheer.

The room turns blurry.

Adam blinks and Steph's standing in front of him.

"Steph," Adam says. Across the room, he sees Rob Thigpen talking to Alton Di Sousa by the door. "Hey."

Steph says, "Where's Victoria?"

Adam shrugs. "We broke up."

"Then why the hell are you here?" She looks at Janie Ng, who has her arm around Adam now. "You brought *Janie Ng* to formal?"

Adam nods. "Uh-huh."

"And me," Leanne says.

(Which isn't in any way true, but at this point in the night, who cares?)

Steph's eyes bulge. "You took *two* girls to formal?"

"Math genius," Adam says. "Nice work."

Steph opens her mouth. Starts to say something. Stops. Just kinda stands there looking dumb. Then Rob Thigpen shows up with a beer in one hand and a Smirnoff Ice in the other.

"What's up?" he says. "What'd I miss?"

"World War Three, I think," Paul says.

Everyone laughs. Steph kind of blushes and shuts up, for now. She walks away. Janie sidles closer to Adam. Kisses his neck. Pretty soon they're making out, and Adam's torn between:

wanting the world to see him making out with Janie Ng

and

that little plastic motel key card burning a hole in his pocket.

"Careful, Janie," Rob says. "Slumming with the help can be fun, but you'd hate to make a habit of it."

(The *help?*)

(The help.)

Adam stops kissing Janie. Turns to Rob Thigpen. "Call me 'the help' again," he says. "I dare you."

Then Leanne grabs him and sticks her tongue in his mouth, while Janie's kissing his neck again. Adam lets Leanne kiss him.

Adam rolls with it.

Adam *likes* it.

Adam doesn't hear Rob's response. Doesn't care.

Rob turns and walks off. The pill's running through Adam's system and he's on top of the world.

In your fucking face, Thigpen.

Tony Montana.

240.

Janie pulls Adam away from Leanne. Kisses him. "We should go somewhere," she says.

Adam flashes her Paul Nolan's motel key. "Funny you should say that."

Janie smiles, wide. Takes Adam's hand and drags him through the room to the door.

Then Janie looks back through the room at Leanne. Leanne's kinda sitting on the bed looking pouty. Looking neglected. Looking lost. Janie calls her name. "You coming?"

Leanne looks at Janie. Looks at Adam. "Hell yes."

Adam and Janie watch Leanne wade through the crowd. As she gets close to the doorway, Janie squeezes Adam's hand. "Told you I'd blow your mind tonight."

Leanne smiles at Janie and Adam. Takes Adam's free hand. Adam rolls with it. Lets the girls lead him out of the motel room.

"What's the room number?" Janie asks.

From inside the party, Paul Nolan calls out, "One thirteen."

Everyone laughs. Everyone cheers. Adam smiles at Janie, a little unsteady. "One thirteen," he tells her.

"Well come on, Pizza Man," she says, fixing Adam with the sexiest eyes he's ever seen. "Lead the way."

241.

Achievement Unlocked: Threesome.

242.

I mean, real talk? It's not exactly porno-grade.

(Adam's a virgin, after all.)

There's a lot of fumbling with condoms. A lot of giggling. A lot of kissing and apologizing and giggling some more.

And it's over all too soon, the first time.

(But the girls are too messed up to care.)

The second time, though, it lasts a little longer. And in between, Adam lies back and watches Janie and Leanne fool around and—

(tries not to think about Victoria)

—thinks about how awesome this is all going to sound when people at Nixon hear about it on Monday morning. How cool it's going to sound on Twitter.

(#PizzaMan)

(#winning)

Thinks, *If I wasn't a god before, I am now.*

(And pretty soon he's ready to go again.)

243.

After the second time, the girls pass out. Adam lies there and stares up at the ceiling and thinks:

> *So that's sex.*
> *(What the hell's all the fuss about?)*
> And thinks:
> *I just got lucky with two goddesses.*
> > And thinks:
> *(There's no way Victoria doesn't hear about this.)*

244.

The day after is deadly.

Adam and Janie and Leanne wake up sweaty and sticky and with *killer* hangovers. They take a shower together and fool around a little, but, you know, it's morning. It's daylight.

The magic's kinda gone.

(Anyway, it's not about the sex, really. It's about the *having* sex. It's about the losing your virginity. It's about everyone in the party seeing you leave with Janie Ng and Leanne Grayson and knowing you're god material. It's about the Facebook updates, the tweets, the pictures on Instagram. It's about every guy in the school wanting to be you and every girl in the school wondering what you have that make Janie Ng *and* Leanne Grayson want to do you. It's about the power. The prestige. It's about the achievement.

The achievement happened. It's over. Adam Higgs is the Man.)

(Adam Higgs feels fucking empty.)

They get dressed and check out, and Janie and Leanne call a cab. Adam waits with them outside the lobby, the big trucks roaring past on their way to the bridge. "We should do this again sometime," Janie says.

Leanne laughs. "Seriously."

"Next time I'll be better," Adam tells them.

The girls laugh. "We can teach you," Janie says. "That's what we're here for."

"Awesome," Adam says. "Perfect."

(Except it's not awesome and perfect. It's booze and drugs and two girls Adam hardly even knows. And there's no satisfaction here, just this pathological need to keep going, keep moving, keep pushing the envelope. Keep winning, whatever the hell that means.

Still, Adam tells the girls he wants to see them again, because:)

(What guy says no to on-demand threesomes?)

The cab comes, and Adam kisses Leanne and Janie both good-bye—

(and enjoys the look of envy on the cab driver's face)

—and then he walks to the bus stop and spends the rest of the day riding public transit in a hungover state, replaying the night's events in his head and wondering why in the hell he doesn't feel happier.

245.

By Monday morning, word's got around.

Adam Higgs is the Man.

Everyone—

(*everyone*)

—knows about Janie and Leanne.

Adam Higgs is everywhere. Front-page news. The editor of the yearbook comes up to Adam at his locker, tells him he's giving Pizza Man his own page in this year's edition. Guys stop Adam in the hall, shake his hand, slap him five. Girls follow Adam with their eyes as he walks down the hall. Everyone wants to know Adam.

Everyone wants to hear the story.

Everyone's talking.

Of course Victoria's going to hear.

"Heard you got those hot chicks you were after," she tells Adam. "Two at a time, even."

Adam just kind of blinks and doesn't say anything. It's midafternoon between periods. He's been numb since lunchtime. "Victoria," he says finally. "Shit."

"Good to know I didn't mean that much to you after all," Victoria says. She can't meet his eyes.

"It's not even like that," Adam says. "I didn't—"

Victoria pushes past him. "Have fun, Adam," she says. "Don't get any STDs."

Then she's gone.

And that's pretty much the end of Adam and Victoria.

246.

Victoria Lemieux's relationship status on Facebook goes from "It's complicated" to "Single."

Then she unfriends Adam.

Unfollows him on Twitter.

Blocks his texts.

Won't take his calls.

It's.

Over.

"Of course she's pissed," Steph says. "That stunt you pulled with Leanne and Janie was a real dick move, Adam."

"What the hell," Adam says. "We were broken up already."

"Yeah, for like a week," Steph says. "Not even. And then you had to go off and sleep with a couple of sluts like you didn't even care about her."

"Janie and Leanne aren't sluts," Adam says.

Steph gives him a look like he's the dumbest kid in the world. "Adam. They had a threesome with you. In a Super 8."

"Whatever," Adam says. "We were broken up."

"She *loved* you."

"I loved her," Adam says.

"Bullshit," Steph tells him. "You love Paul Nolan and Sara Bryant and Jessie McGill. You love being loved." She shakes her head. "There's something wrong with you, Adam."

"What am I supposed to do?" he says. "Torpedo my whole reputation?"

Steph rolls her eyes. "Of course not," she says. "Just enjoy your popularity, I guess."

"Thanks," Adam tells her. "At least Sam will be happy for me."

247.

This is it.

God mode.

The guys want to be you and the girls want to be with you.

This is Tony Montana in his mansion, Michelle Pfeiffer on his arm, a Porsche in the driveway, and a *tiger* in the yard.

(You watched the movie like you were supposed to, right?)

This is winning.

This is Pizza Man.

This is real life.

248.

Janie Ng and Leanne Grayson find Adam at his locker, Friday after school. Janie grabs his ass, sidles in close. "Got plans for the weekend?"

Adam shrugs. "Homework," he says. "You know how it goes."

It's busy season. Midway through the term. Wayne and Lisa and Devon are busting their asses to keep up with the workload. And it's not like Adam got much homework done on formal weekend.

(Neither did Wayne, for that matter. He comes up to Adam Monday morning at Cardigan's.

"Holy shit, man," he says. "I can't believe that party. Did you really screw Janie Ng and Leanne Grayson at the same time?"

Adam shrugs. "I can't really remember," he says. "What about you? Did you get to fuck a popular kid?"

Wayne grins, sheepish. Looks down at the ground. "I took her to bed."

"And?"

"And, well, we made out and stuff." He blushes. "I didn't have a condom, so we had to go find a condom, and then, well, by the time I got back to the room and stuff, well . . ."

Adam waits.

Wayne grins again, shakes his head. "By the time I got back, I was, you know."

He shrugs. "I was too drunk to pump."

Adam bursts out laughing. Can't hold it in. Wayne doesn't mind. He's laughing too.

"Sara didn't care too much," he says. "She said I could make it up to her."

Adam does a double-take. "Whoa. You're seeing her again?"

"This weekend. She's really nice. And *hot*."

"That's for sure," Adam says.

"Not as hot as Janie and Leanne, though," Wayne says. "That must have been a trip."

"It was something," Adam tells him. "Believe that.")

(That was a really long sidebar. Sorry. The point is, Adam didn't get anything done last weekend and neither did Wayne. So they both have some serious catching up to do. Except Janie and Leanne are here at Adam's locker, looking at him like they have something better in mind.)

"My parents are out of town," Janie tells him.

Leanne giggles. "They have a water bed," she says.

Adam looks at the girls. They're still smoking hot. They're still goddesses. He's got homework piled up. But what guy turns down Janie Ng *and* Leanne Grayson?

Fuck it, Adam thinks. "I'm in."

Janie grins. "Rest up, tiger." She kisses him. Lots of tongue. "You have a long weekend ahead of you."

249.

"A threesome," Sam says. "Holy shit."

They're out for pizza. Pepperoni, extra cheese, and a pitcher of Coca-Cola.

(Adam's taking a little bit of a party break.)

Sam pours himself more Coke and chews thoughtfully. He's not as excited as Adam figured he would be. Not as impressed.

"How'd Victoria take it?" Sam wants to know.

Adam looks around the restaurant. There's some runty kid with a pockmarked face clearing tables. He looks sad. He looks pathetic.

He looks a little bit like Adam.

(*Pizza Man.*)

Adam shakes his head. Looks at Sam. "Jesus Christ," he says. "Why is everyone always asking me about Victoria?"

250.

After their second or third time together, Leanne Grayson opts out of the threesome.

Ménage à trois becomes *ménage à deux.*

"Someone called her a slut in the hall," Janie tells Adam. "Some senior bitch. She doesn't want to, you know, get a reputation."

"Oh," Adam says. "Shit."

Janie grins. "Anyway, she knows you like me better," she says. "She didn't want to be a third wheel."

"Right," Adam says.

"Enough talking." Janie reaches for Adam. Pulls on his zipper. "Come here, Pizza Man."

251.

"What's wrong?" Janie says.

They're on her parents' water bed. Janie's in some sexy black bra and panties. She's smoking hot. She's DTF. But Adam's, uh . . .

("This usually never happens.")

("It's not you, it's me.")

("*Sorry.*")

Adam's distracted.

(Adam doesn't want to be here.)

(Adam's sick of this.)

(Adam wants Victoria.)

"Sorry," Adam tells Janie. "I just have a lot on my mind."

Janie frowns. The water bed jiggles beneath her. Janie jiggles too. Adam watches her. Thinks,

What the hell is wrong with me?

Janie reaches over the side of the bed. Comes back with a little baggie of pills and a smile. "This'll help you," she says. "Take one of these and let me blow your mind again."

Adam looks at her. Looks at the pills.

Adam thinks, *If I wuss out now and she tells the whole school I couldn't make it happen, I'll never live it down.*

(*Don't you fucking dare.*)

Adam says, "Let me see those pills."

Janie hands over the baggie.

Janie giggles.

252.

The pills help. Within a half hour, Adam's floating on a cloud. Janie's floating beside him. She's still wearing that sexy black underwear—

(until she isn't)

—and every time she touches Adam it feels like a sparkler. He stops thinking about Victoria. He stops thinking about homework.

He enjoys the ride.

253.

It's the comedown that's the problem.

It's the lying awake in bed exhausted but unable to sleep that's the problem.

It's the waking up the next day so depressed you want to kill yourself that's the problem.

It's the feeling so haggard that you don't get any homework done all weekend that's the problem.

It's the giving up Sunday night around midnight and crying yourself to sleep thinking about Victoria.

· *That's* the problem.

254.

Fortunately, none of the popular kids have assignments due Monday. This is a good thing, because Adam gets literally nothing done by Monday morning—

(well, he and Janie work through a box of condoms, but they don't give grades for that)

(and if they did give grades for sex, Adam figures he'd still be only like a C, C-plus at best)

(also, he feels like he's been hit by a moving truck)

(also, he forgot to do his economics homework. And today of all days, Mr. Soulyuk decides to check it)

Adam doesn't even try to hide it. Soulyuk screws up his face. Gives Adam the old disappointed-teacher look—

(maybe you know it)

—"Adam Higgs," he says. "This is a first."

"Sorry, sir," Adam says. "I had a busy weekend."

"No kidding," Soulyuk says. "You look like a zombie."

Laughter from some of the kids who stay connected, who know just why Adam looks like a zombie. Adam is too tired to care.

"We all need a mulligan now and then," Soulyuk says. "Just don't let it happen again."

"No, sir," Adam says. "I won't."

255.

Victoria's still dodging Adam's calls. She won't answer his texts. And Facebook? Forget it.

He finds her in the hall one day. Creeps her locker until she comes around. She's got that big lug with her, the football player—

(Chad)

—and he's hanging around just a little too close, saying something about a party at Tyler's. Adam breaks in. "Can we talk?"

Victoria shakes her head. Looks away. "I can't do this right now, Adam."

"I'm sorry," Adam tells her. "You were right about everything. Just give me another shot and I'll do better. I promise."

Victoria still can't meet his eye. "I'm sorry, Adam," she says. "I just can't."

"You can," Adam says. "You have to. I—"

Chad steps up. "She doesn't want to talk to you, man," he says. "Why don't you just leave her alone?"

Adam looks at Victoria. She's still looking as far away from Adam as possible. She's trying not to cry. "I'm so sorry," Adam tells her.

Chad puts his hand out. Blocks Adam's chest. "Just back off, man."

Adam looks at Chad. At Chad's meaty, football-player

hand. He's not getting through Chad. He knows this. Anyway, people are starting to watch. Starting to stare.

Fighting is *not* cool.

"You're a real dick, you know that?" Adam says.

Chad shrugs. Puts his arm around Victoria. "Whatever you say."

256.

No Victoria.

It's over.

Finished.

Done.

So . . .

Adam sticks with Janie.

Hey, she's a goddess. And she's making his rep. Guys see Janie on Adam's arm as he walks through the hall and they *know* he's legit.

Besides, the sex is amazing—

(when the pills are involved)

—and Adam's getting better all the time.

(Although it's not like he and Janie have much to talk about when they're not as high as airplanes. They pretty much get high and have sex and watch TV and eat pizza, and sometimes Janie talks about going camping with Leanne and what kind of car her parents are going to buy next, and even though she's really nice and really hot and smart and everything, Adam

just

doesn't

care.)

257.

The thing is, Janie's not dumb.

(We've established this.)

She figures out pretty quickly that Adam's going through the motions. I mean, she's thinking relationship. He's thinking—

(what is he thinking?)

(sex?)

(drugs?)

(rock-star status?)

Whatever he's thinking, it's sure not boyfriend/girlfriend, lovey-dovey thoughts. He's thinking business. He's thinking winning. He's thinking takeover.

And Janie knows this. She knows when he blows her off Monday through Thursday nights to do homework.

("It's my *job*, Janie.")

She knows when he won't text back to her smiley faces.

("I just got distracted.")

She knows when it takes the pills to kick in before he'll even look at her.

("Stuff on my mind.")

And when he brings Sara Bryant's geography project to the hotel room Janie rents them for the long weekend, she knows for damn certain.

(This is the big fight. This is the one where Janie's dressed up for dinner out somewhere fancy downtown, dress, heels, the rest of it, and Adam's hungover as fuck, sitting at the hotel room desk in his underwear, grinding out five mediocre pages on coal mining. This is the one where Janie gets mad.

"All you do is homework, Adam," she says. "Seriously, what's up with you? I got us this hotel room so we could do something special and you—"

"I just have to get this finished," he tells her. "It's due Tuesday and Sara will freak if I don't get it done."

"What do you care?" Janie says. "Why are you still doing this homework stuff, anyway?"

Adam shrugs. "Homework got me here," he tells her. "I can't give it up now."

"Sure you can," Janie says. "Just tell them you're not going to do it." She looks at him. "Or are you afraid you'll lose all your friends if they don't need you to do their bitch work anymore?"

Adam looks up from Sara's paper for the first time. "I don't want to talk about it," he says.

"I'm totally right, aren't I?" Janie says. "You're so obsessed with being a big shot that you can't even enjoy the good things in your life."

"Bullshit," Adam says.

"No, *you're* bullshit," Janie says. "Popularity is bullshit. You have to stop caring about what people think."

"Whatever," Adam says. "Just let me finish this paper, okay?"

Janie sighs. "Fine," she says. She stands there a moment. Then she smiles at him, wicked. "*Pizza Man.*")

258.

Adam flips out at Janie.

Loses it.

"What's the matter?" she says. "You are the Pizza Man, aren't you? Isn't that who you want to be?"

"Not when you say it like that," Adam tells her. "Not with that fucking, like, *tone*."

Janie looks at Adam. Looks at Sara Bryant's geography paper. Looks at her own reflection in the mirror.

(Dress. Makeup. Heels.)

(A goddess.)

"Screw this," Janie says. "Keep the room if you want. I'm outta here."

And she's gone.

(Like I said, Janie's not dumb.)

259.

Adam keeps the hotel room. Adam finishes Sara Bryant's geography paper. Adam wonders if letting Janie walk out was a tactical error. If it'll have a harmful effect on his reputation.

Then Adam thinks, *Who cares?*

He thinks, *I'll fix this, somehow.*

He thinks, *Finally, I can sleep.*

Adam sleeps.

260.

"So what's the deal?" Brian says. "You get with those two hotties, or what?"

They're driving out to meet Bondy for the weekly ID pickup. It's a slow week, only three orders. It's been a slow month.

(Apparently everyone at Nixon has a fake ID by this point. Business is trending down. The market, she is saturated.)

Adam looks out the window at the factories and train yards alongside the expressway. "Yeah," he says. "I guess I did."

Brian laughs. "You're such a pimp. How was it?"

Adam shrugs. "It was good."

Brian glances across the car at Adam. "Just good?" he says, grinning. "Bullshit. I bet it was pornographic."

Adam just smiles. Doesn't say anything. Since Janie walked out, he's been kinda meh. The Janie stuff, it's had a definite effect on his standing at Nixon.

(I mean, he's still popular. People still notice when he walks down the hall. But the threesome stuff is old news at this point. And Janie Ng *dumped* him.

This morning, Paul Nolan made a comment about Adam's watch, some throwaway joke. All in fun, obviously—

(it's some shitty Timex)

—but the message is clear.

Adam's stock is declining, just a little.)

(And Rob Thigpen's still riding high.)

"We need a new income stream," Adam tells Brian. "Something to keep us on top of the game."

Brian frowns. "Homework and two hot chicks on your jock isn't enough?"

"Tony Montana didn't stop," Adam says. "This ID thing's nearly played out. You want to go back to running pizzas?"

Brian shakes his head. "Hell no."

"Good," Adam says. "Because I have our next big idea."

261.

Pills, Adam's thinking.

Yeah. Real *Scarface* shit.

Brian isn't feeling it at first.

"It makes perfect sense," Adam tells him. "All the popular kids are into the stuff. They have to get it from somewhere."

"Shit," Brian says. "I dunno. That's some heavy-duty territory you're talking about moving into right there."

Maybe, Adam thinks. But maybe it's the logical progression. Homework. Booze. IDs. The only other things Nixon kids need are drugs and sex—

(and pimpin' ain't easy)

(pills, on the other hand? Super easy. Every popular kid in the school pops a pill Friday night. Adam's seen it. But they have to get their pills from somewhere.

Why not from Adam Higgs?)

"Because it's fucking illegal, is why," Brian says. "Like, hard core, break the law, they'll throw us in jail if they catch us."

"So we won't get caught," Adam tells him. "We'll keep our mouths shut. You ever watch movies? Ever watch *Scarface?* It's when you get stupid that you get caught. We just won't get stupid."

Brian shakes his head. "I don't know, man," he says. "Easier said than done."

"Look," Adam says. "When I first started at Nixon, you told me I had to get ballsy to succeed. Summer's coming. You want to drive pizzas around while everyone else is getting fucked up at parties?"

Brian stares out the window. "Shit," he says.

"Just work with me," Adam tells him. "Your cousin offered to hook me up, back in the day. We talk to him, feel him out. It's just talk.

"Come on," Adam says. "When have I let you down before?"

262.

Adam and Brian meet up with Tommy a few days later.

Tommy lives in an apartment on the west side of town, in the ghetto underneath the bridge to Detroit. Brian looks back twice at his shitty Sunfire as he and Adam walk up to the building.

Adam gives him a look. Brian shrugs. "In this neighborhood?" he says. "That thing's as good as a Bentley."

Tommy's apartment is on the eighth floor. It's a long-ass ride in a smelly, graffiti-stained elevator. The lights flicker. The elevator shudders.

It ain't confidence-inspiring.

Tommy's waiting for them at the door. He's scrawnier than Adam remembers. Pale, with a patchy goatee and a stained wifebeater. He grins at Adam and Brian, kind of unfocused.

(*High.*)

"You guys," he says. "How's it going?"

Tommy's living room has a big flat-screen TV on the wall and a nice leather sofa. The window looks out over the river. Adam looks around, feels a little more confident in Tommy's ability to provide.

"You were going to hook me up with some hot high school honeys," Tommy says. "You never called me back, though."

Adam shrugs. "They're overrated."

Tommy looks at him. "Yeah," he says. "I guess they are.

So what's up? You guys looking for more booze, or what?"

Adam sits. The sofa is nice. Butter-soft. "We need something a little harder."

"Harder." Tommy picks up a bong. Takes a rip. Offers it to Brian. Brian shakes him off. "You want drugs?" Tommy says.

Tommy looks at Brian again. Brian doesn't say anything. Brian hasn't said anything since he got off the elevator.

"Pills," Adam tells Tommy. "How many can you get us?"

Tommy looks at him. Cocks his head. "How many do you want?"

"Lots," Adam says.

Tommy lights up again. Studies Adam as he inhales. "This isn't just for some party, I guess," he says.

Adam shakes his head. "Nope."

"'Nope.'" Tommy looks at him some more. Then he laughs. "Ice-cold, you are. You want to be a drug dealer. Bona fide."

"My whole school's on this stuff," Adam tells him. "They have to get it from somewhere."

"Somewhere," Tommy says. "That's the problem. Somewhere is Jamal."

"Who the hell is Jamal?" Adam says.

Tommy looks at the bong one more time. Like he's debating firing up again. Then he stands. "Come on," he says. "I'll show you Jamal."

263.

They ride into downtown in Tommy's five-liter Mustang. It roars. It rumbles. It's hard to converse.

"All of your little friends get their pills from Jamal," Tommy's yelling over the engine. "Hell, *I* get my pills from Jamal."

"I'm just talking about Nixon," Adam yells back. "I don't want the city. What the hell's this guy going to care?"

"Gee, I dunno," Tommy says. "Rich kids, pretty girls, lots of parties. I'd say he won't like it."

"Screw him," Adam says. "It's a free market."

Tommy laughs. "Yeah," he says. "Okay. You tell Jamal that. There he is now."

He pulls the Mustang into a parking lot. Kills the engine and points out the window. A strip club in daylight, the most depressing sight known to man. A cream-colored Lexus sedan with blingy chrome rims. A big Lebanese dude with tats and a shaved head and *muscle.* "Jamal," Tommy says.

Adam looks at the guy. Adam thinks, *That's a fucking drug dealer.* Adam thinks, *This is way over my head.*

Adam thinks:

Scary.

But then Adam thinks about breaking things off with Janie. He thinks about how Victoria's never coming back. He thinks about how, for the first time ever, Pizza Man Enterprises actually *lost* Likes on Facebook.

People have their IDs.

They can get their own booze.

Adam's not pulling threesomes with goddesses anymore.

He needs something to stay in the game.

Because:

As soon as the hustle stops, god status disappears. And Adam cannot have that.

Adam wants . . .

Well, he wanted to *win*.

Now he wants to TAKE OVER.

So, fuck Jamal.

264.

"Fuck Jamal," Adam tells Tommy. "This isn't the movies. I'm not afraid of him."

Tommy looks at Adam. Looks at Jamal. Laughs and fires up the Mustang again. "Ice-cold," he says, idling out of the lot. "Ice-fucking-cold."

265.

Tommy drives them back to the west side. Parks the Mustang and just looks at Adam. "I know a guy who runs separate from Jamal," he says finally. "I think I can swing something. If you're serious."

Adam glances at Brian in the backseat. "We're serious," he says.

"Cash in advance," Tommy says. "And keep my name out of it. The last thing I need is Jamal on *my* ass."

"Don't sweat it," Adam tells him. "We'll stay cool."

Tommy climbs out of the car. "You sure you know what you're doing, kid?"

Adam looks at him.

(*No.*)

(*Shut up.*)

"Yeah," Adam says.

(*Taking over.*)

Adam grins. "Tony Montana."

266.

"We're actually doing this, huh?" Brian says.

It's a couple days later. They're driving away from Tommy's apartment. They've just traded a serious pile of cash for a Ziploc bag filled with pills. Adam has the bag stuffed in the glove box. Brian, he notices, is driving *exactly* the speed limit.

"How do you feel about it?" Adam asks him.

Brian purses his lips. Pulls out to pass a tractor trailer coming down off the bridge and nearly gets creamed by another one. "Shit," he says, diving back to the slow lane. "I dunno."

"It's just pills," Adam tells him. "Harmless. It's not cocaine or anything."

"It's still drugs," Brian says.

"It's going to make us rich," Adam says. "We're going to take over. You'll see."

Brian drives. Brian sighs. "Yeah," he says. "Maybe."

"Just you wait," Adam tells him. "Just you wait."

267.

Okay, so Adam has the product. Now he needs the clientele.

Jessie McGill has a chemistry assignment due. Adam finishes it over the weekend. Hands it over Monday morning.

Jessie takes the paper, gives him a quick hug. "Thanks, Pizza Man." She pulls out her purse. "I have a French assignment coming up. You know any French?"

Adam shrugs. "*Un petit peu.*"

Jessie laughs. "I guess you'll do anything for a price, huh?"

"I guess so," Adam says. He lowers his voice. "Speaking of, where do you get your drugs?"

Jessie's eyes go wide. "Pardon?"

"Pills," Adam says. "I came into a few. If you know anybody who's interested."

"Whoa," Jessie says. "You're dealing now?"

Adam grins at her. "I'll do anything for a price."

268.

It's not long before word gets around.

"I hear you're selling," Sara Bryant tells Adam. "Any good?"

"Top of the line," Adam tells her. "Tested them myself."

(*Test* is a funny word for it, he thinks, given that the test pretty much consisted of hooking up with Audrey Klein and tripping balls all weekend, but the high was amazing.)

(So was Audrey Klein.)

(The comedown, not so much.)

Sara makes a face. "Audrey Klein?" she says. "I thought you were mixed up with Janie and Leanne."

"Got old," Adam tells her. "Why, you jealous?"

"Hell no," Sara says. "Some people have standards."

"And how's Wayne?" Adam says. "You still mixed up in *that* sordid affair?"

Sara frowns. "Oh, quit being so superficial, Pizza Man. Not everyone cares about being popular."

"I take it you're still going out with him, then," Adam says.

"He's taking me to dinner on Friday," Sara says. "Then we're hitting Crash. Which is why I need your hookup, so are you selling or no?"

"I'm selling," Adam tells her. "How many do you need?"

269.

Sara buys. Jessie buys. Paul Nolan and Alton Di Sousa buy.

Rob Thigpen drops by Cardigan's. "Hear you're holding, Pizza Man," he tells Adam. "Can I score something?"

Adam gives Rob a big, cheesy fake smile. Adam says: "Of course, buddy. How many do you need?"

Rob buys like five. "Just enough to get me through the weekend."

Adam charges him double.

Then he puts a blast out on Facebook. *Party favors*, he writes. *Inquire within.*

Pretty clear, he figures.

Kids get the point.

They inquire within.

Instant messages on Facebook. Texts. Phone calls. The supply is good. The price is right.

Everyone wants a taste of the stuff that made Janie Ng and Leanne Grayson turn Adam Higgs into a god.

It's not long before the first supply is depleted. Some of that's Adam, if he's being honest. He's giving out tasters. Free samples. He's partying, a little.

(Hey, girls love a god. And Adam's getting decent at the whole sex thing. He worked for this. Why not enjoy it?)

270.

Sam calls Adam. Leaves a message on his phone.

Adam's in the back of a cab when he gets it. He's lost in some suburb in the south end of town, looking for some sophomore's party. He thinks the girl might have left a message with her address. He's scrolling through when Sam's voice comes on.

"Uh, hey, Adam," Sam says. He clears his throat. "Haven't heard from you in a while, but, uh, the hockey game is next week."

Shit, Adam thinks. *Right*.

"I was thinking we could just meet up at the bus loop and take the tunnel bus over," Sam says. "Like, after you get done with school or something? It's probably good if we get there a little early, because, you know, sometimes these places aren't exactly wheelchair friendly, right?"

Adam thinks about taking the bus with Sam. Wheeling him into the hockey arena, trying to navigate about a million and a half people. Trying to get home at the end of the night.

Crap, he thinks. *What was I thinking?*

"Anyway," Sam says, his voice artificial, like he's trying to be cheerful. "Give me a shout and we'll work out the details, okay?

"Hope you're doing good," Sam says.

"Later," Sam says.

Adam looks out the window of the cab. It's nothing but identical McMansions for miles. The cab idles forward. The phone is hot against his ear.

The answering machine prompts him to save or delete.

Adam deletes the message.

He keeps looking for the sophomore's address.

271.

You already know what's going to happen, right?
I mean, I shouldn't have to spell it out for you.

272.

Tommy looks surprised when Adam and Brian pay him their next visit. "You need more already?"

Adam grins at him. "What did I tell you?"

"I guess I should have listened," Tommy says. He goes into his bedroom and comes out with another Ziploc bag. "I thought you kids were a couple of screwups."

"Screwups?" Adam laughs at him. "Fuck that. We're taking over."

"Uh-huh," Tommy says. "You hear from Jamal yet?"

"Dude doesn't even know we exist."

"Oh, he knows," Tommy says. "Jamal knows everything that goes on in this town. Just don't lead his ass back to me."

"You'll be fine," Adam tells him. "Get another package ready for us. Two weeks."

273.

"You thinking about a new car?" Adam asks Brian as they dodge more eighteen-wheelers on the drive home from Tommy's. The Sunfire is wheezing, rattling, squealing, *dying*.

Brian frowns. "What's wrong with my car?" he says. "I like it."

"The money we're going to be making, you could pick up something sweet. A Camaro, maybe. Something *pimp*."

"I'm not really a car guy," Brian says. "Anyway, I'm more concerned with not getting killed."

Brian looks at Adam. "Jamal's scary, man."

"You're scary," Adam tells him.

"Jamal's huge."

"*You're* huge."

"Not as big as Jamal," Brian says. "I heard he stabbed a guy once. Anyway," he sighs. "Dude, I'm really not sure about this."

"I know," Adam says. "You keep saying that."

"This money we're making, it's *drug* money."

"You'd rather be making pizza money?"

"Fuck," Brian says. "I don't know. I'm just worried, man. I don't want to get my ass beat or end up in jail."

"You just gotta be ballsy," Adam tells him. "We'll be fine."

Brian drives a mile or so. "I hope so," he says finally. "I really hope so, man."

274.

The product keeps moving.

Pizza Man is a machine.

Anyone who bought homework, or booze, or a fake ID, Adam pitches the new scheme. *Party favors. Rock out this weekend like a god.*

Some kids aren't into it. Some say no to drugs. Adam respects that. No need for the hard sell. There are more than enough buyers as is.

He gets Amanda Rimes, Brian's girlfriend, to sell to the sophomore kids. Distributes from his locker at lunchtime, at Cardigan's after school. It's decent money. It's not Mercedes money. It fills the fake ID gap, though, and the girls seem to love it. Adam hits a lot of parties.

(More than the rest of Nixon's ruling class *combined.*)

Adam's *busy.*

So's the rest of his team.

"Just pick up a couple of my assignments," Adam tells Wayne. "Just once. And maybe next week too. I'm swamped with this party-favor stuff."

Wayne looks at Adam. Frowns. "You sure about this, man? Maybe we need to scale back a little."

"Are you kidding?" Adam asks him. "Do you know who I am to these people?"

"You're a god," Devon says. "You slept with Janie Ng and

Leanne Grayson at the same time. People love you. So why keep pushing?"

"They don't love me," Adam tells him. "They love what I do for them. I have to keep going until they respect me."

"Okay." Wayne kind of frowns. "I just, you know, I need a break too. I'm supposed to go out with Sara this weekend and you're piling it on, man."

"We *all* need a break," Lisa says. "This workload is ridiculous, Adam."

"I know, guys. I'm sorry," Adam says. "We're all working hard here."

"Are we?" Lisa rolls her eyes. "All you do lately is party and hook up with sophomore girls, from the looks of it."

"I have other business," Adam tells her. "It's not just the homework. Listen, I'll try and find help, though. Keep it together until things calm down again and I'll make it worth your while."

"Yeah?" Lisa says. "How?"

"Two hundred dollars," Adam says. "Each. Monthly bonus."

Lisa rolls her eyes again. "Weak."

"You don't want it?" Adam says.

"She didn't say that." Wayne sighs. "We just really need a break, Adam. Cut us some slack."

"I *know*," Adam says. "I'm working on it, okay?"

"Okay," they tell him. They sigh and nod and promise to keep at it. They're tired, but the machine keeps rolling. The money's too good. The perks. The popularity. They can't look Adam in the eye, though, as they're walking away. None of them can.

275.

The machine doesn't stop rolling. The game doesn't just end. The thing about a takeover is you can't just quit halfway. Even if you want to, even if you wish you could just sit down and shut up and just be satisfied—

(with Victoria)

(with middling popularity)

(with a little bit of cash and a few decent friends)

—there's no stopping, not once you've tasted success. Not once you know what it feels like to be a god. Not when this has been your rightful place all along.

The homework keeps getting done. The pills practically sell themselves. The money keeps coming. The girls—

(Ashley Cody

Toni Crowson

Elizabeth O'Brien

Andrea Stevens

Stacey Roy

Allison um, Allison something—

(they all kind of blur together))

It goes on and on and on. Adam has more fun than anyone. More hookups than anyone. And he makes sure everyone sees it.

(Especially Rob Thigpen.)

(#rockstar)

(#TonyMontana)

The nights are long. Sleep is minimal. The parties are epic and the comedowns are brutal. The texts keep rolling in. IM. Facebook. Twitter. Ceaseless. Incessant. Someone always wants more.

There's always another opportunity. Another party. Another pretty girl. There's always another dollar to be made, another favor to be curried.

The game continues, long after you've won.

The machine keeps rolling, until

pretty soon

you're not even sure you can control it anymore.

276.

Sam finally gets ahold of Adam.

"Holy crap, buddy," he says. "Check your messages much? Where the hell have you been?"

Adam sighs. Looks across at his desk.

A stack of homework assignments.

A baggie of pills.

A box of condoms.

(*I should really hide this stuff*, he thinks.)

"Where have I been?" he asks Sam. "You wouldn't believe me if I told you."

"I just wanted to make sure you didn't forget about the game," Sam says. "I hate to be a nag, but it's next Thursday."

"Yeah," Adam says. "Next Thursday night. Definitely."

"You're cool with taking the bus?"

(*Since I still don't have a Porsche*, Adam thinks.)

"Definitely," Adam says. "I'll meet you at the bus loop after school. Four o'clock."

"Four o'clock," Sam says. "See you there."

"Definitely," Adam says.

277.

Poor Sam.

278.

"Jamal's pissed," Janie says.

Her parents are out of town. Adam has a shit ton of homework jobs, but . . .

Janie's parents are out of town.

Adam's lying there on Janie's mom and dad's water bed, staring straight into space as the ceiling spins above him, feeling Janie's hand on his chest as she lies curled up beside him.

(They broke up, a while back, Adam and Janie—

(you remember)

—but, you know.

Nothing is forever.

Especially when there are drugs involved.)

"Paul told Jamal we're all buying from you now." Janie runs her fingers across Adam's chest, and the way the drugs are working, her touch feels like electricity. "Jamal didn't like it. He got pissed. He wanted to know where you live."

"Forget Jamal," Adam tells Janie. "I'm not afraid of him."

"He's, like, a gangster," Janie says. "Maybe you should be afraid of him."

"What is this, a movie?" Adam says. "What's he going to do?"

"I heard he stabbed somebody," Janie says.

"Whatever," Adam says.

Janie's silent for a while. She's still touching Adam's chest and he lies there and looks at the ceiling and enjoys her electric touch.

Then Janie sits up and looks at Adam. "If we break up again, does that mean I have to pay full price for your pills?"

279.

"Dude," Brian says. "I know you're living large and everything, but you gotta ease off on the free samples. It's seriously cutting into our profit."

They're making another run back to Tommy's place. Brian's been trying to figure out the math. The math came in real short. Adam knows why.

Janie Ng.

And Audrey Klein.

And another sophomore, Kaylee Preston.

And maybe a few freebees for Paul Nolan and Alton Di Sousa at a party.

("Thanks, Adam.")

It's an investment, right?

(An investment in what?)

Popularity don't pay the bills.

"Sorry, man," Adam tells Brian. "Take it out of my share. I'll pay it back."

Brian thinks about it. Brian sighs. "Fine," he says. "I guess that works."

280.

Never mind the money. The machine is chewing Adam up. Wayne and Lisa and Devon are taking on most of the homework at this point. The partying, the pills, the comedown, it's too much. Little by little, the machine's falling apart.

"What's happening, Adam?" Ms. Garvey says as she hands back the latest geography assignments. "I didn't get a paper from you. Did you forget?"

Adam didn't forget. He was finishing Rob Thigpen's and Alton Di Sousa's projects instead. "I'm sorry, Ms. Garvey," Adam tells her. "I've been busy."

"Get it to me by Friday," Garvey tells him, "or I have to give you a zero."

Adam tells her he will. Adam fully intends to. Adam's off the pills, off Janie Ng, off Kaylee Preston.

Adam's on homework.

100 percent.

Then Lisa Choi quits.

281.

"It's nothing personal," Lisa says. "I'm just tired of this, man."

"I'll get you help," Adam tells her. "I'll pull my share again. Hire another employee. Just give me a little time."

Lisa shakes her head. "It isn't fun anymore, Adam. I don't need it."

"The money—"

"Forget the money," Lisa says. "You could pay me double and I'd still walk."

"Why?"

"It's just . . ." Lisa sighs. "It's *you*, man. You're just kind of an asshole. You work us to the bone while you're off hooking up and partying and whatever. You take half our money and you don't even earn it.

"Hell," Lisa says, "Wayne handles half of the meetings these days, even. What's to stop us from doing something like this on our own, anyway?"

"Don't you dare," Adam tells her. "Don't you *dare*, Lisa. I'll—"

"You'll what? Relax, Pizza Man." Lisa shrugs. "I just want my life back."

282.

And that's that. Lisa hands in her last assignments, takes her final day's pay, and walks out of Cardigan's and out of this story. Just like Victoria, she doesn't look back.

"Forget her," Adam tells Wayne and Devon. "We don't need her."

Wayne and Devon share a look. "We kinda do, Adam," Devon says. "We're swamped."

Wayne nods. "All due respect, but I don't think I can keep this up any longer."

"It's too much," Devon says. "Humans weren't made to do this much homework."

"Don't you guys start," Adam says.

"We just need help," Wayne says. "Figure something out, *please*. I'm not sure how much more we can take."

283.

"Not interested."

Adam stares at the kid. Can't believe it. "Not interested," he says. "What the hell are you talking about?"

The kid's name is Cameron Cardinal. He's a sophomore, but he's supposed to be brilliant. His Facebook page says he wants to be an accountant, so Adam knows he likes money, and he's always wearing Lacoste and Ralph Lauren to school—

(even though his stuff looks like he bought it at the discount store and might even be fake).

Adam finds him checking his stock portfolio in the computer lab. He lays out the whole spiel, emphasis on the money. Emphasis on the hype new gear in Cameron's future. Then he sits back and waits for the kid to take the bait.

But Cameron doesn't even think about it. He shakes his head. "Too risky," he tells Adam. "If I get caught, it's over. Accounting firms take cheating seriously."

"It's not really cheating," Adam says. "Besides, it's not like you're going to get caught. We've been doing it for months and nobody suspects a thing."

Cameron shakes his head. "Can't do it, man. Sorry."

Then he turns back to the computer screen.

Adam watches him for a minute. Finally, Cameron turns back around. Looks at Adam.

"Did you really start calling yourself Pizza Man?" he says.

284.

"Craaaaaap," Wayne says. "We don't have *any* help?"

"We have me," Adam tells him. "I'm back in the game. I'll take on the extra workload. I'll be fine."

"We're still behind," Devon says. "There's too much work for three people. We're dying, man."

"Just do what you can," Adam says. "I'll handle the leftovers, okay?"

Wayne looks at Devon. They both sigh. "Yeah, Adam," Wayne says. "Okay."

285.

Thursday after school—

(after Cardigan's)

—Adam calls Sam. Bails on the hockey game.

(You knew it was coming.)

"I'm just swamped," Adam tells him. "I forgot about this geography project. Can't you just take someone else?"

Sam doesn't answer for a minute. "Adam, I'm at the bus loop," he says finally. "Who am I supposed to take?"

"I'll make it up to you," Adam says. "I swear."

"The season's almost over," Sam says. "And this is the *Leafs*, Adam."

Adam looks around. Closes his eyes. Wishes this phone call would just end.

Then he has an idea.

"I'll throw you a party," Adam says. "The biggest you've ever seen. I'll bring every girl I can find. It'll be better than any stupid hockey game, I swear to god.

"You're going to love it," Adam says.

"I promise," Adam says.

Sam is silent a long time. "You're really not coming?"

Adam shakes his head. "I'm sorry," he says.

"Fuck," Sam says.

286.

And that's how Adam finds himself locked in his room Thursday night, a huge stack of homework jobs sitting between his present state—

(stress)

(chaos)

(flux)

(madness)

—and Ms. Garvey's geography project

(due tomorrow).

At this point, it's midnight. Mrs. Stewart has English projects due tomorrow and half the damn school's paying Adam to finish them. And he's nowhere near done.

(And he's exhausted.)

(*Sorry, Ms. Garvey. Guess I'm taking the zero on that geography thing.*)

Adam decides he's cool with the zero. He's fine with the zero. What's one zero, anyway? He'll clear five hundred bucks, easy, with the work he's putting in. Nobody pays him for his own grades.

He'll work out the last of these English assignments and use the money to throw Sam the biggest party ever—

(maybe even find him a girlfriend)

—and show Sam that his little brother has attained the god status that should have been Sam's destiny. Show Sam his little brother's living on some Tony Montana shit now. He's not a loser anymore.

(#victorylap)

Except then Adam moves a stack of assignments and unearths the career guide Bonnie Dubois gave him. And he thinks about how eager she was to help him.

(How pleased the vice principal was with his grades.)

(How excited Victoria was when she talked about college.)

Shit, Adam thinks. He picks up the phone.

"I need something to keep me focused," he tells Brian. "I have, like, a million projects tonight. Can you help?"

287.

Brian shows up an hour and a half later. "Ritalin," he says, handing Adam a pill bottle. "Only thing I could score at this hour."

He holds up a plastic 7-Eleven bag. "And some Red Bull. Because sleep is overrated."

"You're a lifesaver," Adam tells him. "How much?"

"Thirty bucks." Brian looks at him. "You sure you're all right?"

"I'm good," Adam tells him, handing Brian the cash. "Just got a ton of crap on my plate, but what else is new, right?"

"Yeah," Brian says. "Right."

288.

Sleep *is* overrated.

Adam pops some Ritalin, downs a Red Bull, and grinds out the English assignments by about four thirty in the morning. Spends the rest of the night writing about tectonic plates. Finishes around dawn, reads it over. Figures, it's not bad.

Figures, it might even be coherent.

Steph stares at Adam over breakfast. "What the hell happened to you?"

"Big project," he tells her. "Long night."

"You look like a corpse," she says. Then she frowns. "Wait. Weren't you supposed to go to that hockey game with Sam last night?"

"I had to reschedule," Adam tells her. "I'm going to throw him a party instead. The hotel at the casino, next weekend. Tell your friends."

Steph stares. "Seriously?"

Adam shrugs.

"Wow." Steph sighs. "I hope it's all worth it, Adam."

Adam yawns. "It's everything I ever wanted."

289.

Adam gets the English assignments back to their owners first thing in the morning. Gets paid, too—
       (at this point, he has a shoe box full of cash in his locker, stacks of twenties. He hasn't hit a bank in a while.)
       —then he hands the geography assignment in. Ms. Garvey looks at him funny. "Everything okay, Adam?"
       "Of course," Adam tells her.
       "This isn't like you," Garvey says. "You're usually so conscientious."
       "I'm just busy, miss," Adam tells her.
       She doesn't believe him, he can tell. "Anything you want to talk about?"
       "I'm fine," Adam tells her. "Really."
       She kind of waffles there, doesn't really know what to say. What can she say? He handed in the assignment, didn't he? Even if he looks—
       (and feels)
           —like he's been hit by a truck, he's still rolling. And now he can go home and sleep.

Except:
Then Adam walks into economics and Mr. Soulyuk is handing out the midterm.
       (*Shiiiiiiiiiiiiiiiiiiiiiiiiiiiiiiit.*)

"Hope everyone had a chance to study," Soulyuk's saying. "I didn't exactly make this an easy one."

290.

So, you know, that sucks.

      The midterm looks like it's written in Swahili.

      Not that Adam can really focus anyway.

            Too much Red Bull.

            Not enough sleep.

He's.

      Screwed.

291.

Something has to change.
  This isn't working, Adam thinks—
  (as he stumbles out of the economics midterm fully aware
  he just bombed)
  (feeling like he's just been *hit* by a bomb).
Something has to change.

292.

But what, though?
>The partying?
>The girls?
>The popularity?
>The pills?
>None of it is conducive to getting homework done, sure.
None of it is going to get Adam those honor-roll grades. None of
it's getting him into college.
>But this was never about college.
>It was never about grades.
>It was about partying. And girls. And popularity.
>*Nothing has to change*, Adam thinks.
>(*All I really need is Ritalin. Red Bull. And another employee.*)

293.

Brian hooks up the Ritalin.

Adam can score Red Bull on his own.

The new employee?

Has to be George Dubois.

He's Bonnie Dubois's kid, but he's the only candidate Adam can find. And Adam needs help. Now.

George is sitting at his locker when Adam finds him. He's reading a music magazine. "Want a job?" Adam asks him.

George's eyes go wide. "The homework thing, really?"

"So you know about it," Adam says.

"Everyone knows about it," George says. "It's the coolest thing ever."

"It's pretty rad," Adam says. "You want in?"

George grins. "Hell yes."

"You'd have to start right away."

"Just give me the work," George says.

"And you have to keep your mouth shut," Adam says. "Don't tell anyone. Especially don't tell your mom."

"I won't tell anyone," George says. "I won't let you down."

"Good," Adam says. "Meet me at Cardigan's after school."

He shakes George's hand.

Wonders:

How long before I start to regret this?

294.

Adam gives George Lisa's old beat. Physics with a side of sophomore.

"Awesome," George says. "I love physics."

Adam slaps him on the back. "Go make me proud, buddy."

Wayne lingers after George is gone. "You sure this is cool, man?" he asks Adam. "You know his mom is—"

"You got any better ideas?" Adam says. "He's pumped to be part of the team. And he's ready to work. This is good for us, trust me."

Wayne thinks about it. "I just hope this doesn't blow up in our faces."

Wayne looks skeptical. But Wayne defers to Adam anyway. And just as Wayne is about to reluctantly agree to the George Dubois thing, Wayne and Adam see Brian's Sunfire pull into the Cardigan's lot. Watch Brian climb out.

Brian looks scared.

Brian looks hurt.

Brian's *bleeding.*

295.

"Jesus Christ," Adam says. "What the hell happened to you?"

Brian leans against the hood of his car, kind of hunched over, holding his right arm. He has a black eye. A bloody nose. He's been tuned up.

"Jamal," Brian says.

296.

"I was dropping off some supply," Brian tells Adam and Wayne—
(who is kind of lingering wide-eyed in the background,
shifting his weight and looking altogether terrified)
—"A couple of sophomores, Tammy and Ryan," Brian
says. "They're throwing a kegger or something. You know?"

"Sure," Adam says.

"Jamal was there," Brian says. "When I walked back to
my car. He had his homeboy with him, some big, ugly dude."

"Uh-huh," Adam says.

Brian spits blood. "They pretty much just kicked the shit
out of me, man. Took the rest of my pills, my money, everything.
Told me if I knew what was good I would give up the pill game.
Shit, man."

Adam nods. "Shit."

"What are we going to do?" Brian says.

Adam looks at him. Brian looks at him back, blood drip-
ping from his nose.

Brian looks *stressed*.

Adam pulls out his wallet. Peels off some money. "That
should cover you," he says, "for what they robbed."

Brian holds up his hands. Tries to shake off the money.
Adam presses it into his hand and Brian gives up and takes it.
"Fine," he says, shoving the cash into his pocket. "But what are we
going to *do*?"

"You want revenge?" Adam says.

Brian looks at him. "No, man," he says. "I don't want to start a war with some Lebanese gangster. I just want to know if enough is enough."

Adam looks around the parking lot. "Enough is never enough," he says.

Brian sighs. "So you still want to deal. After all of this."

"We'll watch our backs," Adam tells him. "We'll be careful. You don't want to go back to Pizza Hut, do you?"

"At this point," Brian says, "I don't even care."

297.

But Brian sticks around.

"Take a break," Adam tells him. "Go behind the scenes for a while. Let me handle the product. Just drive."

Brian closes his eyes. "Shit, man."

"I need you," Adam tells him. "I can't do this by myself."

"You need my car," Brian says.

"I need *you*," Adam tells him. "You've been here from the start. Don't walk away now."

Wayne steps up from the background. "I have a car," he tells Adam. "Well, my mom has a car. If you need it."

Brian looks at Wayne. Sighs again. "Fuck it," he says. "I can still drive, I guess."

298.

The pills keep selling. Brian drives and divides the pills. Adam sells them. Splits the share with Brian—

(Fifty-fifty, which is kind of wack now that Brian isn't actually selling. But he did take a beating, so maybe he earned it.)

—and handles the homework side of things. Speaking of which, George Dubois is an absolute champ. Works hard. Works *smart*—

(throws in the odd typo and grammatical error, hits the target grade without getting too fancy).

(The kid *gets it*.)

"This is the coolest thing ever," he tells Adam. "Pizza Man. I thought you were an urban legend or something."

"Not a legend," Adam tells him. "I'm me."

"You slept with Janie Ng and Leanne Grayson," George says. "You hooked Wayne Tristovsky up with Sara *freaking* Bryant. You're the Pizza Man. You're like a god or something."

"That's the idea," Adam tells him.

"I just always wanted to be a part of your team," George says. "I'm so glad you picked me, with my mom being who she is and all."

"Yeah, well," Adam says, "we're lucky to have you. Keep working hard and there's no limit where you can go. I'm living proof."

A cream-colored Lexus with big chrome rims drives past on the street in front of Cardigan's.

(Drives

s   l   o   w   )

Adam shakes his head clear. "Living proof," he tells George.

299.

A cream-colored Lexus with big chrome rims.
Jamal's car.

300.

Maybe it's paranoia. Maybe it's real. Adam starts seeing that cream Lexus more and more.

Usually, it's drifting by in traffic, in the corner of Adam's eye. Usually, he turns to look for it and it's gone.

Sometimes, though, it's there. Sometimes he sees it idling at the stoplight at the end of Nixon's lush green front lawn. Sometimes it drives past as Adam walks home from school.

Sometimes, he looks out the window during geography class and that big Lexus is parked across the street.

Sometimes, Jamal's out there, leaning on the hood, staring up at the school with a gleaming white grin on his face, searching the windows like he can find Adam's face in the glass.

Sometimes, Adam gets scared.

301.

But not always.

Most of the time, Adam convinces himself he's seeing things. Convinces himself he can hide from Jamal.

He walks home on back roads. Sneaks out of school. Sometimes he has Wayne handle the meetings at Cardigan's, just so he can fly under the radar.

"Christ, man," Brian says as Adam slips into his Sunfire a couple blocks from school. "How is this even worth it anymore?"

Adam has the nicest watch in the school—

(TAG Heuer)

—financed by the pills they've been selling. He's dating—

(sleeping with)

—Alexis Van Deusen, the head cheerleader, now. She's a senior.

Adam's saving up for a car.

"Hell yes it's worth it," Adam tells Brian.

Adam can afford to be scared.

302.

Adam comes home from Tommy's one day with *literally* a million pills in his backpack.

(Not literally.)

Brian drops him off outside his house and Adam takes his overflowing backpack from the trunk of the Sunfire and walks up the drive and . . .

Victoria's there.

303.

She still takes Adam's breath away.

She's standing by the side door like she's been waiting for a while. She's not smiling. She looks nervous. Adam takes one look at her, and he figures out the whole story.

(*She finally broke up with Chad.*)

(*She totally wants you.*)

(*She finally realized she wants to be with a god.*)

Adam can't keep from smiling. He tries to sound casual. "Hey," he tells Victoria. "You want to come inside?"

304.

Adam lets Victoria into the house—

(His dad's gone out somewhere, thank god.)

(Adam's not really up for that level of mortification right now.)

Shows her the shitty kitchen and the shitty living room, the shitty computer and the shitty TV. Offers her a glass of shitty tap water. Victoria shakes it off. Looks around.

"So this is where you live," she says.

Adam nods. "Uh-huh."

"It's not so bad," she says. "You don't have to be so ashamed of it."

Adam looks around. Shrugs. It's a shitty little house and they both know it. It's no place for a god.

"I won't be here too much longer," Adam tells her. "Anyway, what's up? What can I do for you?"

Victoria fiddles with some cutlery on the kitchen table. Worries a place mat with her fingers. She can't look at Adam. Time passes. The question lingers.

Adam takes a couple steps toward Victoria. Moves in to wrap his arms around her, to kiss her. He's a god now. He's confident.

(Maybe she wants to sleep with him, even.)

"It's okay," he tells her. "You don't have to be embarrassed. I'm just glad you came back."

He reaches out to pull her closer to him, to kiss her. Victoria stiffens at his touch. Draws back. "Adam, are you dealing?" she says quickly.

Adam blinks. Adam hesitates. "Um, why?" Adam says. "Do you want to score or something?"

"What?" She looks at him. "Oh my god. No, Adam, I don't want to score." She shakes her head. "Jesus. Steph told me you were selling drugs and I thought she was crazy, but it's true, isn't it?"

Adam shrugs. "Does it matter?"

"That's a yes," Victoria says. "Oh my god. What's *wrong* with you, Adam?"

"It's just for a little while," Adam tells her. "The money's good. Pretty soon I'll have enough for tuition."

"Tuition?" Victoria says. "College? You're a freaking drug dealer, Adam. Are you using, too?"

Adam stares at her. "It's just a little bit," he says finally. "Not much. You know, on weekends or whatever."

"You need help, Adam," Victoria tells him. "You need someone to help you. Get out of this craziness and go talk to somebody. This isn't normal."

"I don't need help," Adam tells her. "I'm a god, Victoria. I'm totally winning. What would I ever want to change for?"

"You're not winning," Victoria says. "You're ruining your life, Adam. Let me help you before you crash and burn."

Adam looks at her. "You want to help me," he says. "That's why you're here."

"I do," she says. "You have to give up all this bullshit. No more homework. No drugs. Nothing. Okay?"

She's still smoking hot. And right now, all Adam can think about is how bad she must want him. How much she must love him, to come crawling back.

"Okay," Adam says. "Whatever you say. You can help me."

She looks at him. "Do you promise?"

"I promise," he says.

(He'll say anything at this point.)

(They can work out the gory details later.)

Victoria hugs him, tight. Adam hugs her back, feels the curves of her body, her warmth, and it's all familiar and wonderful and awesome, better than any other girl he's been with—

(even Janie Ng and Leanne Grayson)

—and Adam holds on to Victoria for a minute or two, and then he looks down at her and does what feels natural.

(It feels perfect.)

He kisses her.

305.

Victoria goes stiff. "Adam."

Adam opens his eyes. "What?" He doesn't let her go.

"Adam, no." She squirms out of the hug. "I can't do this. I'm sorry."

"I thought you wanted to help me," Adam says. "You said you loved me."

"I do love you," she says. "I do want to help you. As your friend, Adam. As someone who cares about you."

"You're still with Chad," Adam says. "Admit it. You always liked him, even when we were together."

"That's a lie," she says. "I liked you. I loved you. I was happy with you. But you chose, I dunno . . ."

She gestures to his clothes, his shoes, the TAG Heuer on his wrist.

"So you went running to Chad," Adam says. "The big, dumb high school quarterback."

Victoria shrugs. "He is what he is, Adam. And he's happy that way."

Adam says nothing.

Victoria looks at Adam. "Let me help you," she says. "*Please.*"

She's more beautiful now than ever, maybe. And she loves him. She'll stick by him and help him dismantle the whole machine and get him out of this whole sordid mess.

She'll be there for him. She'll do this. She can save him.

Adam knows this.

306.

And then? Adam thinks.

After she gets Adam out of the homework scheme, and the drugs and the parties and everything else?

After she's killed and buried the Pizza Man?

What then?

307.

Nothing.

    No friends. No parties. No popularity.

    Adam won't even get the girl.

(Chad will.)

308.

Adam shakes his head. "I can't do it," he says. "Sorry."

Victoria deflates. "You *can*," she says. "I know you can. You just have to—"

"I'm sorry." Adam walks to the door. Opens it.

"I think we're done here," Adam says.

(Ice-cold.)

309.

So, forget Victoria.

    She's gone forever, but who cares, really?

    Adam's still winning.

    He's still a god.

    (And gods don't waste time on frigid little freshmen.)

    (Gods take over, don't they?)

    Adam's taking over.

310.

So Adam throws Sam that party.

      Figures it's better than a stupid hockey game.

      (Hey, the Red Wings lost anyway.)

      Figures Sam will enjoy getting out of the house, getting a taste of the good life again. Figures it'll be a nice break from the doughnut shop and that shitty apartment.

      Adam puts a blast out on Facebook. Invites everyone he knows. Books a suite at the casino hotel and tells Paul Nolan and Alton Di Sousa to round up every college girl they can find.

      (Figures maybe Sam will get lucky.)

      (Or as lucky as Sam can get.)

      It'll be the party of the year.

      Everybody will be there.

      Sam will have a blast.

      He'll forget about the hockey game.

      (Adam hopes.)

311.

(Probably, Adam knows this is all wrong, somewhere deep inside.

Probably, he knows that a high school party—

(no matter how amazing)

—is a shitty substitute for a hockey game with his older brother.

(Even if the Red Wings lost.)

Probably, he knows that Sam would have a good time at the party, and maybe Adam even knows that he doesn't actually care.

He's not throwing the party for Sam.

Somewhere deep inside himself, he knows this.

Probably.)

312.

Anyway, the party is off the chain.

Everybody's there.

All the gods.

All the goddesses.

The suite is amazing. It's, like, two bedrooms. Two bathrooms. Floor-to-ceiling windows with a sweeping view of the river. Of Detroit.

(Somewhere in the distance, you can see the hockey arena where the Red Wings play.)

(If you're looking.)

Adam arrives early with Brian and Tommy. Brian and Tommy bring booze and weed and pills—

(everything's on Adam tonight)

—and the guests start arriving. The music starts bumping. The party's already raging when Sam texts from downstairs.

Adam excuses himself from Alton Di Sousa and a couple college girls. Takes the elevator to the lobby and finds Sam waiting in his wheelchair inside the front doors. He looks small and kind of frail and there's a food stain on his shirt.

"Hey," Adam says. "You made it. Awesome."

"Yeah," Sam says.

"Tonight's going to kick ass," Adam says. "Believe me. You'll see."

(He took a pill earlier. It's just starting to kick in.)

Sam follows Adam through the lobby to the elevators. Looks around at the gleaming metal, the polished stone. Everything swank and sleek and modern. Everything money.

"How much did this cost you?" Sam says.

"Don't worry about it," Adam tells him. "It's all on me tonight. Anything you want, I promise."

Sam looks around some more. He doesn't say anything.

"Hey," Adam says. "Did you have fun at the game? Did you wear that jersey I bought you?"

Sam looks at Adam like he's an alien. "I didn't go," he says. "I couldn't find anyone to go with at the last minute. And I can't just go over to Detroit by myself."

Adam frowns. "Well, shit," he says.

"Yeah," Sam says.

Neither of them says anything for a minute. Adam just stares out the glass elevator at the city lights beyond. The way the drugs are kicking in, the whole night looks magical.

(Even Sam has to be impressed.)

Then the elevator dings. The doors slide open. You can already hear the music from Adam's suite.

Adam grins at Sam. "Party of the year," he says. "See if I'm lying."

313.

The party's going full steam when Adam and Sam get back. Paul Nolan and Alton Di Sousa are dancing with a bunch of girls. Wayne Tristovsky and Sara Bryant are making out in a corner. Brian and Amanda Rimes are dancing.

(Even Tommy's found himself a hot high school honey at last.)

Adam ushers Sam inside the suite. Gets him a drink. Calls over the gods and introduces Sam to every one of them.

"Oh, shit," Paul says. "You're that hockey player." He looks at Adam. "Dude, you never told us you were related to this guy."

Adam looks at Sam. "I mean, shit," he says. "Of course I am."

Paul slaps Sam on the back. "You were the greatest, man. You could have turned pro."

Sam gives Paul a smile back. Sam doesn't drink his drink. "Thanks," Sam says. "Thanks, man."

314.

Rob Thigpen stays away, Adam notices.

He doesn't come anywhere near Sam, and with good reason, Adam figures. The bastard probably feels guilty about what his brother did to Sam.

(Adam didn't even invite him to the party, but of course he showed up.)

(And you can't very well turn a god away at the door.)

(Not even if his brother ruined your brother's life—

—and by extension, your own.)

315.

"How does it feel to be related to the Pizza Man?" someone asks Sam.

Adam forces a laugh. "Come on," he says. "This night's about Sam, not that Pizza Man stuff."

It's too late, though. Sam looks at Adam. "The Pizza Man?" he says. "Who the hell is that?"

"Pizza Man Enterprises," someone says, pointing at Adam. "He's the fucking Tony Montana of Nixon Collegiate. Tony Soprano shit. Boss."

Sam looks at Adam.

Adam shrugs.

"I'm the Pizza Man," Adam says. "Surprise."

Sam shakes his head. "What does that even mean?"

"It means . . ." Adam trails off. Can't think straight anyway. He looks around the party. "This," he says, gesturing. "It means *this*."

Sam doesn't look impressed. "Oh," he says.

"*Anyway*," Adam says. "Can we get this man some girls, please?"

316.

Paul Nolan brings a couple of his college friends over.

They're smoking hot.

They look like real women.

All the other girls look like kids playing dress-up, by comparison.

Adam forgets their names as soon as he's introduced. He tells the girls all about Sam and his hockey career. About how Sam was a god back at Riverside High. The girls are into it. They look impressed.

"What do you do now?" one of them asks.

"Sam's making moves," Adam tells them. "He's got big things popping, believe me."

Sam gives Adam another funny look. "I work at the doughnut shop," he says. "Across from city hall."

The girls laugh like it's all a big joke.

Then they realize Sam's serious.

The girls wander off.

317.

The girls wander over to Rob Thigpen. Rob chats them up. The girls laugh at whatever he says.

     The girls stick around.

     They don't wander off.

318.

Adam and Sam hang out for a bit.

"You want another drink?" Adam asks Sam.

Sam looks at his cup. It's half-full.

"I'm good," Sam says. "Thanks."

They kind of stand around together in a corner of the suite, staring out at the chaos. Loud music. Drugs. Hookups.

Best. Party. Ever.

Then Brian disengages from Amanda and motions to Adam from across the room.

"One sec," Adam tells Sam. "I'll be right back."

He wades through the sea of people to where Brian stands by the window. Brian looks worried.

(Brian always looks worried.)

"What if Jamal hears about this?" Brian says. "What if he shows up?"

"He's not going to show up," Adam tells him.

"The whole school knows about this party," Brian says. "Jamal will find out."

Adam shakes his head. Slaps Brian on the back. "You're fucking up my high," Adam says. "Would it kill you to have a little fun?"

319.

Adam is intercepted on his way back toward Sam.

It's one of the college girls.

(Rebecca?)

(Rachel?)

"Are you really the Pizza Man?" Rebecca/Rachel says.

Adam glances at Sam. Sam's alone in the corner. He's not talking to anybody. Nobody's talking to him.

Adam looks at Rebecca/Rachel. Then back at Sam.

(Rebecca/Rachel is smoking hot.)

(Sam's all alone.)

(Shit.)

Adam grabs a freshman girl walking by. "Go talk to that guy in the corner," he tells her.

The girl screws up her face. "Who, the guy in the wheel-chair?"

"That's my brother," Adam says. "His name's Sam."

The girl looks the other way. "My friends are all over there."

"Just for a little while," Adam tells her. He pulls out a baggie of pills. "I'll make it worth your while."

The girl looks at the baggie. Then at Sam. Sighs.

"Fine," she says.

Rebecca/Rachel is still there when Adam sends the freshman away. "So you *are* the Pizza Man," she says. "The guy they're all talking about."

"Only if they're saying good things," Adam says. "Is your name Rebecca or Rachel?"

Rebecca/Rachel laughs. "It's Aimee," she says.

320.

Adam's still talking to Aimee when the first noise complaint comes.

Brian handles it.

"The hotel manager," he tells Adam. "He told me if we don't turn down the music he will call security."

Adam looks around. The party is bumping. It's maybe a little loud. "I paid a thousand dollars for this room," Adam says. "The manager won't do shit."

Aimee watches Brian walk off. Wraps her arms around Adam's neck.

"You have any more of those pills?" Aimee says.

"I sure do," Adam tells her. Then he spies Sam across the room. The freshman is nowhere to be found. Sam's alone again. He's just chilling in his wheelchair, not having any fun.

Adam sighs. "Give me one second," he tells Aimee. "I'll be right back."

Aimee pouts. "Don't be too long."

321.

Adam pushes through the crowd to Sam.

(Leaves Aimee behind.)

(Reluctantly.)

Sam's still just kind of hanging out. His glass is still half-full. Someone spilled their drink on him. Sam smells like beer.

"Hey," Adam says. "How're you doing?"

Sam looks at him. "I'm about ready to go home," he says. "Can you just get me out of here?"

Adam glances back at Aimee. Rob Thigpen's talking to her. She's not looking at Adam.

"*Adam.*"

Sam has a look on his face like he knows exactly what Adam's thinking.

"I just want to go home," Sam says. "Can you help me, please?"

Aimee's laughing at something Rob says. She has her hand on his arm. Adam watches her across the room. Feels his frustration growing.

"This party's so epic," he tells Sam. "Why don't you just, I dunno, mingle or something? Meet people. Have another drink."

Sam looks at Adam. Sam shakes his head. "I'll just go," he says. "Forget it. Stay here."

Sam starts to wheel himself away. He doesn't get very far

before he starts bumping into people. His wheelchair's a damn hazard. It's fucking unwieldy. Adam watches his brother struggle. Watches Rob Thigpen flirt with the college girl.

Adam feels his high suddenly vanish.

(The world just seems so unfair.)

"This is your party," he tells Sam, "and you're not even grateful."

Sam stops trying to wheel his way through the crowd. He looks back at Adam. Makes a face. "Are you kidding me, bro?"

"This is about the hockey game, isn't it?" Adam says. "You're still pissed that I had to bail on you."

Sam shakes his head. "This isn't about the hockey game, Adam," he says. "This is about what the hell is wrong with you."

"I thought you'd be proud of me," Adam tells him. "You should be proud of me right now. I did this for you."

"Proud of you," Sam says. "For what? Paying a thousand dollars so your friends could get trashed in some fancy hotel room?"

(Well, yeah, Adam thinks.)

"This isn't normal," Sam says. "I don't know what happened to you, but it's really not cool."

"What happened to me?" Adam says. He steps closer to Sam. Leans down. He's yelling over the music.

(People are starting to stare.)

"I'm the most popular guy at Nixon," Adam tells Sam. "That's what happened to me. You told me to go out and take what life had to offer. Guess what, Sam? I did it."

Sam just looks at him. "I don't give a fuck if you're popular or not," he says. "In fact, if this is how it's going to be when you have friends, I wish you were still a loser. This isn't for me. This is for your needy fucking ego."

"Fuck you," Adam says. "You can wheel yourself home."

"Whatever," Sam says. "Enjoy your night."

He wheels past Adam. Bumps into, like, three sopho-more girls and keeps going.

"Fuck it," Adam says, watching him go. "Fucking cripple."

322.

Sam's halfway to the door when Rob Thigpen reappears.

Adam's watching Sam wheel his way through the crowd. He doesn't see Rob.

Rob's dragging the college girl, Aimee, toward the alcohol. He doesn't see Adam. Or maybe he does, and he just doesn't care.

Either way, he bumps into Adam.

Hits him, not hard—

(certainly not hard enough to paralyze anyone)

—but hard enough to knock Adam off balance.

Adam turns. "What the fuck?"

Adam sees Rob and Aimee. Aimee's holding Rob's hand. She's laughing. Rob's laughing too.

(Everyone's laughing.)

(Everyone's always laughing.)

(No matter what Adam does, they never stop laughing.)

323.

Adam loses it.

Adam hits his breaking point.

Adam watches Rob Thigpen drag Aimee toward the booze—

(Adam's booze)

(Adam's girl)

(Adam's god status, if Sam wasn't such a cripple)

(if Rob Thigpen's brother hadn't made him that way)

—and Adam's suddenly sick. Suddenly tired.

Adam's suddenly mad.

He follows Rob Thigpen and Aimee through the crowd. Pushes his way toward them. Rob's got his back turned when Adam arrives.

"Hey, *fucker*," Adam says to him. Then he shoves him from behind.

324.

Rob stumbles. Nearly falls. Catches himself on a counter and pulls himself up. He turns around and sees Adam, and smiles.

It's an unpleasant smile.

"Pizza Man," he says. "What the fuck?"

Adam stares at him.

Adam knows this is wrong.

He knows this is suicide, what he's about to do.

But Adam can't help himself. This is for Sam.

325.

Actually, fuck it.
        This is for Adam.

326.

Adam hits Rob.
> (Cue record scratch.)
> Adam hits Rob and the air is sucked out of the room.
> Adam hits Rob and everybody shuts up.
> Adam hits Rob and the party stops.

327.

Adam hits Rob and keeps hitting him.
    (It's like every last little slight
    joke
    insult
    has been bottled up inside him and is now pouring
                            crashing
                                roiling
                                     out.)
    Adam keeps hitting Rob. He doesn't explain himself. He hits Rob until his fists are bloody and sore and Rob's flat on his back on the ground, shielding his face.
    (Rob doesn't fight back. Rob doesn't have time. Rob's taken off guard by the first punch, and Adam doesn't slow down with the second
    or the third
    or, like, the eighteenth.)
    Someone's grabbing at Adam. Holding his arms, dragging him up and away from Rob Thigpen. Adam wrenches free. Adam goes after Rob again.
    Someone screams.
    (It could be Aimee.)
    (It could be anybody.)
    Rob's laid out on the ground. His face is bruised. His nose is bloody. He's not fighting back. Adam's kicking his ass.

Somewhere inside, Adam realizes it feels good.

(*Take that, you rich piece of shit.*)

(*Take that, you asshole.*)

(*Take this back to your brother, for ruining my life.*)

Adam keeps hitting Rob Thigpen. Feels like his hands are breaking. His knuckles brush something, and he looks over and sees it.

A beer bottle, empty.

Adam reaches for it. Closes his fingers around it.

He raises the bottle above his head.

Above Rob Thigpen's head.

328.

Someone grabs Adam before he can hit Rob with the bottle. It's Brian.

"*Adam*." Brian drags him away. "*Jesus Christ*, Adam, what the hell is wrong with you?"

"That fucker did it," Adam tells him. "He fucking ruined my life. His brother's the asshole who put Sam in a wheelchair."

Brian pulls Adam back. "Calm down," he tells Adam. "Just calm the fuck down, okay?"

Adam struggles loose. Starts toward Rob again. Brian grabs for him, and Adam comes around, swinging. Catches Brian square in the nose. Brian goes down, and Adam's free again.

He turns back to Rob Thigpen, but it's too late at this point. The whole party's crowded around him—

(checking out the damage).

There's no getting through. Whatever damage Adam planned for Rob, it's been done. And anyway, security's coming in through the door.

Another noise complaint.

The party is officially over. GTFO.

329.

Adam watches Paul Nolan and Alton Di Sousa drag Rob Thigpen out of the hotel room.

"Serves you right, asshole," he calls out after Rob. "Your brother's a cheap piece of shit and you know it."

Rob Thigpen doesn't answer. Nobody answers. They're too busy getting the hell out of the hotel room before security calls the cops.

The room clears out fast. Paul and Alton take Rob Thigpen away. Aimee disappears. Tommy's a ghost. Even Sam is gone. Brian struggles to his feet, holding his nose. He doesn't look at Adam as he brushes past him.

"Dude." Adam reaches out for him. "Dude, I'm sorry. I blacked out or something."

Brian's shirt is bloody. His nose is a mess. "Fuck off," he tells Adam. Then he walks away.

Pretty soon, the room is empty. "I paid a thousand bucks for this room," Adam tells the security guards. "I want a fucking refund for this."

The guards look around the room. Then they look at Adam.

Then they laugh.

330.

Suicide.
　　　(#ItsOver)

331.

"It wasn't even Rob's brother," Steph says. "Jesus, Adam, it was, like, his cousin or something. Rob doesn't even know the guy."

Adam looks up from the kitchen table, where he's icing his hands. His hands are sore and bruised black and swollen from the fight with Rob Thigpen.

(From the one-sided ass-kicking.)

(Adam's still kind of proud.)

Adam looks at Steph. "It doesn't matter," he says. "It was a fucking Thigpen who did it. Rob had it coming, no matter how he's related."

Steph sighs. "I just don't get it, Adam," she says. "You worked so hard to be popular. Why the hell would you just throw it away?"

Adam goes back to the kitchen. Gets more ice for his hands. "I didn't throw it away," he tells Steph. "I'm bigger than that asshole.

"Nixon needs me," Adam tells Steph. "You'll see."

332.

And she will.

They all will.

Nobody's talking to Adam. Nobody wants to be friends. He's used up his party invites, his daps and hugs in the hall. Those pretty Nixon girls have stopped throwing themselves at him.

(Even Brian won't return Adam's calls.)

Adam's alone.

He lies awake nights and thinks about *Scarface*. It's not a pleasant thought anymore. It doesn't seem like such a good idea now. Tony Montana isn't much of a hero, in the end.

(Spoiler alert: Tony Montana dies. It's a really fucking chaotic, fantastic scene. Colombians. Assault rifles. *"Say hello to my little friend."* You should probably watch it if you haven't already.)

Adam doesn't want to die. Adam doesn't even want to be a god anymore. He's through with winning. He just wants to take over. Sell enough pills to move out of Remington Park and get an apartment with an eighty-inch TV and a stripper pole in the bedroom.

Victoria's gone.

Sam won't talk to him.

His grades are a sinking ship.

But the gods still need him. All of Nixon does.

(And fuck homework, at this point. It's pills Nixon
wants.)

(The machine keeps rolling.)

(Pizza Man won't die.)

333.

Adam puts a blast on Facebook.
    Pizza Man pill sale, he writes. *Bargain prices. Buy now.*
    Then he sits back and waits for his phone to blow up.

334.

And it does.

There are enough kids at Nixon who think Rob Thigpen's a dick.

A bunch of others who, frankly, don't care.

(People want to score. The Pizza Man's a good hookup. It's just business, man. Everything else is bullshit.)

Adam logs a whack of solid orders. Then he picks up his phone and calls Tommy.

335.

"Shit, man," Tommy says. "I heard you went dark at that party. Heard you kicked somebody's ass pretty hard."

"Some punk," Adam tells him. "The bastard had it coming. Anyway, listen, I need a re-up."

Tommy goes quiet. Adam coughs. "You there?"

"I'm here," Tommy says. "I'm just— Dude, I'm thinking you might want to take a break for a while. What I heard about Jamal, he's looking for you."

"Fuck Jamal," Adam tells him. "What is this, the movies? You have my supply or no?"

Tommy hesitates again. "I'm skipping town," he says finally. "Getting a head start on summer vacation. Come by tomorrow morning—early—and I'll set you up."

"I'm bringing cash," Adam tells him. "Give me all that you have."

336.

Tomorrow morning.

Adam amasses every last dollar he has.

Figures, Tommy's leaving town, this might be his last shot. Stock up on supply now, and go looking for a supplier.

Bypass Tommy.

Bypass Jamal.

Take over Nixon, one pill at a time.

337.

Only:

Adam needs a ride to Tommy's. And Brian's still not picking up his phone.

(What Adam figures, Brian might never answer that phone again, if he knows it's Adam calling.)

(Which is fine. Adam was starting to resent paying the guy 50 percent just for driving.)

(But now Adam doesn't have a driver.)

(And people want their pills.)

(The customer is always right.)

(Right?)

Adam finds the bus schedule on Google. Tommy's place is two bus rides from Remington Park. Adam figures he can get up early, head to Tommy's on the first bus, and still make it back to Nixon in time for second period.

It all works. Except:

Jessie McGill has a chem assignment she needs back. And Paul Nolan's history paper is due too.

(Even if the gods hate Adam, they're still paying him, right?)

Both jobs need to close out before school starts tomorrow. No way Adam can make it to the west side and back in time. Not if he's taking the bus.

Luckily:

Wayne's mom has a car.

Wayne can drive.

338.

Except Wayne can't drive.

"Sorry, dude," he says. "My mom's going to Detroit tomorrow. Needs her car all day."

"Crap," Adam says. "Thanks anyway."

"Maybe on Wednesday, though?"

"Wednesday's not soon enough," Adam says. "Thanks anyway."

339.

At first, Adam's like:

I'll just, like, rent a freaking car.

(Or steal one.)

(Or borrow one.)

(Or *buy* one.)

But nobody's going to give Adam a car on such short notice. Especially since he only has his learner's permit.

So then, Adam's like:

What the hell, let the customers wait for their pills. Who cares?

But Adam's not in the business of disappointing his customers. Not after the Rob Thigpen debacle.

(His girlfriend? Sure. His employees? Why not? His friends and family? Duh. But *never* the customers.)

(Anyway, who knows how long Tommy's skipping town?)

Adam needs a driver.

Today.

340.

"Wanna cut class?" Adam asks George Dubois.

It's the next morning. Adam gives Paul and Jessie their assignments back, and George is there, too, running a couple of sophomore English papers through Adam for approval. And Adam looks at George, and thinks for a minute—

(not long enough)

—and then he pops the question.

"I need to get to the west side of town," he tells George. "Just for, like, twenty minutes."

George frowns. "You can't go at lunch?"

"I need to get there this morning," Adam tells him. "I need to go now."

"So, I don't get it," George says. "What do you need me for?"

"Your mom drives to school, right?" Adam says. "Can you get her keys?"

341.

Turns out George has a spare key to his mom's Buick in his back pocket. And George is ready to roll.

"Holy shit," he says. "You're making a drug deal? This is so gangster."

"It's just a re-up," Adam tells him. "It's not really that glamorous."

"How much are you buying?" George asks him. "Can I see the money?"

Adam looks around. Unzips his backpack and gives George a peek. "Holy shit," George says, his eyes wide. "How much is in there?"

(All of it, is the answer.)

"Enough to buy enough pills to put us both in jail," Adam says. "So keep your mouth shut. You sure your mom won't miss the car?"

"She has a meeting first period," George says. "She won't even know."

"Excellent," Adam says. "So let's go."

342.

The deal plays without incident. Tommy's bags are already packed. His apartment is empty. He looks like he's itching to leave.

"Little vacation," he tells Adam and George. "You know how it goes."

Adam looks around. "Looks like you're leaving for good."

"Maybe," Tommy says. "Who knows?"

"Where are you going?" George asks him. He's giddy, nervous, bouncing around. Tommy just looks at him.

(George is the wrong guy for a drug deal.)

"Anyway." Tommy pulls out a bag. A big bag. It's filled with about fifteen smaller bags of pills. "Here's the stuff," he says. "You run out, I got a number you can call. Just don't let Jamal catch you."

"He's not going to catch me," Adam tells him. He takes the bag. Stuffs it into his backpack. Hands over the money.

"Have a nice trip," Adam tells him.

343.

"Dude, you gotta calm down," Adam tells George as they walk back to the car. "You couldn't be more suspicious if you were wearing an 'I'm a Drug Dealer' T-shirt."

"I'm sorry, man," George says. "I'm just, like, excited. This is the most badass thing I ever did in my life."

They're crossing the street to the parking lot where they left the Buick. George is still bouncing around. "I wish I was you, man," he says. "I bet it gets easier. Does it get easier?"

Adam's about to tell him, yeah, it gets easier. Yeah, this stuff is simple. Then Adam sees a cream-colored Lexus pull into the lot ahead of them.

"No," Adam says. "It never does."

344.

The Lexus parks at the other end of the lot. The doors open and two men climb out. One of them is Jamal. The other guy should be an offensive lineman.

"Hurry up." Adam grabs George, pulls him toward the Buick. "Get in the car and start driving."

George is pissing himself. "Who is *that?*"

"Nobody," Adam tells him. "Let's go."

They book it for the car.

They don't make it.

Jamal intercepts them ten feet from the Buick. Grabs Adam and George by the collars and practically lifts them off their feet. "Whoa," he says. "Slow down, little homies."

He turns them around, one meaty paw apiece. He's grinning a great-white-shark grin.

"Holy shit," George says. "What the hell is *happening?*"

"Just be cool," Adam tells him.

"Yeah," Jamal says. "Just be cool, man. I just want to talk to you."

He grins at Adam. "Adam, right?"

Adam shrugs. Tries to look mean. Tries not to look like he's a half second away from pissing himself.

(Actually, scratch that. Adam isn't really scared, per se. I mean, of course he's scared. *You* find yourself face-to-face with a guy like Jamal and tell me you aren't scared. But fear isn't the overriding emotion here. No way. Not by a long shot. What Adam's feeling most here is . . .

Anger.

Anger at himself for letting them get caught.

Anger at George for not running to the Buick fast enough.

Anger at Jamal for showing up outside Tommy's, of all places.

Anger at the whole goddamn universe, pretty much. For fucking him over.

For not letting him win.)

Jamal looks at George. "And who the fuck are you?"

"I don't know," George says. "I'm just George. I don't know anything, I swear."

"Shut up," Adam tells him. "Let me handle this."

"What brings you to the west side, little homies?" Jamal says. "Didn't anyone tell you this is my territory?"

"We're just running an errand," Adam tells him. "Nothing to do with you."

Jamal chuckles. "Something tells me all of your errands have something to do with me." He picks up Adam's backpack where it dropped to the pavement. "So let's see what kind of errands you and homeboy are running."

Jamal has to let go of Adam to pick up the backpack. Adam thinks about running. Before he's even aware of the thought, though, Jamal's big linebacker friend is up on him. There's no escape, Adam realizes. There's just playing this thing out.

Jamal unzips the backpack and peers inside, and Adam can literally *see* the moment when Jamal finds the pills. His posture shifts. His breath catches. His shark grin gets bigger, and Adam knows he's screwed.

"This is a lot of weight, man," Jamal says. "Fuck you up a long time, you get caught riding with this."

George is openly crying now.

"I'mma do you a favor," Jamal says.

Adam waits for it.

"Don't want you little homies doing anything crazy," Jamal says. "Get yourself caught with this stuff and fuck up your whole lives and shit, know what I'm saying?"

Adam shakes his head. "Come on, man."

"Hate to see you kids do something stupid," Jamal says. "So I'mma take this weight off your hands, okay?"

"You can't do that," Adam tells him. "That stuff is mine. I paid—"

"Homey." Jamal leans in real close. "I don't give a *fuck*."

345.

Jamal shoulders the backpack. "Let's take a walk, little homies."

It's not a request. There's no room for negotiation. Jamal takes Adam and the linebacker takes George, and they walk into a back alley behind some shithole bar and Adam knows what's coming.

"Go easy on my buddy," he tells Jamal. "He isn't part of this."

"Rolls with you, though," Jamal says. "That makes him an accessory. Better teach him a lesson, just in case."

"Come on," Adam says. "You don't have to—"

He never finishes the sentence. The linebacker cold-cocks him—

(POW)

—and down Adam goes.

346.

It's not much of a fight. Five minutes, maybe. Adam gets his shots in, for all the good it does. Jamal's big. His buddy's bigger. Adam isn't exactly a tower of power.

George gets the same treatment. Except George doesn't get any shots in. Not that it does him any good. Five minutes and they're both curled up into little balls on the pavement, begging Jamal and his buddy to stop.

Jamal and his buddy do stop. "Remember, little homies," Jamal says. "Stay out of the deep end."

He spits on the ground, a few inches from Adam's face. Adam lies on the ground and stares at the loogie on the gritty pavement. The ruined remains of his TAG Heuer a few feet away.

Jamal and his buddy walk away with Adam's backpack. They climb into the cream-colored Lexus and drive off. Adam just lies there. Listens to George crying and feels a perverse satisfaction that—

(at least)

—he isn't crying himself.

347.

Disaster, obv.

The backpack is gone. The pills are gone. Adam's savings are, effectively, gone.

(Hell, even the TAG Heuer is destroyed.)

And George is fucked up, too.

Disaster.

348.

Adam leans against a dumpster and looks himself over. His Rag & Bone jeans are torn and he's missing a shirtsleeve. His knuckles are scraped and his eye feels swollen. His mouth tastes like blood.

He's alive, though, right?

(Shut up.)

And he can rebuild, right?

(Can he?)

Adam pulls himself to his feet. Fuck yes, he can. What's he lost, really?

(a shitload of money)

(a sack full of drugs)

(self-respect)

Nothing. He can find a new pill connection. He can make back the drug money selling pills through the summer. He can rebuild.

Nobody even saw them get their asses kicked.

It's not so bad, right?

(Right?)

349.

By the time Adam pulls George to his feet, he's feeling better about the whole situation.

(What's a drug dealer's life without an ass-kicking now and then? Hell, even Tony Montana had to take a few punches. Right now, Adam figures he should be happy he's not watching George get sawed in half by a chainsaw in some shitty motel somewhere. It's all good.)

(It's. All. Good.)

George sniffs. Wipes snot from his face and his sleeve comes back bloody. "I want to go home," he says.

"You want to get cleaned up first?" Adam asks him. "There's a McDonald's right there. We should probably—"

"I just want to go home," George says. "Okay?"

Adam looks at him. Shrugs. "Okay."

They walk to the Buick. It's tough going. They're both kind of unsteady. George's lower lip is trembling and his eyes are bleary. He looks like a kid who just got beat up in an alley.

"Whatever you need to make this thing right," Adam tells him. "Money, pills, girls—you name it, I'll make it happen, okay?"

George shakes his head. "I don't want anything."

He climbs into the car. Adam climbs in beside him. Sits in the passenger seat, watches George as he drives, and tries to convince himself everything will be fine. Tries to convince himself this is all just a minor setback.

You're still the Pizza Man, he tells himself. *It's. All. Good.*

The minute George pulls into the Nixon parking lot, though, Adam realizes he's fucked.

George slows down on the gas and kind of lets out a moan. The Buick just drifts into the faculty lot. Adam follows George's gaze. Sees what George sees.

Bonnie Dubois and Mr. Acton are standing in the middle of the faculty lot, watching the Buick pull in. Neither of them look happy.

And it all comes crashing down again.

It's all bad.

350.

It plays out pretty much how you'd expect.

Adam and George sit in the Buick for a little while. George stares out the window at his mom and Mr. Acton. George is pale. Adam looks at George and knows:

1. George is going to get out of the car.
2. Bonnie is going to see how messed up he is.
3. Bonnie's going to lose her shit.
4. George is going to cave.

He's going to tell Bonnie everything he knows. And given that George knows a shitload, Adam knows:

5. He's screwed.

"Listen to me," Adam says. "I know you're going to cave on me. I don't blame you. Just, you know, do me a favor, okay?"

George stares out the front window, his hands glued on the steering wheel. "What?" he says.

"Just leave the rest of them out of it," Adam says. "Wayne and Devon and Lisa. Don't fuck up their lives too, okay?"

George blinks. Finally looks at Adam. "I won't tell them anything," he says. "Swear to god."

Adam says. "Just put it on me, okay?"

"Yeah," George says. "Of course."

Then George climbs out of the car.

351.

And from there, it's on.

Bonnie Dubois takes one look at George and starts bawling. Mr. Acton looks at Adam, and Adam just shrugs.

"We got beat up," he says. "We cut class and went to McDonald's and some punks beat us up."

"Some 'punks,'" Acton says. "Did you know them?"

"Never saw them before in my life," Adam says.

Acton looks at George. "Is this true?"

George kind of hesitates. George can't answer. George looks at Adam and then quickly away. Mr. Acton nods like he knows what's coming.

"Okay," Acton says.

They walk inside the school. Into the administrative office. Acton takes George and Bonnie into his office and leaves Adam outside. Adam sits there by the secretaries' desks and waits as George spills his guts to the VP. Adam feels . . .

Adam feels calm.

Relieved.

Adam feels like every ball he's been trying to juggle is hitting the ground and there's nothing he can do now but watch the destruction.

Like he can finally just sleep and not care anymore.

Like Pizza Man is dead.

Adam feels . . .

peaceful.

352.

And eventually, the VP's door opens, and Acton comes out with George and Bonnie behind him. Acton walks to the secretaries' desks and nobody is looking at Adam.

"Miranda, would you give the police a call?" Acton says. "Tell them we need a couple officers down here."

The secretary reaches for the phone. Acton finally looks at Adam. "Well," he says. "I guess we need to have a talk."

Adam looks at him. Looks at George, who can't meet his eye. Looks at Bonnie, who glares at him like he's the scum of the earth.

Adam stands. "Yeah," he says. "I guess we do."

353.

Adam never finds out what George Dubois told Mr. Acton. It's not much, though.

> (Shout-out to George.)

Acton pulls Adam into his office and grills him about the drugs, and Adam channels every cop show he ever watched and keeps his mouth shut and asks for his lawyer.

They don't get him a lawyer. He doesn't know any lawyers, anyway—

> (except Sara Bryant's dad, and that might be a *tiny* conflict of interest)

—but he does keep his mouth shut until the police search his locker.

> (Which sounds like a big deal, but it really isn't: since Jamal stole all of the pills, the police have nothing to connect Adam to any drug dealing.)
>
> (Bonus.)
>
> (They do find a shoe box full of money. And even if the police don't think it's enough to prove the drug stuff, the VP isn't ready to give up just yet.)
>
> (Especially after he finds a couple of assignments in Adam's locker.)

"So what's all this, then?" Acton says. One assignment is an English paper for some goofy sophomore kid. The other's Rob Thigpen's latest econ lab.

(Fucking Rob Thigpen.)

"Tutoring," Adam tells the VP. "I was helping some kids out with their homework and stuff."

Understatement of the year.

The VP isn't buying it. He calls Rob Thigpen and the goofy sophomore down to his office. Leaves Adam to sit out by the secretaries again and hope his clients keep their mouths shut.

Rob Thigpen comes out ten minutes later. His eye is still swollen, and his face is all bruised. He doesn't say anything at first. Then he looks at Adam. "I didn't say a damn thing," he says.

Adam glances at the secretaries. "Me either."

Rob nods. "So let's hope that twerp in there keeps his mouth shut," he says. "Maybe you'll walk away from this, Pizza Man."

"It's not Pizza Man anymore," Adam tells him.

"Oh, it better be," Rob Thigpen says. "Now, more than ever."

354.

The sophomore stays in the VP's office a long time. Adam and Rob sit on the bench and don't talk to each other and wait.

Then Acton's door opens and the VP's standing there with his hands on his hips, looking at Rob and Adam, and he drags them both back into his office.

"This is a crock of shit," he tells them when they're all standing in front of his desk. "Your stories don't match up in the slightest. I want to know what's going on here, and I want to know now."

"I was tutoring these guys," Adam says. "What's the big deal?"

"Bull," Acton tells him. "You're a liar and a drug dealer."

"So call the cops back," Adam says. "Maybe they'll arrest me this time."

Acton's face goes red. "You little shit," he says. "I know something's going on here. I'm going to find out what it is."

"In the meantime, can you send Rob and this guy back to class?" Adam says. "They had nothing to do with whatever you're talking about."

The VP stares at Adam, the muscles in his neck as tense as frozen ropes. Finally, he shakes his head. "Get out of here," he tells Rob and the sophomore.

"You stay put until your parents get here," he tells Adam.

355.

Big deal.

"Adam, honey?" his mom says, when she arrives with Adam's dad. "What's the matter?"

"Your son is a liar and a criminal," Acton tells her. "I want him off school property immediately."

Adam's dad bristles. "Is this true, Adam?"

Adam shrugs. "Maybe," he says. "Or maybe I'm an honors student who happens to be tutoring a couple other students for some money. Maybe I cut class today to get breakfast and got jumped by a drug dealer and his friend."

Adam looks at the vice principal across his big desk. "Maybe my friend thought he saw something he didn't when the dealer stole my backpack. Maybe he came up with a crazy story to explain why he borrowed his mom's car, and you're jumping to some equally crazy conclusions."

Mr. Acton stares back at Adam. "You were a burnout and a loser at Riverside," he says. "You think that doesn't count for anything?"

"I pull straight A's at Nixon," Adam says. "Doesn't *that* count for anything?"

Acton doesn't say anything. Adam's mom and dad just watch.

"If you have something you can prove, then prove it," Adam tells Acton. "If not, give me a detention for cutting class and let me get back to work."

"It makes sense to me," Adam's dad says. "Do you have anything you can prove, Mr. Acton?"

Acton doesn't even look at him. "Adam, if you think for one minute I believe this crock of shit, you're a fool," he says, standing. "But you're right, I can't prove anything, so go on. Get out of here."

Adam stands. "Finally."

"Just know that I'll be watching you," Acton says. "I'll be checking up on you, and I will catch you, someday soon."

"Uh-huh," Adam says. "Good luck with that."

Adam walks out of the office. Leaves Acton fuming by the door. Adam's parents follow him out. "It's not true, is it?" his mom says as they walk into the hall. "None of what that man says is true, right?"

She's stopped in the hallway now, looking at Adam, and Adam knows he's home free. He knows Mr. Acton will never catch him, knows he can walk down the hallway and into economics class and, yeah, he still flunked the midterm, and yeah, the homework scheme is shot, but he kept his mouth shut, at least, and the gods will respect that. In a couple of weeks, Rob Thigpen's face will heal, and everyone will forget about the party at the casino, and Pizza Man will be a legend again.

He's home free.

He made it.

He *won*.

356.

Except:

(In the movies, this is the part where Victoria comes out of a classroom and comes walking down the hall, and Adam locks eyes with her and instantly sees the error of his ways, and this big, redeeming moment happens with the music swelling and Adam copping to everything, but—)

(This isn't the movies.)

(Victoria doesn't magically, melodramatically appear.)

Adam looks past his mom. Down the hall. It's the same hall he walked down a thousand times, holding hands with Victoria.

(And for everything else that Adam's accomplished here, Nixon *is* Victoria.)

It's the same hall he and Wayne ran down when they stole the Applied Science exam. It's the same hall that consigned Ryan Grant—

(the stoner)

(the burnout)

(the loser)

—to Maryvale Tech.

And Adam looks at that hallway and thinks about Ryan Grant at Maryvale, probably getting his ass kicked, no friends, pretty much just biding his time before prison, and Adam figures:

Shit.

Adam figures, even if he can live with the cheating and the lying and the drug dealing and everything else—

(even if he can rationalize all of that stuff)

—there's no rationalizing what he did to Ryan Grant. Adam can't explain Ryan Grant to Victoria. Or himself. He can't justify it. Can't forget about it.

He can't live with it.

Adam's mom is still looking at him. She's still waiting for an answer. And Adam looks off down that hallway and he—

—shakes his head and gives in. "I'm sorry, Mom," he says. "I'm really sorry."

357.

Adam still doesn't cop to the homework stuff.

(Which drives the VP nuts.)

He keeps his mouth shut. Because even though there's something appealing about tearing the whole school down to the core, leaving nothing but scorched earth and fallen gods when he finally packs up for Maryvale—

When it comes down to it, Adam doesn't really want to get Wayne and Devon—

(and hell, even Lisa)

—involved in his mess. He's seen how *Goodfellas* ends. He's not that guy.

(#StopSnitching)

358.

Adam doesn't cop to the drug stuff, either.

(Which drives the VP even nuttier.)

He doesn't cop to the fake ID stuff, or the booze.

(He takes Pizza Man Enterprises off Facebook, and the VP is too clueless to find it anyway.)

Ultimately, all Acton has against Adam is that one Applied Science exam. It should be a suspension, for an honor-roll kid. But Acton throws the proverbial book.

And that proverbial book knocks Adam

all

the

way

to Maryvale.

359.

If Adam was a god at Nixon, he's THE GOD at Maryvale.

Zeus.

Odin.

Captain America.

(Pizza Man.)

Everyone at Maryvale knows Pizza Man. They know about the homework and the exam and the fake IDs and the booze, and they sure as hell know about the drugs.

(Some of them even know about the threesome.)

At Maryvale, Adam's a hero. Fist pounds. High fives. Everyone wants to be friends. Everyone wants a hookup. Everyone has a buddy they want Adam to meet.

Adam's done with it.

Adam smiles and nods and says thank you a lot. Adam puts his head down and doesn't talk much. Adam tries to keep to himself.

Pizza Man is dead and gone.

Adam Higgs just wants to survive.

360.

After a couple weeks, everyone at Maryvale decides Pizza Man the legend is much cooler than Adam Higgs the person. They leave him alone.

Mostly.

Ryan Grant's friends don't leave him alone. Ryan Grant's friends come and find Adam. Ryan Grant's friends pay Adam back for what he did to Ryan.

Adam lets it happen. Hey—once you've had your ass kicked by a big-ass drug dealer, a couple of angry high school kids don't matter so much. Adam keeps his head down. Tries not to find himself in any empty bathrooms. Tries not to let his mom see the black eyes and bruises.

For the most part, it works.

361.

Time passes. The semester ends and summer arrives.

    (Not that it means much.)

    Adam's grounded.

    (Indefinitely.)

    No Xbox. No iPhone. No MacBook Pro. No rap music and no gangster movies, just Mom's old Neil Young CDs and, you know . . .

books.

    It's a long summer. But Adam's mostly at peace with it. I'm not going to lie; he's not a monk. Sometimes he thinks about Janie Ng and Leanne Grayson together in that Super 8 bed. Sometimes, he dreams about walking into a party and hearing the cheers, seeing smiling faces. Sometimes he misses being a god.

    Sometimes—

    (all the time)

    —he misses Victoria.

    But he's relieved, too. He sleeps a lot. He doesn't stress about Rob Thigpen and Paul Nolan and Sara *freaking* Bryant. He doesn't have to worry about being popular anymore.

    So he doesn't.

    He just sits in his room.

    He just . . .

is.

362.

Adam's parents get sick of him lurking around the house. His mom makes him get a job at the Tastee Freez down the street. It's okay. It's pretty meh.

(It's a goofy hat and an apron and a lot of soft-serve ice cream.)

It's better than sitting in your room all day, though, even if the money barely buys you a B-minus homework assignment from the Pizza Man. Adam treats work like he treated Maryvale.

He keeps his head down and just does it.

He has nothing to say.

363.

Then, one day in August:

Adam's working in the back of that stupid, oversize Tastee Freez ice cream cone and he hears a couple familiar voices outside. Looks out the window and sees Rob Thigpen's daddy's BMW 335i in the lot.

(Shit.)

Rob Thigpen comes up to the window. Paul Nolan and Sara Bryant and Jessie McGill are there too. They stand and jostle by the counter, studying the menu, and Adam's first instinct is to run and hide.

But he doesn't.

"Hey, guys," he says, stepping up to the counter. "Can I take your order?"

Paul Nolan steps up. "Yeah, I—" He stops. "Adam?" He turns to Rob and Sara and Jessie. "Guys, look who it is."

Adam leans out of the booth. Waves. "What's up?"

"*Pizza Man.*" Jessie McGill comes up. "We heard you were in prison or something."

"Or, like, dead," Sara Bryant says.

"Not dead," Adam tells them. "Maryvale. Pretty much the same thing."

He looks at Rob Thigpen. Rob's face has healed fine. He looks normal again.

(He still looks like a dick.)

"I'm sorry, man," Adam tells him. "I don't know what I was thinking. I just blacked out at that party or something. I'm sorry."

"It's cool," Rob tells him. Gives him that cocky smirk. "If somebody slept with my sister, I'd want to kick their ass too."

Adam doesn't say anything. Decides he doesn't feel so bad about the fight after all.

(Rob's still a dick.)

"You going to Janie's party tonight?" Jessie says.

Adam shakes his head. "I'm grounded for life."

"So sneak out," Paul says.

"You should totally come," Jessie says. "You're a legend now."

"Pizza Man," Paul says.

"*Pizza Man*," Jessie says.

"Everyone would lose their shit if you showed," Sara says. "For real."

364.

A Nixon party.
    Gods and goddesses.
    ("You're a legend now, Pizza Man.")
        It's
                so
                        tempting.

365.

Adam lies on his bed until his parents go to sleep. Then he sneaks out.

The whole party goes nuts when Adam walks in the door. People cheer. Someone hands him a beer. A couple girls want a pic on their iPhones. Adam poses, kind of sheepish.

(Adam thinks, *If my parents see this* . . .)

Paul and Alton and Jessie and Janie and Leanne are there. Wayne *freaking* Tristovsky's in a corner with Sara Bryant. Red cups everywhere. Weed smoke in the air.

(*Jamal's stuff?* Adam wonders.)

Music blasting. People grinding on each other. Making out. It's the hottest party in town and Adam's the guest of honor.

He lasts maybe ten minutes, tops.

366.

Paul Nolan's in the middle of telling Adam a story. Some pretty sophomore is pulling Adam out to the dance floor. It's so easy.

Nothing's changed.

Adam puts down his beer. "Sorry, Paul," he says. "I'll be right back."

He kind of shrugs and tells the pretty sophomore, "One minute," leaves them both standing there like—

(*Wait, what?*)

—and pushes through the crowd and out the front door. He makes it to the sidewalk in front of Janie's house before someone calls his name. "*Adam.*"

Adam stops. Looks back and it's Victoria coming out after him.

Damn it, she's still breathtaking. She's in a green summer sundress and her skin is tanned and she looks

absolutely

radiant.

"Where are you going?" she says. "You just got here."

Adam says nothing. He just looks at her, and it's like every mistake he ever made smacking him in the face—

(Victoria frowns. "Adam?")

—and he just shakes his head. He can't say anything, can't even *look* at her without feeling like the world's biggest chump.

(Without wanting to throw himself in front of a bus.)

"Hey," Victoria says. "Are you okay?"

Adam just shakes his head again. "I doubt it," Adam says.

Then he's crying.

367.

Victoria lets him cry. She hugs him tight and holds on to him and lets him blubber and sob and get it all out. And when he's cried as much as he's going to cry, he tells her everything. Pizza Man. Sam. Rob Thigpen. Jamal. Maryvale.

Victoria listens.

"I'm such a tool," Adam tells her. "I was the dumbest kid at Nixon."

Victoria kisses his cheek. "Shut up," she says. "I'm just glad you're okay."

368.

The door opens behind them. Chad pokes his head out. "Hey," he says. "What's up?"

Victoria looks up. "Just give us a minute, 'kay?"

Chad looks at Adam. Shrugs. The door closes, and Victoria sighs. "I guess I should get back," she says. "Sure you don't want to stay?"

"I'm supposed to be grounded," Adam says.

"Yikes." Victoria makes a face. "I guess you should go."

"I guess so."

Victoria stands. Adam stands too. He doesn't want to go. He doesn't give two shits about the party. But Victoria?

He's feeling it like a knife in his heart.

"I guess I'll see you around," Adam says. Their eyes meet, and Victoria looks away quickly.

"I'd like that," she says.

They hug again. Adam clings to her like a lifeline, like he always does. It's over too soon, like it always is. He makes himself let go and walks away toward the road, and just before he hits the sidewalk, she calls out behind him. "Adam?"

Adam turns. She's standing in the doorway, backlit from the party behind her. She fidgets a little. Smiles a little. "Call me sometime?" she says.

Adam hesitates. Adam nods. "I will," he says. Then he grins at her. "Assuming my mom ever gives me back my phone."

369.

Adam leaves the party, but he doesn't go home.

Not yet.

He gets on a bus and rides all the way downtown. Gets off at the bus loop and wades through the crowds of drunk people, the lineup outside Crash and Voodoo and every other dope spot. Walks until he reaches city hall and the doughnut shop across the street.

Sam's doughnut shop.

Sam's clearing tables when Adam walks in. He's wearing his silly hat and tie and he's wheeling dirty coffee mugs from the tables to the counter, and the light is too-bright fluorescent and it all suddenly looks so unbearably real that Adam nearly walks out again.

But he doesn't.

He stands at the counter and waits for Sam to see him, and when Sam does see him, he hesitates for a second and then wheels himself over.

"Hey," he says. "Adam."

"Hey, Sam," Adam says.

"I thought you were grounded," Sam says. "Steph said Mom and Dad have you on lockdown."

"I snuck out," Adam says. "There was this party."

Sam's face gets tense. "Oh."

"I didn't stay for very long," Adam says. "I couldn't do it.

I couldn't go back to that—" He looks for the right word. "That bullshit."

"Oh," Sam says again. "Yeah."

"Look, I'm sorry," Adam says. "I was trying to impress you. I thought you'd be proud of me or something."

He pauses.

"I just didn't want you to be ashamed of me," Adam says. "I didn't want you to think you had a loser kid brother."

Sam shakes his head. "I was proud of you when I saw you with Victoria," he says. "When I saw how happy you looked with her, man."

Adam thinks about Victoria in that green dress at the party. Feels it like a ragged wound again.

"I just wanted you to be happy, chill out, relax a little bit," Sam says. "Meet some friends, find a girl, make some memories. The rest of it? Shit."

Adam looks around the empty doughnut shop and thinks about those useless hockey tickets. He thinks about Sam at the party with beer spilled on his shirt.

He thinks about calling Sam a cripple.

He's blinking back tears again.

"I fucked everything up," Adam says. "You didn't ever get to be a god. I just wanted to give you something to be happy about."

"I'm happy," Sam says. "You don't think I'm happy?"

"You work at a doughnut shop," Adam says. "You live in a shitty apartment. You can't use your legs, for god's sake."

Sam shrugs. "Yeah," he says, "but I have a life, though."

"Where?" Adam says. "I don't see it."

"You haven't seen much, the last few months," Sam says. "I'm playing basketball again this summer. I met a girl. I'm not entirely dependent on your exploits to keep me off suicide watch, little brother."

Adam doesn't say anything.

"And it's a good thing, too," Sam says after a moment. "If all I had to live for were my kid brother's tales from the Tastee Freez, I'd slit my wrists in a millisecond."

"Don't say that," Adam says. "Jesus."

"Why not?" Sam says. "Cut too close to the bone?"

Adam looks at him. Sam doesn't look so angry anymore, or even disappointed.

(He doesn't even look silly in that dumb hat and tie.)

Sam just looks like Sam.

Solid. Secure. Happy.

"Come by the apartment the next time you're not grounded," Sam says. "Just because you're a legend now doesn't mean I can't kick your ass on PlayStation, Pizza Man."

Adam smiles, finally.

Adam laughs.

"Don't call me that," Adam says.

370.

So that's that.

Summer ends. Adam's parents get the school board to release him from Maryvale. He's a good student. His grades are decent and he doesn't fight. The vice principal has never heard of him.

(At Maryvale, that's a good thing.)

The school board agrees to let Adam back into the wild. They tell him he can go back to Nixon if he wants. Adam thinks about it for about fifteen seconds. Then he shakes his head no.

They put him into a school on the south end of town instead. Massey High. It's not far from Remington Park, and the principal agrees to take Adam on, after some serious negotiation.

So, there it is.

First day of school and Adam walks into Massey and knows literally nobody. Some of the kids know Pizza Man—

(word gets around)

—but he's not the guy they think he is, not anymore. He's no legend. He's no rainmaker. He's certainly not a *god*.

He's just Adam Higgs now.

He's kind of a loser again.

371.

And he's okay with it.

ACKNOWLEDGMENTS

I wrote the first draft of this book a little more than twelve years ago. It was the first novel I ever wrote. It was awful. The fact that you're holding it in your hands right now is a testament to the courage and fortitude of my teachers, both at Kennedy Collegiate and Riverside Secondary in Windsor, Ontario, and at the Universities of Guelph and British Columbia.

It's also a testament to my wonderful agent, Stacia Decker at the Donald Maass Agency, and my fantastic editor, Kristen Pettit at HarperTeen, whose insights and enthusiasm turned the forgotten scribblings of some misguided emo kid into one kick-ass book.

I owe a ton of thanks to everyone at HarperTeen, too, especially Elizabeth Lynch and the copyeditors and proofreaders who saved me from public embarrassment on many an occasion. Any embarrassment that remains is mine to bear, and mine alone.

Thanks to my friends, especially Maciejka Gorzelnik and Shannon Kyla, for story consultation, fact-finding, and general inspiration.

And thanks to my family, whose love and support carried me through my wayward youth, and imbued in me the courage to follow my dreams. Mom, Dad, Andrew, and Terry, I love you all.

P.S. Readers familiar with Don Winslow's work will probably notice that this book owes a lot stylistically to his novels *Savages* and *Kings of Cool*, both of which are incredible, and which revolutionized the way I looked at this story. If you haven't read them, you have homework tonight.